The Sacred Mountain

An account of the successful ascent of

Mount Everest in 1924 by Reverend Morton Tutter

as told to the author shortly before

Reverend Tutter's death

Stan Huncilman

To Phil Brown, who never let me forget the fun and folly that is also part of mountaineering

CONTENTS

ACKNOWLEDGMENTS

Thanks to Hot-legs and Fantastic for their
comments and suggestions.

1

THE BROADHURST

"Ladies and gentlemen, welcome to the Broadhurst Theater. Tonight I have the pleasure of introducing one of the world's great mountaineers. A man that has dedicated himself to the greatest natural challenge that exists on this earth. His past two expeditions have set records and humbled the fiercest critics. He has battled forces that have destroyed armies and survived. He has gone where most mountaineers can only dream of going. He has that special quality that leads a man to the top of the mountain. He is a man that never looks back until he is on the summit! Ladies and gentlemen, I give you the man who will conquer Everest, Mr. George Mallory."

My mind wandered back to my time in Tibet. It had been a life of adventure. Regrettably, Mallory was going on and on, listing facts and achievements of the two previous expeditions, endless elevations and comparisons of snow conditions. He sounded more like a bureaucrat than a mountain climber. I was yawning when Mallory began to answer questions from the audience.

"Mr. Mallory, am I to understand that these expeditions are not for all mankind but rather about fulfilling British destiny?"

"England and the world share the same destiny—but England has taken the initiative," replied Mallory.

"What is your position on the use of oxygen? And is that belief the reason why Mr. George Finch has been excluded from future expeditions?"

"Mr. Finch is a brilliant man and an exceptional climber. Unfortunately, the climbing members are chosen by the expedition organizer, the Royal Geographical Society, not by the climbers. I for one feel that mountaineering is a true test of the human spirit, and I intend to forgo oxygen."

Sally whispered, "Is Mr. Mallory married? He is so dull that I can't imagine he has a wife."

"He is."

"Unbelievable. England must be a lonely place. I'm very tired, Morton. Can we go?"

"Soon. I promise," I said.

"But why climb Everest?" came the question.

"Because it is there," he replied.

"That is reason enough to risk your life?"

"What better reason to risk one's life than the pursuit of this ultimate challenge? Yes, I'll climb it because it is there!" said Mallory. He thanked the audience and stepped back from the podium. With that phrase, Mallory had struck a chord in an American psyche that yearned to conquer new frontiers. The audience, which had been lukewarm, stood and gave him thunderous applause. Adventure! Mallory was a different sort of man. He didn't want to talk about what he wanted to do, he just wanted to do it: climb Mount Everest.

And he hadn't said it outright, but the whole world knew it—they were coming to America again for help. Not for men, just for money. And up until those final words, I don't think any American cared.

"Oh, Morton, doesn't it seem so dangerous! Why would any man want to do it? Just think of my father and all the good he does. Isn't that more important? And it isn't dangerous," said Sally as we waited for a cab.

I was still thinking, *Why did I do it? Why did I marry her?* Aloud I said, "For some men, there is a fire inside, a drive that pushes them. Think of your father and his never-ending service to the poor."

"Oh yes, Father is always helping the needy."

He has helped them, all right, as long as he can take his cut. And if I sing my psalms right, someday it will all be mine.

"Yes, he is driven, or guided, by our Lord to help the poor. This Mallory, he has been chosen by the Lord to climb Mount Everest. Do you see?"

"Why, yes I do, my love. God has made him a mountaineering soldier. But who will he save on the mountain? It's very cold and empty there. Remember those photographs he showed us."

"I don't think he will save anyone. He is going because he is driven."

"But you said he was like Father."

"He is like your father because he has drive."

"Father doesn't drive. He hates the automobile."

"No, Sally, he is like your father in that God has given both of them tasks. If Mallory finds souls on the mountain, then he can ask your father's advice. Now do you see?"

"I think so. It is like Father's sermon about the snowflakes."

"Snowflakes?"

"You don't remember? It's Father's favorite winter sermon, the one about how each of us is unique but at the same time we—"

"Oh yes, now I remember it. 'The Individual and Identity.' But what does that have to do with Mount Everest?" I asked.

"Well, isn't the mountain covered in snow?"

"Of course. Now I see what you mean," I sighed.

Friends approached us, and thankfully she lost interest in the subject.

Until that moment, I had never given much thought to returning to Tibet. The congregation would be mine when my father-in-law retired in a few years. All I had to do was stay married to Sally. I loved the ministry and—no doubt—my wife, but if the devil ever wanted a way to drive a man to drink, Sally would be it. Mallory had revived my wanderlust. But what good, upstanding Christian family would allow their son-in-law to travel to the other side of the world? Sally had never even gone camping; she hated the outdoors.

An expedition to Everest—the chance of a lifetime. But what about Sally?

Step one: I'll promise to meet her in Paris on the way back. She'll be so happy, she'll let me go anywhere.

"Say, Sally, would you mind if I spoke to Mr. Mallory for a moment? I won't be long. Here's cab fare. I'll be home as soon as possible," I said as I put the money in her coat pocket. But she didn't hear me, as she was already in conversation with her friends. I was through the theater doors before she had a chance to let my comment sink in. I found Mallory surrounded by the Appalachian Alpine Club, going on and on about their most memorable moments of fright on the mountain. If I waited patiently, I might never get to speak to him. I needed to get his attention.

"Mr. Mallory, our church is prepared to lend assistance to your expedition. Would you have time to meet with me?" I asked as I shoved my card into his hand. I turned and started away but paused when I felt a hand touch my shoulder.

"Excuse me, Mr.—Reverend—Tutter. May I speak with you for a moment? This is quite a surprise. I mean, a donation from a church. I hadn't expected a church to take an interest."

I hadn't expected it to either. An idea was just forming in my mind as he spoke.

"When would you like to meet?" he said, extending his hand.

"Would 10:00 a.m. tomorrow be too early? I'm visiting hospitals tomorrow. The church isn't far from here. I trust that an explorer can find his way."

"I'm a mountaineer, not a Livingston—but I'll be there." He nodded, then turned back to the crowd.

"You told Mr. Mallory what?" my father-in-law asked.

"I told him the church was considering donating to the expedition. Tibet is a closed society, but eventually it will open and we'll have an inside track when missionaries are allowed. We have the money, and it's time we started a missionary program."

"Why do we need that? Even if we did sponsor missionaries, Tibet is an isolated country, sparsely populated. Not a lot of promise there. Whereas when I think of Nigeria—now that is a place with potential. Money and time better spent."

The old man was a pragmatist. I was going to have to work if I wanted this excursion. I didn't think that a man who took on a challenge "because it is there" was going to sell the idea. "Jesus never worried if there were enough loaves."

He frowned.

"God made the world in six days, but our work as humans is never ending and must be prioritized. At this time I believe our priorities are here in the city."

Just then George Mallory walked into the office. "Mr. Mallory, right on time. This is my father-in-law, Reverend Edward Lutz." As they exchanged greetings I was thinking of how to get Mallory off the "because it is there" song and dance.

"Mr. Mallory, Morton tells me that you are planning to climb Mount Everest."

"That's true. I'm here to raise money for what will be our third and certainly our successful attempt."

"Third attempt? You are determined, aren't you. The ability to carry on in spite of the odds is a virtue."

"I agree."

"Mr. Mallory, I don't know what Morton promised you. It was only a minute ago that I first heard your name and your mission."

"I see," said Mallory as he glanced at me. "The reverend told me that this church was interested in contributing to our expedition."

"That would be highly unusual for any church, I think. Mountaineering is hardly feeding the poor, wouldn't you agree, Mr. Mallory?"

"Mountaineering has benefits other than the act of reaching the summit, but I can't say that it helps feed the poor. I think there has been a misunderstanding. Last night was very hectic. It has been a pleasure, Reverend Lutz. Good day," said Mallory as he turned and headed for the door.

"Because it is there!" I shouted. "That's why we need to contribute— because it is there. Mr. Mallory, please don't leave," I said as I moved between him and the door. "Don't you see, Dad? The expedition is like God's love: It's there, but we have to rise up and take it for it to be part of us. To reach the eternal love of God is the greatest challenge in the universe, and Everest is the greatest challenge on earth. If we can put men on top of Everest, then we can bring God to the heart of every man and woman on earth whom our church can reach."

"Your son-in-law is an enthusiastic man. Your church is fortunate. Now I must be going. Good day," said Mallory as he waited for me to step aside.

"Just a moment, Mr. Mallory," said Lutz. "Morton has a point. Everest and God—I like it. Last year Reverend Morehouse's congregation sponsored a fellow's trip to the Holy Land—or was it Turkey—to look for the Ark. I don't know if he's found anything, but it sure has put Morehouse on the map. The way he talks, you'd think the entire congregation were involved, though I believe only a few of the members went along."

"That's interesting, Reverend, but Mount Everest isn't Noah's Ark," said Mallory.

"No, but it could be. How much money have you raised so far, Mr. Mallory?"

"Not as much as I had expected."

"Did you ever stop to think that Americans have their own heroes?" Lutz demanded.

"Excuse me?" said Mallory.

"The Great War opened many eyes. America is looking outward and realizes that it has a role to play in the world. Americans no longer think Europe has a monopoly on anything, including exploration."

I didn't understand what Dad was up to and hoped he wasn't planning to have me lead an expedition. I just wanted to get out of town for a while.

"No doubt Americans are entitled to have their heroes, sir," said Mallory.

"Exactly. And that is why your fundraising is lacking. Those fellows listening to you are thinking they could do the same thing. Most could not but that doesn't stop them from thinking they could. They're individualists and entrepreneurs. Why, I wouldn't be surprised if P. T. Barnum was sponsoring an expedition to climb Everest and capture an abominable snowman! You are in America, sir: *Carpe opportunitas.*"

"I'm not sure I understand."

"Take advantage of the situation. Appeal to the imagination and watch them reach for the pocketbook. How much longer does your tour last?"

"Five more days."

"You know as well as I do that you won't reach that summit of gold. You are a mountaineer, not a salesman. I can't give the church's money to you, Mr. Mallory, but I can help you. In exchange, you can help us by letting Morton join the expedition as a reporter for our church. If you agree, then on Sunday I will ask for a special contribution for your expedition."

I could see Mallory's muscles twitching. He must have felt he was trapped on a rock face with nowhere to go but up. The old man was good—if he lived long enough, he could lock up the whole world for Jesus. "Dad, I don't think it's appropriate to ask Mr. Mallory to take me along. I was inspired by his talk and by his risking everything to reach the highest point on earth. I thought that somehow our church could help. I never wanted to go along."

"I know that, Morton, but you must go. It's a forgotten corner of the world. Christians need to know what life is like there, so that when the time comes they'll be ready to help. Morton, I can't think of anyone better suited than you to go and then report back to us."

"Reverend Lutz, I am unaccustomed to hearing a man of God speak in such pragmatic terms. It's so American to see the economics in everything, yet until now I had only considered its crass aspects, not the opportunities. I am flattered that you have faith in the expedition and wish to contribute. But I must decline, for I cannot take responsibility for Reverend Tutter. He is a well-intentioned fellow, but this is a mountaineering expedition. We shall camp and climb at extreme elevations and exposures, travel through remote areas, and be far from any assistance—and he is a married man."

"Are you married?" asked Lutz.

"Yes, but my dear wife knew of my obsession before our marriage. And Morton is not prepared for such an undertaking."

"Morton, have you told Mr. Mallory about your life?"

"No."

"Tell him."

I cleared my throat. "I grew up in Tibet—actually western China, but the people were ethnic Tibetans. My father was a missionary. My grandfather was a rancher who realized his son, my dad, needed a better life. He sent him to a boarding school in Boise. Of course they had church on Sunday. Dad told me he remembered his first time in the church. By the time he was seventeen, he knew that he was called to the ministry. He went to Chicago to study to become a minister. Yet he was no city man. He had wanderlust, so he took his Bible and went to China. He met my mother there. She was German and worked at a mission. Mother gave birth to three kids, but I was the only one to make it past the first year. Mother and Dad were so busy proselytizing for the Lord that I spent most of my time with the locals—Tibetans—learning their ways and language during the day. At night I received a Western education.

"One day Dad decided we needed to go to Lhasa. Even though Lhasa was technically closed to most foreigners, he was determined. The three of us, along with enough supplies for six months, piled into a yak-pulled cart and headed off. A month into the journey, we were attacked by Khampas. Bandits.

"They surrounded us and killed Dad. Mom and I were kidnapped. For a while we were together. At first there was talk of a ransom, and then we were on the move constantly because local tribes had begun retaliatory raids. The traveling and lack of food took a toll on her. When the bandits realized that her health was failing, they halted for a few days to let her rest and they gave us extra food. I remember Mom saying that there was compassion in even the coldest heart. She was wrong, for as soon as she got color back in her cheeks, they sold her to Han traders for a horse and sugar."

"Did you, I mean have you ever—"

"Heard from her? No, nothing. From then on, I was a slave. I tended to the sheep and yaks. I was slowly starving and they didn't care. They didn't watch me too carefully, for there was nowhere for me to go. It went on this way for a year or so, till one day I was alone with Rutak. He was your basic filthy, lying brigand, though he cut a fine figure as he sat proudly on his horse. He was out looking for a few stray sheep to pay off a gambling debt, and I was along to herd whatever he found or stole. We came upon an empty tent, which Rutak said wasn't far from some hot springs. No doubt the owners of the tent were there.

"Rutak rifled through the tent, grabbing whatever was colorful or shiny. I didn't want to steal, but I knew he would beat me if I didn't help, so I started taking similar stuff. While he wasn't looking, I took a watch and fountain pens. They were small enough to hide in what clothing I had left. If I ever escaped, I could sell them for food. When he had all he could carry and was getting ready to leave the tent, he saw a pair of boots and told me to get them. It was a lucky break, for if Rutak liked the boots, he might give me his, and at least I'd have a pair of shoes for my effort. As soon as Rutak stuck his head out of the tent, I heard shots. It was the owners. Rutak's demeanor went from warrior to wet dog as he ran for his horse. I was right behind him until I tripped on a tent stake. He had stashed what he could on his horse. When I got to him, he was about to ride off. I tried to pull myself up on the horse, for there was no way to escape the riders on foot. Rutak looked down and smiled.

"'Long shoes, good,' he said as extended his hand to me.

"As soon as I gave him the boots, he kicked me in the head. He was off before I hit the ground, and I was as good as dead. Now Khampas have a reputation as fierce, and there is some truth in it. But once they fill their pockets, there is one thing they truly excel at, and that is a dashing retreat. I never saw him again after that day. I heard other horses approaching, and when I looked up I saw two Caucasian men staring down at me. I was so filthy they didn't notice my blond hair or even my blue eyes. They got off their horses and went in the tent, and when they came out they were yelling at me. They were Germans. The next thing I knew, they were both kicking me. I had the watch and pen, and if they found them they'd kill me. Thank God for blustering cowards like Rutak, who, having made good his escape, stopped and fired a shot at the Germans, once again showing that the Khampa is bravest in retreat. I slipped the watch and pen under a rock before they returned to kicking me.

"*'Dieb, dieb!'* they shouted.

"*'Vater und Mutter tot. Ich bin ein Gefangener,'* I shouted at them again and again until they stopped kicking me.

"'Prisoner? And you are helping him steal? We saw you with the boots trying to get on the horse. You lie!'

"'No, I tried to take the boots back. I tried to stop him when I heard your shots.'

"'Liar.'

"'No, I'm not a thief. I'm an American. My parents were missionaries. Bandits killed my father and traded my mother for a horse.'

"When they finally saw that my hair was blond and that I had blue eyes, they calmed down and listened to my story. They were archaeologists searching for evidence of Alexander the Great's lost armies, which had crossed into Tibet on their way to India and then disappeared. One of them, Hans, was a doctor. He had met my father years before I was born when he had passed by the mission. Luckily they were in the process of returning to Germany, so they took me along with them to Shanghai, and from there I came to America and lived with my aunt and uncle and went to school. I met Sally, my wife, at church one Sunday, and the rest is history."

"Amazing tale of resilience, though hearing of your mother's fate is disturbing. She was never heard of again?" queried Mallory.

"Never. It is a vast, empty land that takes no prisoners."

Mallory's head dropped ever so slightly and he looked sad. "Your mother and father were brave and devoted people. I am impressed by people of faith and courage. Yet even the strongest of us can have weaknesses. I've seen it on the mountain numerous times. We can be so strong and moments later be so fragile."

He raised his eyes to mine.

"We can be so strong. We can be so fragile," Dad said. He took a breath and turned his head toward heaven. "Oh, what a wonderful metaphor for your adventure, and what a perfect theme for Sunday's sermon. You and your team on the mountain, so strong yet so fragile! Oh, the wonders of our Lord. What an inspirational thought for the congregation. I had been thinking of using the threat of the papist influence in Tibet as a theme. Fear is effective even if fraudulent, but your words, Mr. Mallory, are like honey from a silver chalice."

Mallory turned to my father-in-law and stared. I think he was truly awed by what he had just heard.

"Reverend Lutz, am I to believe that you can take that simple phrase, create a Sunday sermon, and expect to raise money with it for our expedition?"

"My dear Mr. Mallory, you are in America. God has blessed America and his blessings will soon be upon you. In this great land, nothing is impossible when one turns to the Lord."

Mallory appeared to listen intently while Dad went on about the wonderful things members of his congregation had done because of God and America. Something changed in Mallory's demeanor. He seemed to see in my father-in-law something other than another crass, money-obsessed American. He saw that Dad was rising to a challenge. It was the same thing Mallory had experienced when he was on a mountain. He ignored the odds and the doubters, for he had a goal and he had faith. Dad was a natural-born salesman, and he was at his best when he was selling hope. Mallory's expedition carried the hopes of the lonely, the poor, the sick, and even the wealthy, for Dad would remind them in his own unique way that every day each of them faced an impossible challenge, just like the English as they climbed to the top of the loneliest and tallest mountain on earth. As I listened to Dad and Mallory, I imagined I saw them face to face, rising high into the clouds, as all of New York stopped and stared and cheered, *Everest! Everest! Everest!*"

"Reverend Tutter. Reverend Tutter." It was Mallory's voice calling me.

"Oh yes, Mr. Mallory. Sorry, my mind was wandering."

"Quite all right. Some of my best students have been daydreamers. After hearing of your early life, I feel that—although your presence as a reporter would be of little interest to us—your language skills, as well as your previous experience with Tibetans, would be of great benefit to the expedition. Although I expect the Everest Committee would object at first, it could be persuaded. I say the Committee, but actually there is only one man that needs to be persuaded and that man is Arthur Hinks, secretary of the Royal Geographical Society. I can get his approval, but I must make clear that you could not in any way consider yourself a member of this expedition with regard to climbing, and you could go only as far as the base camp. All of what I just related to you would be subject to your church contributing a reasonable amount of money to our endeavor. Are you still interested in coming along?"

"Why, of course he is," blurted out Dad as Mallory waited for my answer.

"I am. And I am honored that you find me valuable to the cause," I said.

"Excellent," said Dad. "You won't be disappointed in Morton, Mr. Mallory. And do come on Sunday, for after the service we'll be having my wife's fried chicken, which is the best in New York."

Ah, the power of the pulpit. Reverend Lutz gave the sermon. Afterward, there was a second special collection, and $927.37 was donated to Mallory's expedition. Personally, I think what sold it was when Dad started on about the crevasses that opened and closed: "And so although six may step over this crack safely, the seventh will find that what had been a bridge is gone and is now a void. Such is our world. We follow blindly the path of those before us, for it is the easy thing and safe to do, or so we think, until we fall into the abyss! So as mountaineers rope together, so must we tie ourselves to God's rope...."

"Mrs. Lutz, this is the best fried chicken I've ever eaten. My wife, Ruth, would love it. Would it be too much to request the recipe?" said Mallory before asking Reverend Lutz to pass him another drumstick.

"Why, thank you. The recipe is yours for the asking. It will be only a matter of finding an obliging hen when you return home, Mr. Mallory," Mrs. Lutz beamed.

"Speaking of drumsticks, is it true that Tibetans believe that the Dalai Lama is a god?" asked Lutz.

"Why, yes, Reverend Lutz, they certainly do."

"And they found him as a baby by shaking a bunch of bones?"

"Must you, Mr. Lutz?" said my mother-in-law with a sigh.

"I can't say whether that is the methodology, sir. But one is struck by the peculiarity of finding a god through a roll of the dice, so to speak," said Mallory.

"Brilliant. Morton, make a note of that. Finding God Through a Roll of the Dice—that will make a fine sermon," said Reverend Lutz.

2

CALCUTTA

If Tibet was the roof of the world, Calcutta was surely the basement--a sea of humanity sloshed at the end of the gangplank, with hundreds of shouting voices offering their services. I avoided eye contact with them as I made my way into the crowd on the lookout for a Caucasian, Reverend Thomas Foster, who had arranged to meet me on arrival. That was a mistake, for no sooner had I stepped from the gangplank than a rascal grabbed my ankle. His hands were in my pockets the instant I hit the ground.

"Thief! Get away!" I shouted as I tried to get back on my feet. Not wanting to leave empty handed, he bit my nose and continued to rifle my pockets. I fell back to the ground. If I got up he would keep my nose. "Help, help," I cried again as I tried to pry away his mouth.

"Ye yathesta Amita, eke e loka asuna."

The thief let go and ran off. In his place were a pair of polished shoes, white trousers, and jacket. A thin pale face beneath a pith helmet stared down at me.

"Are you alright? Can you get up? Sorry I'd help you but, well, I've had a fever and if I try to help you I'm afraid I'd simply land on top of you, Reverend Tutter. You are Reverend Tutter aren't you?"

"Why yes I am, how did you know?"

"I had a description of you in a letter from your father-in-law--tall, sandy hair, rugged--and when you started down the gangplank into the crowd without a porter, I knew you had to be an American, an American minister."

"I see," I said as I shook his hand.

"Rickshaw ready, Reverend Foster."

"Thank you, Ganesh. This is Ganesh, Reverend Tutter, the overseer at the mission. He'll take care of your baggage while I'll take you to the mission."

I reached out to shake his hand but he was already fighting his way up the gangplank.

"Never stops, an amazing fellow been with us for fifteen years and I've never seen him sit down. Shall we go?"

"Let me just check my pockets, that thief may have taken something."

"No need to worry if he did we'll get it back."

"Get it back?"

"Yes that was Amita one of the orphans, he's a good kid."

"He tried to rob me!"

"I suppose one could say that, but I think it is more the fact that he has nothing and doesn't understand the nature of property. You see they all share in the dormitory; it's one of the things we emphasize: learn to work together. India is special Reverend Tutter, you'll see. As a matter of fact, you are lucky to have arrived when you did, for Annie Besant is speaking tonight. You must come and hear her. I hope you are up for a long evening. She will discuss the godhead."

"What is the topic again?" I asked, overwhelmed by the sudden mass of humanity around me.

"Krishnamurti."

"Why would I want to hear a lecture on occultism?"

"It is not occultism. It is another way of seeing God."

"Another way? What is wrong with the way you had?"

"If the church is to make lasting progress, we clergy need to understand the thought processes of the people we want to reach."

"What is wrong with telling them that we are better? Isn't that the truth?"

Foster looked as though he had just met the devil.

"Reverend Tutter, you as a servant of our Lord should be the first to know that no man is better than another. We are all equal before God."

"Reverend Foster, we are bringing our teachings to them. Why? Because we have a better way. How can you argue with that?"

"Reverend Tutter, it is so easy to be right. But it is not about right. God is multifaceted and we Christians have ignored this. Here in India, I have seen his truest beauty manifested in thousands of ways, and not just in church. I see our Lord in everything. I hear our Lord everywhere."

Foster has gone feral, I thought. My father had talked about it in China. It was rare but it happened. He had mentioned India, saying that historically the Hindus had absorbed all religions, even Islam. Listening to Foster, I could he tell he was close to the point of no return. His next words told me that he was already a goner.

He took my hands into his and pressed them. "Reverend Tutter, come with me tonight. Come hear Annie Besant. She is presenting the young man

Krishnamurti, the world teacher, who will speak for all people tonight. You must come and hear. Then you will understand."

After being on a ship for a nearly a month, the idea of a lecture wasn't inviting. But Foster had the connections I needed until I reached Tibet, so I agreed to go.

The hall was crowded. Every confused and guilt-ridden European in Calcutta must have been there. Several audience members greeted Foster. Besant rambled on and on about "oneness" and wove her way in and out of "clairvoyant lucidities," as she called them. How people can think that so-called psychic phenomena can be more important than reality, I'll never understand. She finally brought the kid out. A total groomer he was. We had them back in New York. Dad could always tell one when he saw one. "You see, Morton, look how he stands and look at his eyes—the sparkle, the love. God has a plan for that boy." Now a lot of old men—including Annie's buddy, Charles Webster Leadbeater—have plans for boys, but Dad actually believed God sent emissaries in the form of Adonis. "Beauty is God's tonic for the blind," he would say.

The words flowed from the young man's tongue as easily as his coal-black hair rose from his handsome forehead.

Now I've heard a lot of sermons and even given a few, but what made this kid unique was how he took a whole lot of nonsense and condensed it for Westerners. Hinduism in a box. That was it. If Besant was lucky, she had a meal ticket. This was not for the natives. What Krishnamurti said was bred into them. He had put the uncountable gods and goddesses in a package for export. It just might sell if there were enough idle, neurotic people of means who wanted to sign up for an exotic hobby. I had spent enough time in China to be able to see what this country had exported a thousand years before. Buddhism had been their first go at it, and it had worked pretty well, but there's always room for improvement, even in religion. Krishnamurti had the gift, all right, but something told me he didn't want to sell it.

That was obvious at the post-lecture dinner at Foster's. Krishnamurti avoided all talk of religion, joining the conversation only when it turned to food and the latest Indian movies, which he could now afford to see. As the evening went on, I noticed that Foster never ate, and drank only water. The night was unseasonably cool, yet Foster was dripping wet. So that look in his eyes wasn't only from going off the deep end. It was also because he was slowly dying.

Besant had an assistant named Betty Rhodes. She was backstage when Krishnamurti spoke, but luck placed her next to me at dinner. I'm a married man, but beauty is in this world to remind man of God's perfection; Betty's talents and beauty were certainly that. Her mother was a nautch dancer and her father an English officer.

"You see, Mr. Tutter, Miss Besant understands that there is only one true Light in the universe. Her role is to find and bring those who can lead to the forefront. That is why she is so excited about Krishnamurti," she said.

"I can tell a selfless person right off the bat. Her love radiates through me as if I were a leaf on a tree in the sun," I said.

"Oh yes, she touches everyone but does not cling. She will be the last to board the ferry to everlasting love. When she visited my school, I knew I wanted to be with her. Though my mother's unexpected death was a tragedy, it left me free to work with Miss Besant."

"What about your father?"

"He is in England, married and with a family. I think my mother seduced him. For a woman in her profession, it was a way to survive. I was lucky, for he took responsibility for me and saw that I received an education. His only request was that I not become a nautch dancer."

"And did you follow that request?"

"Yes and no."

"The no intrigues me," I said, recalling the perfect hip-to-breast ratio I had spotted earlier.

"I still dance as a way of worship. The word *worship* is a clumsy one. Perhaps *devotion* or *prayer*. Yes, *prayer* is more appropriate. My prayers are dance."

"I see." Suddenly Betty's lovely form evaporated as I thought of her dancing alongside the potato bag Besant. "Does Miss Besant dance with you?"

She recoiled and glanced across the table at Besant. "Oh no, and you mustn't say anything about this to her. I'm afraid she wouldn't understand. You see, it is a form of *devadasi*. She would be very upset, even though it is part of our heritage."

"*Devadasi*. Isn't that a dance?"

"Who told you that?"

"Oh, I saw a movie poster with lovely dancers on it and asked what it was about when I stopped by the Great Eastern Hotel."

"That is a silly movie, not the real dance. Would you like to see real *devadasis*?"

"Why, yes. Are you performing somewhere?"

"It is not a public performance. It is a sacred rite. You must meet me after dinner. I will take you and you will see, you will understand."

About an hour after she had left with the ever-babbling Besant, Betty arrived back at Foster's mission in a rickshaw. Had I not known it was her, she would have been unrecognizable in her makeup and in the clothing she wore beneath her *dupatta*.

"Come now, you will experience the true path to understanding, the path of action and devotion."

I suddenly felt uneasy, "I'm not sure I want to go, Betty. I'm tired and won't appreciate the performance. Perhaps when I return after the expedition."

"You do not need to enjoy it."

"Then why are you taking me?"

"I do not expect you to *understand*, but I hope you will *experience*. You are a Western man. What you know as your body is an illusion. Tonight you will witness breathing the life of the divine."

Hundreds of doors and windows twisted past us as the rickshaw driver's bare feet tapped a steady yet varied beat on the cobblestones of the narrow streets. We were heading north along the Hooghly River. The road stretched farther into the darkness of rural India. We were well into the countryside when the rickshaw turned onto a dirt path and stopped.

"We must walk. He will go no farther. He will wait."

"Why? The path is wide enough. Is it too dark?"

"No, he will not come, for he understands that he cannot know."

"What is that supposed to mean?"

"You see, Morton, you can only exhale. You have never inhaled," she said as she removed her *dupatta*. The moonlight traced her figure through her delicate clothing. "This man is a rickshaw driver. That is all he is allowed to be and he understands that. Leave your shoes in the rickshaw. Come."

"The path is dirt. I can't go barefoot."

"You must remove your shoes. The temple of Kali is sacred." Her persona had changed. It was as if she were taking orders from someone.

I put my shoes in the rickshaw and followed Betty. Her feet seemed to control her. She almost floated down the path. The moonlight seeped through an oily, heavy smoke. We entered a clearing. At the end of it was a temple illuminated by small pyres. That didn't strike me as odd until I noticed that lining the path to the steps were small beehive-shaped huts made from human skulls. As we passed, I saw that some of them had occupants, skinny and naked men with painted faces.

"Betty, who are these—"

She replied impatiently, with an odd heaviness in the movement of her head while her right hand trembled as one finger pointed. "They are the holy ones, the guardians of the temple. Mind the rats, for they are the messengers of the goddess."

"Rats?" I looked about and there were rats everywhere, seemingly oblivious to our passing. I yelled as one darted across my foot. Betty turned to me again, the light from the pyres flickering across her face.

"Do you wish to leave? Are you afraid? The goddess demands complete devotion."

"You said it was a dance, not a religious service."

"It is a dance, the dance of the goddess Kali. Do you think that dance is for entertainment? You are a corpse, Morton. The blood in your veins is putrid, for you can only exhale the illusions of your ego. Are you coming?"

"No, I am returning to Calcutta. I feel dizzy. Maybe it was dinner."

"Morton, you must not go back." Her voice was chilly. "You will learn to breathe."

I turned toward the road. Covered in ash and with necklaces of bones, the skull shack demons stood between me and the rickshaw. There was no doubt about it now; I was leaving. I pushed the skinnier of the two aside and ran for the road. The next thing I knew, I was on the ground with a trident on my neck.

"Morton, I want to give you life. You know life only through fear—fear of the unknown, fear of darkness. Come, let the goddess Kali enter your soul."

This was sounding less and less like a folk dance and more and more like a séance. I wanted to leave, but with a three-pronged spear against my neck, I was trapped. I'd have to bide my time until I had another opportunity. I tried to turn my head to see Betty's face. As I did she suddenly lowered herself, and her beautiful legs were astride me. Lying there I remembered my original motive for coming: seducing Betty. "Sure, I'm sorry. Sometimes when my stomach gets upset, I panic. I didn't mean for you to think I wasn't interested in seeing you dance."

There was a quick hand movement, and the trident was gone. Another hand movement and the bony guys disappeared. Betty got up and I followed her toward the temple. I noticed as we ascended the rat-infested stairs to a large door that the risers were engraved with figures who were standing on what looked like dead people. As we entered, there was a muffled chant from the dimly lit chamber. Slowly, as my eyes adjusted, I saw that the temple contained maybe a dozen other men and women. The women were dressed like Betty. They were all Indians. When they noticed that I was a foreigner, there was a lot of shouting and pointing at me. A tall, muscular man stepped forward and addressed Betty.

"*Ka mati ligu ta tam! Kali muta belika!* He is a white man...*tum huggi apka marra*...this is a sacred site...*puni marra hinditakka.* He must leave on the instant...*nakka mani tabi*...strictly prohibited...*barat nam shakti.*"

Betty must have known this would happen, for as the man continued his diatribe she made eye contact with the others in the chamber. There was no doubt that she was in charge. I noticed that I was an extra male. That meant that Tarzan was going to be the wallflower, and he wasn't happy about it.

"*Kali japna keen git puri hinditalka ghat.* The goddess is witness to this doubter…*kam jetna matti lumgotti hai. Pugree barsaat*…get out!" shouted Betty, pointing to the door.

Tarzan stepped toward her and grabbed her arm.

"*Heeka sannu tomi,*" Betty said.

Tarzan paused for a second and then reached for her other arm.

"*Nabaam heeka sanni tomi tomi!*" came a rumbling command from deep within Betty's lungs.

Suddenly Tarzan started to scream as he reached for his legs. Rats, hundreds of rats, climbed up his legs. He covered his face, as the rats had reached his neck. His muffled cries subsided as he fell to the floor, invisible beneath thousands of swarming rats.

"*Tum nakii boorit,*" said Betty. And the rats left the bleeding man.

Betty had great legs, but I had my limits. I saw this as my chance to make a run for it, as Betty seemed preoccupied with the disintegration of Tarzan. I turned for the door.

"No, Morton, you will stay with us." Her hand was on my shoulder. "Surush sought only power. He lived within his definitions of self. He, too, could only exhale. Do not think that our knowledge is only for those of India. The goddess is all."

I looked in her eyes. I expected to see evil, but instead I saw that she believed what she was saying. I was frightened. "Really, Betty, I don't think I'm ready for something this special. I've been in India only a day. Perhaps if I came back another time—"

She interrupted me. "You must stay, Morton. No harm will come to you. In a moment the dance will start." Betty turned toward the center of the temple and spoke: "*Apka matihia mooghly!*"

Two men came forward, grabbed Surush's lifeless body, and dragged it to an opening in the temple floor, where they dropped it in.

"What did you do with him? Don't you cremate the dead?"

"He doesn't deserve cremation. We threw him in the Hooghly. They will find his body in a few days and assume he was killed by dacoits. Then he will be cremated if his family claims him. All will be as it should. Come, Morton, the dance begins."

The men moved to the edge of the room, and the drumming started, followed by singing. Betty and the other women removed their *dupattas*. Such was their lack of clothing that their jewelry afforded more cover. Torches now illuminated a sculpture of a large black figure standing upon a corpse. This was a large version of the carvings I had seen on the steps when I entered the temple. I stared at the beautiful dancers; if this was a sacred dance that would lead to salvation, then I would be first in line. I lost track of time as the hypnotic drumming filled my mind. The erotic power of Betty's and the other dancers' movements were distractions, temporal pleasures that kept one from seeing the truth. I was crossing a bridge to a new understanding of life. I saw the illusory nature of flesh. That was what Betty had been harping on in the rickshaw on the way to the temple. An hour ago, I would have risked life and limb to sleep with any of the dancers, and now I sat cross-legged, gently swaying, content in the knowledge that all of life was an illusion. Time was nonexistent. Had the rats really killed Surush? Had there even been a Surush?

"Morton, Morton…"

Betty was gently touching my cheek. I opened my eyes, turned my head, and took a deep breath. She sat next to me, still in her dancing costume, silhouetted against the large sculpture. "The dance is over. Everyone has left. I see you are inhaling. The goddess has entered your lungs and will fill your soul. Did you enjoy the dance? I must ask because when I dance I am one with the goddess. I see only her."

"Yes, I did. It was amazing. I have never… Well, it was as if I left my body. The world was an illusion. Time ceased to exist. Is that normal?"

"Of course it is normal. I knew you were special, Morton. So few people, especially men, see the true purpose of the dance."

At that moment my gaze focused on Betty's nearly naked breasts, inches in front of me.

"Oh, Morton, I know your intent."

"And what is that?"

"Of course you desire to seduce me."

Her eyes were those of a vamp and of a mother. I was speechless. Suddenly she began to swell. Her body grew larger and larger, yet so did her seductiveness. I had never looked twice at a large woman in my life, but I sat there, impotent yet longing for a female form that I disdained.

"Morton, you see me, the goddess, the woman, the giver of life, the bearer of rebirth. You cannot seduce. You can only surrender to the weakness of the ego. Come." She took my hand and led me toward the large sculpture. "This is the goddess. She speaks through me." Betty's hands moved across my chest and hips as she led me toward a lumpy mattress below the statue. Then she removed my clothes.

"I have a wife, Betty."

"Your marriage is an illusion. The sacral chakra is your primary compass, Morton. I will lead you to the crown chakra, and then you will know that the distinction of self from the universe is false. We will pierce the maya."

Moments later, she was on top of me. Her body glowing as the room darkened. She became the size of six women, then she was the blood-encrusted black statue that dominated the temple, finally she was the original beautiful Betty I had met at Reverend Foster's. I closed my eyes as points of unfathomable pleasure pricked my body. This was not real. It could not be real. Her lips were redder than the blood that flowed within them. I was smothered yet felt as if I floated.

I took my hands away from Betty and placed them on the mattress. As I did, my right hand touched something. It wasn't stone or wood. It was a human hand, a cold, limp hand! I shouted, clutching the smothering, suffocating figure that had been Betty. Her smile was the same as the smile on the sculpture. Betty was becoming the sculpture again. She twisted as she tried to kiss me.

I tried to get up, but couldn't. "Betty, we are on a dead person. We are making love on a corpse!"

"We are love, we are life, we are the dead, Morton. This moment is a connection to the eternal. Close your eyes and breathe!"

"Breathe! We are having sex on a dead body, and you say to take a deep breath!" I slipped from beneath her and ran for the exit.

"Hakaptam! Pani tompasi!"

The doors slammed shut. I was trapped. I turned toward her. She stood on one foot, with the other behind her knee. She smiled as she gestured for me to return. The sheet over the corpse was gone. It was an old woman's body!

"Morton, you must return. You are so close to understanding the illusion of life and death. Come, lie beneath me once more, my love."

Her voice was a seductive rumble that came from somewhere that had never seen sunlight. Her beauty was irresistible, even though her hair had become a gigantic tangled mass and her fingernails were two inches long. I turned back to the door. It hadn't closed itself. Two ash-covered skull-shack demons were heading toward me with raised tridents. Betty's face now had the look of a glutton who had to have one more bite. Rats had appeared and were poised like retrievers at her feet. I was doomed. Rats! Surush! The Hooghly! I ran for the hole in the floor. A trident passed between my legs, and I tripped, falling headfirst down the hole into putrid blackness. Then I was in water so teeming with microbes that for a moment I felt as if I were in a bottle of soda pop.

I panicked. I needed to breathe. Where was the surface? I exhaled and felt bubbles move past my nose and forehead. I was right side up. I kicked and my head broke the surface. Above, there was the faint light of the temple. I heard voices. The fizzy water was so thick that I floated effortlessly. I was not in the river. Maybe it was only a cesspool. A rock landed in front of my face. Then another. Betty hadn't forgotten me. I had to get out of there. I paused and listened. I heard an echo, the echo of a drain. I wiped the slime from my face and slowly looked around while I treaded water. There it was, a faint light. Was it daylight? A candle?

A current moved toward the light. I started to swim and then I bumped something. No, not something—someone. It was Surush's body, jammed in the sewer. More rocks started falling into the cesspool. A torch landed on the water, illuminating my head. I heard shouting and then a spear landed as the torch sank. I tried to pull the body out of the sewer, but it felt as if it were being held by more than the current. Suddenly the body jolted and then rolled and started to move toward the light. I let go of it, not thinking that the splashing I heard ahead of me had any significance. I was in the sewer. The stench was overwhelming, as I had only enough room to keep my nose above water. The sewer widened as the sunlight grew closer.

Now I was in a cave with sandy banks, and a tangled mangrove kept me from the river. I could make out Surush's body and another body, which lay alongside it. No, it wasn't a body. It was a crocodile! It had pulled his body out of the sewer. Voices emanated from the sewer. The skull-shack demons were coming. Another crocodile had appeared and was headed toward me. If I went to the river, I was a dead man. If I stayed in the sewer, I'd be skewered rat food or end up next to Surush.

The crocodile charged. As I moved toward the sewer, a spear crossed my shoulder and hit the crocodile's jaw, forcing it shut. I jumped onto the back of the stunned creature and grabbed the spear. As I did, the crocodile began to roll. I pushed my thumb into its left eye. The rolling stopped and became an attempted dive, but I pulled back on the spear and kept the animal on the surface. Using the spear, I turned him toward an opening in the mangrove and the river. It was impossible but it was working. Just like the guy at Coney Island, I was riding a crocodile.

As I left the mangrove and entered the Hooghly River, I saw a lone fishing boat in the distance. All I knew was that Calcutta lay downstream. I aimed the crocodile toward the boat. There was a look of amazement in the fisherman's eyes as I approached his boat. I think he took me for a deity before he tried to paddle away. I came alongside the boat, and he hit the crocodile with his paddle, knocking the spear out of the creature's jaw. The beast rolled and then dived as I jumped into the boat. From the temple, I heard Betty's voice. She was screaming something in Hindi at the fisherman. He began to beat me with the paddle.

"Let me on your boat, you fool!" I cried.

"*Mutti harma walla*," he shouted as he beat me with the paddle.

Suddenly the boat rolled, tossing us overboard; the crocodile had rammed the boat! I pulled myself onto the boat, but there was no paddle. It was still in the fisherman's hands. I reached out and tried to take it, but he wouldn't let go. I didn't want him back in the boat, for he would surely push me overboard or take me to Betty. The crocodile had disappeared, but I was afraid to use my hands as paddles. I needed the paddle. I grabbed the paddle again and pulled it toward the boat, smiling and motioning the fellow to come aboard. I had to risk it. I stood as I pulled upward on the paddle until he had a grasp on the gunwale and released the paddle. As his weight rolled the boat, I balanced myself and kicked his head. Caught unaware, he fell backward. I had the paddle and open water. I looked back and there, above the mangrove, was Betty. She stood in the entrance to the sanctum.

"Morton, you have forsaken light! May darkness curse your soul!"

I blew her a kiss as I paddled toward Calcutta. I found a few rags on the boat, enough to fashion a simple loincloth and be decent enough to get to Foster's mission. Because it is hard to distinguish the pious from the insane in Calcutta, I was given several rupees on my walk.

"House wallah, house wallah," I called as I entered the compound. "Ganesh, please gather my things. I must leave for Darjeeling this morning."

"Sahib, where are your clothes? Sahib not here last night. Sahib maybe foolish? Dacoits?"

"What does that word mean?"

"Robbers," said Ganesh.

"Yes, yes, robbers. Dacoits very dangerous, most desperate," I said. By now the entire staff had gathered, and the chatter was in full force.

"Sahib very lucky. Dacoits very desperate people, always killing, killing. Sahib tell police now."

Dacoits, that was the excuse I needed. One of the staff rushed forward with a newspaper, tapping the pictures of dead victims

"Quite true. The papers are always full of pictures of people murdered by dacoits," said Foster, who had appeared, seemingly from nowhere. "You are a lucky man, Morton. Might be best if you went down to the police and made a report. Once they know this is happening, put a lid on it they will. Actually it's not that common; papers tend to use the same photographs again and again. Where did you say it happened, Reverend?"

I had hoped to get away without having to talk. The more I talked, the more the truth would reveal itself. I'd stick to simple lies. "I took a walk. When I decided to return, I realized that I was lost. Must have been later than I thought, for there was no one around. Then I saw a rickshaw driver. I told him Chowringhee Sutter Street. He nodded and I climbed in and we were off. I guess I fell asleep and woke up just as the rickshaw stopped. I opened my eyes, expecting to see the mission, but it was as dark and empty a place as where I had met the rickshaw driver. The next thing I knew, several fellows were on me. Took everything, even my clothes. It was near the river, and I saw lights downstream, which I knew had to be Calcutta. I found a boat and started paddling."

The entire mission staff had gathered around—and why not. How often does one see a sahib in his underwear?

Foster said, "Going out alone in India is seldom a good idea. The transition from urban to rural can be quite sudden here. Not like the straight, well-lit streets of New York, I imagine. After you clean up, we'll go to the police headquarters and make a report."

"Of course," I said. Foster believed me. That was the important part. I'd find a reason to delay the police visit. Now it was time to pack and catch the next train to Darjeeling.

"Go shower and dress, Reverend. We will notify the authorities after breakfast," said Foster.

"But sahib leave with Betty."

Foster's smile vanished. "What's this? You left with Betty?"

It was Ganesh. He must have seen me with Betty. I took Ganesh for an honest fool, but I could be wrong, I had to destroy his credibility instantly.

"No, Ganesh, I did not go with Betty," I said firmly. I waited to see if supporters or witnesses came forward. There was silence.

Ganesh had a momentary look of confusion and then repeated, "Sahib get in rickshaw with woman. Woman had Betty's face."

"Ganesh, you are wrong. I did not go with Betty. A rickshaw stopped when I was on the street. It was Betty. We spoke and she went on her way."

Foster's head was shaking. He was confused—good. Now I had to prove Ganesh a liar. Ganesh had been a waiter during the dinner and had been very attentive, explaining every dish. But he had been curt with Betty. I hoped wasn't the only one who had noticed that I was with Betty.

"Ganesh, last night at dinner, you told me Betty was a prostitute. You said, 'Sahib go with dirty woman. Sahib be man. Sahib give Ganesh baksheesh.' You are angry because I rejected your base and degrading proposition, so now you have decided to lie to get revenge." I paused, I had said enough and I was starting to believe my own lie. I stepped toward Ganesh with all the dignity I could. I put my nose to his face and looked into his eyes.

Foster moved between us as if to prevent a blow. He hesitated and then spoke. "Ganesh, you are to pack your things immediately. Arun will see that you are paid what is owed. You are never to return to the mission. Is that understood?"

"But Reverend Foster—."

"There is no need to explain. Lying and pandering are inexcusable acts," Foster responded.

I thought now might be the moment to inject compassion into the conversation and also cement my alibi. I turned to Ganesh. "I need my luggage taken to the station. And I need a rickshaw. I haven't much time."

"Me, sahib? Sahib said Ganesh is liar," he mumbled.

"Reverend Tutter, surely after what has occurred, you don't want Ganesh to take your things to the station," said Foster.

Ganesh was shaking. I didn't know if it was rage or fear, but I took his hands in mine and brought them together as I bowed my head. "God, you have given me the courage to speak the truth, but you have also given me a greater gift, your wisdom: 'Be kind to one another, tenderhearted, forgiving one another, as God in Christ forgave you.'" I brought his hands to my lips and then released them as I stepped back. There was silence. I glanced at Foster. His eyes were closed in meditation. Ganesh had been humiliated for being honest. His life at the mission was over. I had to leave for Darjeeling as soon as possible. Mallory and the rest of the team were only a day or two from leaving. If I had to make the trek to Everest alone, the going would be extremely tough.

I turned to Foster and said, "Please, as a brother in Christ, forgive Ganesh, for I feel that in his heart he is a good man."

"Two minutes ago you destroyed this man's reputation. Now you say I should keep him."

"Reverend Foster, we are Christian men. Our values are neither inherent nor blood borne. Nor can we drink them as wine, that we might be intoxicated by them. We must strive to live them. We are given words and lessons to guide us. Let his errors be a lesson for us."

"'I say not unto thee, until seven times: but, until seventy times seven,'" said Foster as he took my hand.

Ganesh shouted, "Mr. Tutter, rickshaw ready. Sahib must hurry. Train leave soon."

"Reverend Tutter, it is an honor to know you. I shall never forget you," said Foster as he put his hand on my shoulder. "Ganesh, see to it that Reverend Tutter gets a first-class cabin where the window bars are intact."

"Yes, Reverend Foster."

"Window bars?" I asked.

"One sleeps a bit sounder knowing the bars are all there," said Foster.

"Very well, Reverend Foster. It's been a privilege to meet you and see the mission. When I return to New York, I'm going to recommend that our congregation start a fund for your mission. Good-bye."

3

TRAIN TO DARJEELING

I waited on the platform while Ganesh purchased my ticket. I was surrounded by a hot, malarial bog of humanity. Unbearable humidity. Every living thing was sweating constantly. How could the mind consider anything when there was nothing but heat, constant heat. How could one separate the individual from the environment when there was no escape from the heat? People milled about, most I suspect having no real purpose to their lives—and yet living. A few Europeans were on the platform. I would meet them later on the train. But the Indians, such as Ganesh—I wondered what kept them going. Faith. It wasn't the Western ego. Except Betty. Now there was an ego.

"Reverend Tutter, sahib. First class full."

"What! Why?"

"Darjeeling is hill station. Very beautiful, very popular. Many people going, sahib. You see here, seat posting for 12:00 noon and later. Express train all full. Ganesh has purchased ticket for third class. Not to worry, windows are secure. Sahib sleep on luggage."

"I'll sleep—"

"Yes, no problem. Car is locked at night. If you sleep on luggage, you are safe."

"Are you sure that first class is full?"

"Yes, sahib, you can see postings here. Every line full in first class."

"Wait, these lists are the seat assignments?"

"Yes, they are posted so that those having tickets may find their seats."

"Why doesn't the conductor help them?"

"They are lazy people. Once they post the list, they retire to office for tea."

"Look here, Ganesh, this name has been crossed out."

"That is correction. Many people, many trains."

I glanced over the lists, looking for non-Indian names. I could only hope that they were not familiar with the system. I spotted Crowden, A. I ripped the list from the post and put it in my pocket.

"Ganesh, run to the ticket counter. Say you represent A. Crowden and that the ticket has been lost. Get a replacement. Here are some rupees to bribe the agent."

"Yes, sahib."

An Indian can negotiate a line in minutes when it would take an Anglo an hour. In a flash, Ganesh returned with the ticket.

"Very good, Ganesh. I'm all settled now. We only have to find car 35, compartment 12."

"Tutter, sahib, you are taking seat that is not yours."

"Yes, I am. Come, we have to find my car." The compartment was empty and I took a seat. Ganesh brought in my luggage and then hung about the door. "Baksheesh, Ganesh?" I asked.

"No, sahib, I am only waiting."

"Waiting for what?"

"Only waiting."

"But what are you waiting for?"

"Only waiting, sahib."

"Ganesh, there is nothing to wait for. All my luggage is here. The train is about to leave."

"That is true."

"Then why don't you return to the mission?"

"Very well. I'll return to the mission."

"Ganesh."

"Yes, sahib?"

"Ganesh, I hope that you appreciate the fact that I persuaded Reverend Foster to keep you at the mission. I owe you nothing, yet I felt it was the right thing to do. Every man deserves a second chance. I wish you the best."

"Yes, I am grateful. Sahib is a good man."

I was dumbfounded. I had expected acknowledgment but not praise. He had to be a liar. How could any person, even a Hindu, call me a good man after what I had done to him? I stood and looked him in the eye. "Ganesh, do you believe in God?"

He turned his head from side to side. There was an odd look of contentment on his face. "There is a god and there is God. You see a god and I see God. Reverend Tutter sees salvation. I see eternity."

"Eternity?" The train jolted. It was under way. Ganesh was gone.

"Excuse me, I believe you have my cabin. My ticket has this number on it," came a distinctly American accent hidden behind a large suitcase.

"I don't see how, unless the ticket reservation clerk erred. I checked the platform list before boarding, and my name was there."

"That might be part of the problem. I couldn't find the list. I was told there would be a list on the platform with my cabin number on it. I've never been on an Indian train before. I did find this number inside the station though. There was an emergency at the hotel, so there was no one to escort me, only a rickshaw driver who spoke no English."

"What a horrible introduction to Indian trains. Tell you what. I'll go find a conductor and get it all sorted out. Why don't you put your luggage here and just wait until I return."

"That is very kind of you. I feel a bit overwhelmed, what with the masses of people, the language, and of course the heat."

"I understand," I said and headed toward the front of the train. Ganesh was right. The train was full. A few people were standing in the passageway with their luggage. I figured I would offer the conductor the cost of a ticket when I found him. Actually, there were three conductors, all in one compartment. They were pleading, begging really, their hands upturned. They spoke in Hindi, with an occasional English word for emphasis. I looked into the compartment. It was occupied by a woman with several goats. They were trying to get her and the goats out of the cabin, but she wasn't budging. I picked the fattest conductor, the one with stubble on his cheeks and chin.

"Excuse me. I have a problem with my compartment. A woman with a ticket claims to be assigned to my compartment. I wanted you to look at my ticket. Is there a problem with it?" I gave him my ticket, along with rupees folded under it.

He took the ticket and slipped the cash into his pocket. Looking at the ticket, he shook his head. "There is no problem with your ticket, sir. Most likely it is a problem with her booking. I will speak with the lady. Sometimes the booking is a problem. Unfortunately, this problem cannot be corrected once the train departs. It is quite common, people coming without proper tickets. You are not to worry, sir. She can seek recourse in Calcutta at railway headquarters."

"At least the poor woman can have the problem investigated."

"Yes, sir. The problem is the patience of the people failing to recognize the complexity of the booking process, sir."

I had picked the right conductor. He had a system. I went back to the compartment.

"I spoke to a conductor. He assured me that it can be sorted out easily. He'll be here in a few minutes. My name is Tutter. Reverend Morton Tutter," I said, extending my hand. "You're American. Kansas, I'd say."

"I'm pleased to meet you, Reverend Tutter. I do appreciate your help. My name is Miss Annie Crowden from Des Moines, Iowa. It's not Kansas but it's pretty darn close. It's my first time in India, actually my first time out of Iowa."

"Your accent of course told me that you were an American. But there is a feminine quality about you that I have found to exist in only one place on earth—the American Midwest."

"And what quality is that?"

"A soft-spoken, shy, dutiful demeanor and an understated beauty."

"Oh no. I just try to be polite—"

"You see? That is exactly what I am referring to. Are you on vacation?"

"Oh no, I'm on my way to Darjeeling to teach. My aunt is a missionary and has secured a position for me. And you, Mr. Tutter, are you vacationing?"

"Some might call it that, but I'm part of the Everest expedition. I'm on my way to Darjeeling to meet the rest of the members of my team. From there we will start the trek to Tibet."

"How could one possibly undertake such an adventure? Tibet is so remote. Have they ever seen Americans before?"

"Oh, a few. My parents and myself."

"Really?"

"My parents were missionaries. We lived on the edge of Tibet in China, but the local people were Tibetans."

"Are you eager to return and see old friends?"

"I doubt I'll be seeing old friends, as Everest is in a completely different part of the country. But I joined the expedition in order that I might enter the country as a climber and survey the potential for Christianity. Tibet is a ship in a storm with the souls cast overboard in a pagan sea. The challenge is to take the helm. Then one must nail a cross to the mast, rescue the drowning, and steer the ship into the arms of our Lord."

"How inspirational, Reverend Tutter."

"It is my duty."

"It is a gift to be given such a duty."

There was a knock on the compartment door.

"Tickets, please. Tickets, please."

"Here is the conductor I spoke with. He'll sort this out," I said.

"Oh yes, sir. And you are the lady with the improper ticketing. Ticket, please, madam."

"I don't have an improper ticket. I—

"Miss Crowden, let the conductor sort this out. After all, it is his job," I said.

Annie gave the conductor her ticket. He was a true grifter. Slowly he looked over the ticket. Then he checked his purse before saying, "Excuse me for a moment," while he stepped back into the passageway.

Annie panicked. "Oh no, something must be wrong. Why would he leave?"

"I don't know. But many of these types seem to feel they have more authority than they have."

He returned, slowly rubbing the ticket between a thumb and forefinger. Looking up from the ticket to Annie, he said, "Madam, where did you get your ticket?"

"The hotel desk clerk got it for me. Is there a problem?"

Annie turned to me then to the conductor then back to me. For a moment, I felt a twinge of guilt. I just wanted a private seat. I didn't want to make her cry.

"This ticket was purchased at a private booking office. Those rascals care nothing for the interests of the traveler. This is a used ticket. It is a most common problem. Unfortunately, madam, you are an irregular traveler and must purchase another ticket. You can buy a lady's second-class ticket. Plus there is a fine."

Wow, I thought, *I paid a bribe and got a dramatic performance.* This guy knew his business.

"How can that be? My hotel was—"

"This is India, madam. There are many, many desperate people. You must have a ticket, madam. No exceptions."

"Yes, I know I must have a ticket. I just can't believe the hotel would let something like this happen. But I suppose if a little money can fix it, it's not a problem after all."

"Yes, madam, a little money can fix it," said the conductor as handed her a ticket. "The second-class ladies' car is three cars back, madam. It is best to go before the next stop. Then you will have a seat," he said as he left.

"Miss Crowden, I'm sorry that here you are in a strange land on a mission to help others, and you have been victimized," I said.

"Yes, but one mustn't let the actions of one person tarnish one's image of the rest. I simply must be more watchful. Now, how I can manage to get all my things back to the other car before the next station? Do you think my luggage will be safe there?"

"Why don't you leave your luggage here in my compartment. It's the least I can do for you."

"That is most kind of you. Are you sure it is not an inconvenience?"

"Not at all. I'd offer to let you stay here, but I feel that would not be proper. Please go and find your seat in the ladies' car and after you are settled in, return to my compartment so that I may escort you to the dining car."

"Dinner, that's very generous of you, Reverend. I would like that. Thank you."

There was a knock on my door a couple of hours later, "Reverend

Tutter, are you sure you want to do this? The dinner must be very expensive."

"Nonsense, that's what money is for. Let's eat," I said as I took her hand and stepped through the doorway. In a moment, she had fallen into my arms, her breasts were pressed against me. We rolled forward through the passageway and landed on the floor. The train had stopped. We lay there for a few moments, too confused by what had happened to move. I tried to put my arm around Annie, but she instantly twisted free and jumped to her feet.

"What happened? Are you OK, Reverend Tutter? I felt like I was thrown from a horse and almost landed in a fire," she said, looking at me as she straightened her blouse. She was amazingly calm, unlike the rest of the passengers, for whom the shouting, screaming, and panic was just beginning. Of the chatter around us, I understood just one word, repeated again and again, "Elephant! Tusker! Tusker!"

"I think we've hit an elephant!" I said.

Actually, it was the elephant that had hit us. I learned this after I got off the train and worked my way to the locomotive. The front wheels had been knocked off the tracks. The bull was standing his ground on the tracks some yards ahead. Each time the crew approached the locomotive, the bull would raise his trunk and roar. The crew refused to initiate repairs.

"Elephant very disturbed by train," said the engineer. "He think locomotive elephant also. Very angry. Maybe by tomorrow he relax."

"Tomorrow! I need to be in Darjeeling on time. I'll miss the departure of the expedition."

"Sahib not in Darjeeling on time. Tusker is on tracks. Train wait till tusker leaves. Tusker in musth."

"What is mush?"

"No, sahib. Musth. Tusker in very manly way. He think train is other tusker."

"Nonsense. Get me a gun and I'll send him a message about sitting on the tracks. Where is the conductor?"

"Sahib no kill tusker. Tusker leave soon," said the engineer.

"Where is the conductor?"

"He is having tea in buffet car."

"Tea? Two hundred passengers stranded in the middle of nowhere, and he is having tea?"

"Not stranded, sahib. Just delay. Elephant leave soon."

"The tusker had better be gone before I return," I said as I headed for my cabin. I had a rifle in my luggage. It was time to teach the beast and the lazy trainmen a lesson. "A poke between the eyes with my .30-30 Winchester will put an end to this nonsense," I said aloud.

"You are not seriously planning to dispatch the beast?" came a voice from behind me.

It was a white man's voice. I turned. He was a little man with a large mustache, his eyes barely able to meet mine because of the brim of his pith helmet. "I sure am. I'll be doing the local economy a favor. Nothing wrong with a train being on time," I said.

"I'm afraid that's not permitted," He said as he tapped his crop against his open palm "You are in a reserve forest, and therefore the animal is protected under the Reserve Forest Act," he said as he motioned to an Indian trainman. "Conductor, you will find Sergeant Webster and inform him that Mr.—

"My name is Tutter. Reverend Morton Tutter."

"Very well. See that the Reverend Tutter is not permitted access to his 30-30 or other weapons."

"Yes, sir, right away, chop-chop."

"I'm afraid I shall require you to return to your carriage until the matter is settled," he said.

"And just who are you?" I asked.

"I am First Warden William Terry, warden for the Mahananda Reserve Forest."

"Are you telling me I have to sit and wait until some crazy elephant has decided that the train locomotive is not going to make a pass at his cow?"

"If you wish to put it crudely, yes."

"I don't think you have the authority to do that."

"My dear Mr. Tutter, I do have the authority, and I must remind you that you are in a land of law, not the Wild West, where men settle their differences with six-guns."

"Sitting in the middle of a snake-infested jungle, waiting on a jousting elephant to kill us, is close enough to the Wild West that a six-gun makes a lot of sense. OK, how about I take some of these workers and some pots and pans and we drive him off."

I turned to the crew. They were still staring at the locomotive, gesturing at the wheels and arguing. "What do you say? Are you fellows up to it? If you let this elephant get away with this, it'll become a habit. Your homes and families will be next. Do you want to return to living in caves?"

There was silence and then chatter and head rolling. Finally, I heard, "Sahib must wait. Tusker kill."

"So no one will go with me? Is every last one of you a coward" I moved into the lantern light. "Every one of you is afraid. It's because you believe you are no better than that beast. This is man's world because God willed it so. But man must accept the challenge. In my country, America, we had heroes such as Daniel Boone, Davy Crockett, and Buffalo Bill. They tamed the wilderness. They were American pioneers and role models for those who aspire to bravery and freedom. You men can be such men also." I paused for emphasis and then continued: "God has given free will to man but not to the dumb beasts. They wander in the eternal darkness of ignorance, seeking only to survive and to indulge in, as we see with this tusker, the most base satisfactions. Man has the torch of righteousness, but he must hold it high to let the light shine." I was just getting warmed up when a long, pulsating tonal sound overwhelmed the sermon.

The crew froze and then there were voices: "Tusker angry, tusker attack!"

Terry spoke, "Mr. Tutter, these are railroad employees, not cannon fodder for an American Wild West show. Cease this nonsense at once."

"These are free men, not animals. I believe they are outside of your jurisdiction."

"Preventing the injury or death of innocent men is within any decent man's jurisdiction." Terry turned to the conductor. "You will find Sergeant Watson of the railway police in the last car. Please ask him to come forward."

"Yes, sahib."

"Very well," I said. "I'll go it alone. I'll stare him down just like Daniel Boone did."

"Just like—

"Yep. That is, unless there is some edict that prohibits staring at elephants."

"There is no such edict, though societal mores do not allow the mentally deficient to harm themselves. But as you are an American, perhaps what I perceive as foolhardiness is a normal societal attribute. I am only interested in the protection of the elephant, sir."

"Oh, Warden Terry, isn't it amazing to see an elephant charging a train and winning! He is so proud standing there," said Annie with a sigh. For all her virtue, Annie was standing pretty close to Terry. Maybe she found his calm arrogance comforting in a time of confusion. I needed to remember that.

"It's not pride, Mrs. Crowden, it's merely male instinct in crude display. 'And God said, Let us make man in our image, after our likeness: and let them have dominion over the fish of the sea, and over the fowl of the air, and over the cattle, and over all the earth, and over every creeping thing that creepeth upon the earth.' I am the Lord's servant, Mrs. Crowden, and I intend to have this train arrive on time."

"Reverend Tutter, 'Let the waters bring forth abundantly the moving creature that hath life, and fowl *that* may fly above the earth in the open firmament of heaven,'" Annie cried as I stared down the tracks at the shadowy image of the bull. "Let him be!"

"I'm afraid your friend is set on some sort of religious crusade, madam," I heard Terry say to Annie as I marched into darkness.

The bull wasn't far—maybe twenty five yards—and he was standing square in the middle of the tracks. I kept my gaze fixed on his eyes. He was focused on me. That was good. His trunk and tail moved slightly. I didn't know for sure what this meant. Many a dog with a wagging tail has tried to bite me. I stopped six feet in front of him; any closer and I would be between his tusks. I kept my gaze fixed. Suddenly he stopped moving. He raised his head and stiffened his ears. I leaned forward, craning my neck, though I kept my arms down. I moved my head forward slowly, as if drilling into his brain. He did not move.

I shuffled slightly forward. I had to make him move back. I moved forward again. He lowered his head, his ears went back, and he stepped backward. *Retreat, beast, retreat in the name of God*, I said silently. I shuffled forward again. He was submitting. *Annie had better go back to Sunday school and learn how to interpret the scriptures*. The bull had stepped off the tracks and was backing down the grade. I was eye level with him when suddenly that odd pulsating tonal sound returned. It came from the bull. In an instant his ears were fully spread. He grabbed a bush and ripped it from the ground. I heard Terry in the background, laughing.

"I hope God has given you wings, Reverend Tutter, for you will need them."

The bull shook his mighty head and tossed the bush to the ground in defiance. I stepped back and tried to turn, but as I did, his trunk hit my leg, knocking me to the ground. I heard Annie scream. I lay trapped on the ground as he stood with one foot hovering over my chest while he raised his trunk and trumpeted victory. Then he stepped back and wrapped his trunk around my legs. In an instant I was hanging upside down. He swung me as one would a pocket watch. "Let me go, you stupid beast!" I shouted.

"I say, Reverend, best use Bengali with the old boy!" yelled the warden with a laugh.

The beast had raised me to eye level, as if to wish me a devil's farewell, when my rabbit's foot tumbled from my pants pocket, bounced off my hand and into his face, and then rolled across the ground. The bull reared back on his hind legs, crashed back on his front legs, and dropping me as he lowered his head, turned and trotted away. I was alive! My rabbit's foot had saved my life. I was shaken but OK. Luckily, no one else had been in a position to see what had happened.

"Well, Reverend Tutter, it seems the bull took pity on you, though God only knows why he should have," said Terry as he stood above me.

"Stop it! Can't you see he might be hurt? Reverend Tutter, are you OK?" asked Annie.

I would capitalize on Annie's compassion later, in a more private setting; for the moment, I had to pull the rug out from under Terry's ego. "I'm just dusty, Miss Crowden. I knew I could count on the Lord to protect me, and he did, though I'm starting to think he may have other priorities. Perhaps I should be more patient in the future."

"You were lucky he dropped you."

"It wasn't luck. It was the Lord. When the beast swung me, my crucifix dangled in front of him. He had no choice but to drop me. He was powerless, as we all are, in the face of the Lord."

Terry laughed. "Rubbish. I don't know what happened, but to tell us a crucifix frightened a musth bull elephant is ludicrous."

"Do you have a better explanation, Mr. Terry? When the elephant grabbed Reverend Tutter, you said that no power on earth could save him now," said Annie.

As I picked myself up from the ground, I said, ""If ye have faith as a grain of mustard seed, ye shall say unto this mountain, Remove hence to yonder place; and it shall remove; and nothing shall be impossible unto you.""

Annie threw her arms around me. "Oh yes, Reverend Tutter, nothing is impossible!"

"Miss Crowden, I believe we were on our way to dinner. Are you still hungry?"

"I am."

"Reverend Tutter, thank you. The dinner was wonderful, better than I could have imagined. I've never eaten a real meal, I mean a first-class meal, in a dining car or a fancy restaurant. To be in India with the fancy tables and the waiters in uniforms—it's like a play. It will make the night in the cattle car pass a little easier."

"Is it that bad?"

"It's crowded with women and children. Nature abhors a vacuum. If I don't fill my entire seat, someone else will. I had my feet up while reading, and when I put them down, I stepped on a woman lying on the floor!"

"You mean you won't have a seat when you return?"

"Oh no, it just means I have to melt into it. That's all. And now I must be getting back to my seat. I'm tired and it's embarrassing when I fall asleep at the table. Reverend Tutter, you have been so kind and generous. Thank you."

"It was my pleasure. I'll accompany you back to your seat."

"I'm afraid you can't do that."

"Why not?"

"Because I am in the ladies' car. Men are prohibited.

"Funny, the conductor told me, 'You will be protected from mischief.' But I'm not so sure a little mischief wouldn't be less troublesome than all the screaming children."

"Oh dear. I was imagining something quite different."

"Reverend Tutter, if you are anything like my five brothers, you were thinking of a harem, and a harem it is not. It is more of a three-ring circus composed of climbing kids, tired mothers, and food. I just remembered something. Before I return to my car, may I get my journal from your compartment?"

"Of course."

"I find reflecting on the day to be inspirational."

"So you find the evening the best time for reflection?" I asked as I opened my compartment door.

"Oh yes, I see it as a time of peace and order, when God's wisdom and plan become clear. I find mornings to be chaotic. Now, let's see, I know it is in one of these suitcases. I had it last night. Maybe it's this one up here," she said as she reached for a suitcase on the overhead storage shelf.

I stepped behind her, as if to help. "Annie," I whispered.

"Oh, never mind. I can remember my thoughts and write them down in the morning,"

As she turned and stepped toward the compartment door, there was a knock.

"It must be the conductor, I bet he has found you a private compartment and is looking for you," I said. As I unlocked the door, it came swinging toward me. I fell back against Annie, and we both fell to the floor. There above me were three skinny men with fabric covering their heads and faces. I pushed myself off Annie and stood up to challenge them until I saw their knives. One of them pulled the door closed while the second waved his knife. We were trapped. The third began to open the suitcases.

"Reverend Tutter, they're robbers! Stop them," Annie said as she kicked me.

"Don't be afraid, once I get the knife they'll run like dogs," I shouted as I lunged for the knife. I missed it and felt it touch my throat. Then I must have fainted, because the next thing I saw was a hand with long fingers and long fingernails holding a bowl above me. A pungent liquid dripped from the bowl onto my forehead.

"What's going on?" I cried as I pushed the bowl and hands away.

I heard Annie's voice. "Reverend Tutter, you are conscious. You had blood on your neck, so I went to find a doctor—"

"What?"

"The thieves had knives, don't you remember? Your throat was cut."

The long fingers were once again holding the bowl above my head. "Don't touch me!" I shouted at the man with a painted face and long, matted hair and beads around his neck.

"Reverend Tutter, he is a doctor. I brought him here to help," said Annie.

"He doesn't look like a doctor. How do you know he is a doctor?"

"The conductor said so. And he is wearing glasses. As a matter of fact, he is the only Indian I've seen on this train wearing glasses. That must mean something."

"It means he's wearing glasses—that's what it means. Do you think a real doctor would have a red stripe on his forehead and yellow writing on his cheeks?" I said as I felt the doctor gently grasp my wrist.

"Hey, what are you doing? Let go of me!"

"I am checking the kapha dosha. You are dominated by this dosha; that is why that rascal's knife didn't kill you. You have thick skin, a well-developed body, and excellent muscular function. But your vata dosha is very weak. This will cause anxiety and nervousness. No doubt that is why you fainted."

"I didn't faint. After the thief's knife missed he hit me on the head with his other hand. He knocked me out!"

"No, Mr. Reverend, it is the dosha. I knew it the moment I saw you. Now will you allow me to continue with the thalam treatment? It is lasting only twenty minutes and is economical."

"You want to drip oil on my head and have me pay you for it?" I said as I got up and stood in front of the mirror. "It's nothing a bandanna can't fix," I said. "I don't need your services. You can go."

"Very well, then. I will charge only for the examination. Dr. Babuwala is very reasonable always."

"You want me to pay you?"

"I came because I was requested, and of course it is my duty as a professional to help the injured."

"You're nothing but a charlatan."

"Then I'll pay him," said Annie. "How much do you want, Dr. Babuwala?"

"As you like, madam, as you like," he said, cupping his hands before her.

Annie must have paid plenty, because he never even bothered to count the coins in his hands; he just smiled and left.

A guard and the conductor stood in the doorway. "Sir," the conductor said, "you were very foolish. You must never open door at night in a first-class cabin. Mr. Tutter, there are many poor people in India, and they are constantly conspiring against the lawful inhabitants of our country. They stand ready to initiate a desperate action once the opportunity is present. That is why there are bars and locks in the first-class compartments. We have armed guards on the train. They are constantly watching for these rascals, but it takes only a moment to succumb to their nefarious activity if you are careless."

"I understand." I looked at the guard, who was rolling his head in agreement. His rifle was so long that it would be impossible to handle in a passageway or compartment. He could be on the lookout for dacoits, but he couldn't be everywhere. "You are quite right. I will be more careful. Thank you."

"You are welcome, sir. Good night. Madam, good night."

I turned to Annie. "What happened?"

"Well, you fainted—"

"I didn't faint. That fellow's fist knocked me unconscious when I tried to grab the knife," I said.

"And the thieves were searching our luggage," she continued. "Well, two of them were, and one was shaking a knife at me while he stood over you."

"Was I robbed?"

"They started with mine. You can see how things are scattered around the compartment. I'm sure they were disappointed to find a suitcase with four dozen Bibles inside. Look, one of them hit me upside the head with one of them. All they found was a watch and a necklace."

"What about my luggage? Did they rob me?" I asked as I checked my jacket pocket; my wallet was still there.

"They started to search your things, but like I said, one of them hit me with a Bible. I was standing over here, and when he started to hit me again, that was when I noticed the emergency brake. So as I raised one arm to block the Bible, I leaned over and pulled the brake with the other. In the chaos that followed, they panicked and left."

"Well, my valuables are safe; that is the most important thing," I said.

"I'm afraid I lost my watch and necklace though."

"They weren't able to catch the thieves?"

"No. And the conductor recommended that I return to the ladies' car. He said it was safer," Annie was repacking her scattered belongings. "Well, I'm ready for bed. Good night, Reverend Tutter."

I made a last-ditch effort. "Are you sure it is safe in the women's car? After all, it is one large compartment."

"The conductor said that because it is an open car, the thieves cannot get you alone. And of course men are barred."

"Ah yes, the men are barred. No doubt that is the proper way in this pagan land," I said.

"I do believe, Reverend Tutter, that people can be moral even though they are not Christian. I have found that, for the most part, Indian men are gentlemen."

I stepped into the passageway. "Very well. Good night, Mrs. Crowden."

4

DARJEELING

I arrived in Darjeeling with just one day to spare. I had planned it that way; by arriving late, I avoided socializing more than necessary and forewent the possibility of igniting any antagonism, which could end with my being excluded from the trip. I was an outsider who had bought his way in. I had no guarantee I would stay in.

Better-qualified men had been dropped already. The official reason Mr. Finch had been excluded was that he had kept his lecture proceeds and was divorced, but it was really about his being Australian. Only the royal family had kept Finch as part of the expedition in 1922. For this 1924 expedition, Mallory had insisted that Finch be part of the party, but to no avail. Mallory had told me that Hinks was the reason Finch had been excluded, but amazingly Hinks never complained about me wanting to be part of the expedition. Though Mallory had never said it, I thought that he and Hinks had such low regard for Americans that they felt I would be lucky to complete the march to base camp. Unlike Finch, who had nearly reached the summit in 1922, I was no threat to English pride. I knew little about the English, except what my uncle had told me: "Perfidious Albion must never be trusted." In retrospect, my concerns were for naught, as I came to realize the group had very little interest in me.

As Annie and I stood outside the rail station, waiting for her contact from the mission to arrive, I heard a voice call my name.

"Is that one of the climbers, Reverend?" asked Annie.

"Yes, it's Mr. Mallory, the lead climber. Well it looks like I won't have time to escort you to the mission, as it seems they are well under way. I must remain here and get up to speed as soon as possible. I will see you before we leave though."

"I understand, Reverend Tutter. Until later," said Annie.

"Reverend Tutter, what a surprise! We had all but given up on you," called Mallory from a storage shed across the tracks. I crossed the tracks and greeted him.

Mallory said, "Mr. Shebbeare, optimist that he is, has sent your kit on to Kalimpong, along with the rest of the equipment. But I'm afraid we've made no provision for your personal porter. I'm sure you'll agree it was only fair that we not take on the expense for an extra man, and of course there was the thought you might never arrive."

"But I'll need a porter."

"Afraid I can't help you with sorting out a chap, but I think you'll find Shebby of help with that; he has a way with those fellows. I'll introduce you. Come along."

Shebbeare was in front of a warehouse, gesturing and shouting to several coolies, who were about to carry off the last of the supplies. He spoke a few words of Tibetan and Hindi, but it was his demeanor that struck me. He was quite at ease with the coolies. It was not just his smile. It was his posture. He actually took on their gestures and movements when he interacted with them. It was obvious that the porters liked him.

"I say, Shebby, this is Reverend Tutter, the American. Seems he needs a Sherpa. Would you point him in the right direction? I must find General Bruce before he departs," said Mallory.

"Mr. Tutter, the American cowboy. So you took on a bull elephant, did you?"

"You heard? Why, I've just arrived."

"You made quite an impression. Word of miracles travels fast here. You ought to be careful about making an impression on the natives. You might find yourself locked in a temple, performing miracles, for the rest of your life. It must be an American trait. I remember in the Great War, a chap from Ohio charged a Jerry tank at Villers-Bretonneux. It crushed the poor fellow. Tragic. Were you in the war, Reverend Tutter?"

"No, I was in the seminary."

"Pacifist like Howard Somervell, are you?"

"No."

"I see. Nevertheless, you are quite lucky. I've seen a number of people killed by bulls in musth. Quite literally a Jekyll and Hyde experience. A rarity of nature, a beast so generally pleasant going quite mad."

"You seem fond of them."

"I am. I worked with them for years in the Forestry Department. Pity we won't be using them on the expedition. I daresay General Bruce would make a go of them if he could. See himself as Hannibal crossing the Himalayas. But we'll be sticking to mules, horses, and yaks. Less likely to crush the porters. Not to mention that those lamas might find them to be incarnations of some bloody fools and forbid their use. Mr. Mallory said you needed a Sherpa."

"Yes, a Sherpa or a porter."

"Don't recommend a porter. Best to have a chap who has seen snow, and that would be a Sherpa. You're early, so they'll still be sober. Mind you, we've picked the best and healthiest. Why, Dr. Hingston even checked them for worms. Make sure you make them take off their shoes and gloves—some of the blokes are missing toes and fingers. Personally, I find those things to be quite useful."

"Sober," I repeated.

"Yes, they love their *thoo-n*, rice beer. Head over to the market plaza. That is where they congregate."

"I thought Mallory was going to arrange all of this."

"You can grouse, Reverend, but the fact is that if you want a man, you'll have to go and find him. Mr. Mallory had little say in the logistics. He is a climber, which is a good thing because the man can't tell a spanner from a coffeepot. It was me and Colonel Norton who handled the kits. By the way, did you bring a tent? I didn't see one in your kit."

"A tent? No, I assumed I would be sharing one."

"There was nothing on my list about that. Not to worry. When you go find a Sherpa, you'll see that there are old survey tents available—quite good, actually—very popular with the traders and bandits. Do you want to take Karma Paul along with you to translate? He knows the fellows and will steer you in the right direction."

"Who's that?"

"Our sirdar, top-notch fellow. He's right over there with Colonel Norton." He motioned the man over.

We shook hands as Shebbeare made the introductions, "Karma Paul, this is Reverend Tutter, a member of the expedition. Sort of a goodwill guest, I suppose. Are you a climber, Reverend? I don't recall seeing equipment slated for you."

"I don't plan on climbing. I'm only documenting the land and people we encounter so that our missionaries will be prepared when Tibet is opened to foreigners. But of course I will assist if necessary."

"Ah yes. Perhaps a bit of preaching too? I was warned I might have to make room for Bibles."

"No Bibles other than mine and a couple of extras."

"Very well. Karma Paul, would you be so kind as to accompany Reverend Tutter so that he may find a Sherpa?" asked Shebbeare.

"I am helping Colonel Norton organize the porters, but I can take him to the market, where he can find them," said Karma Paul.

"That's all I need," I said in Tibetan.

"You speak Tibetan? Where did you learn?"

"In Amdo. My parents were missionaries."

"Christian missionaries?"

"Yes, why?" I asked.

"Missionaries raised me after I became an orphan."

"Really?"

"Yes. Here in Darjeeling, Christian missionaries took me in. They were good people, but I am still a Buddhist."

"I see."

"Did you come to convert the Tibetan people? You must not do that. The lamas are very strict. If they catch you, you will be punished."

"Oh no, I'm a guest of the expedition as a result of my congregation's contribution to the expedition. My church wants me to give a full report and description of Tibet and its people when I return. I'll describe the hardships of the people that are the result of their pagan lives, but I'm not here to proselytize. The report will be factual."

"'Their pagan lives.' You surely are a Bible thumper," said Shebbeare as he stroked his beard.

"Not at all. I only comment on the fact that culture contributes to progress and religion contributes to culture. Some are better than others; that should be obvious to anyone living above a feudal existence."

"I've never considered choosing a religion. It is something that you got when you were born, that's all. One is the same as another, I daresay."

Shebbeare was a hardworking man dedicated to his duties. He seemed to have little interest in esoteric thought, which made him a good choice to manage logistics. We said good-bye, and I left for the marketplace with Karma Paul.

"You will not find a Sherpa," he said.

"But Mr. Shebbeare said I would."

Karma Paul stopped and looked me directly in the eye. "The only Sherpas still here are men with no families or homes. That is why they stay. They are not good men. You bring bad luck upon yourself if you hire one. Look there," he said, pointing across the street. "You see those men standing by the tea shop? Once they climbed mountains, but now they only want *rakshi*. That man with the big smile, his name is Pasang but we call him Sportsman."

"Why?"

"He was a monk, but he was very bad and was banished from the monastery. Now he is a Sherpa and lives only for rakshi, women, and gambling. He is lost man"

A loud voice interrupted our conversation. "You there, stop where you are!"

I looked at Karma Paul. He looked at the shouting man and then at me. "It's our leader, General Bruce," he said.

"You're the American, aren't you?" he said, extending a hand.

"I am."

"Come along, soldier."

"I'm afraid I can't, sir. I need to hire a Sherpa."

Shebbeare stood at the general's side. "Do as General Bruce says, Reverend. You're in His Majesty's army now," he said with a laugh.

General Bruce said, "Nonsense, hiring a Sherpa can wait. It's imperative for all members of the expedition to meet at the Gymkhana and touch glasses. We'll be leaving soon, and this is the last place for a man and his mates to have a drink that won't contain fly specks or sand. Karma Paul, go and get the coolies under way; mustn't waste any more time, chop-chop."

"Yes, General, right this moment, sir, chop-chop," said Karma Paul.

"But if I don't find a Sherpa soon, they'll all be gone," I pleaded.

"Best come along, Reverend Tutter, or the general will call his Gurkhas."

"Now, Shebby, this is a social, not a military, affair. Nevertheless, every member is hereby ordered to attend," he roared as he turned to two uniformed Gurkhas standing behind him. "Tingbo, Manslu, go and find the others and send them to the club, on the double, chop-chop," he roared again.

5

THE GYMKHANA

The gymkhana was like being in paradise, above the clouds. No minister could have aspired to a greater building. Instead of angels, there were dozens of men whose function was to make it apparent that they were unnecessarily employed. The wood panels were adorned with weapons and animal trophies. It was a Rajhalla, a beacon of Britannia on the edge of the unknown. It was the perfect location for the final motivating speeches before setting off to conquer Everest.

"Impressive, isn't it?" said General Bruce as he gestured around the interior. "Daresay it's the finest gymkhana in all India. I presented that fellow to the club myself. He was nearly 50 stone, all muscle, impressive fangs, don't you think? He was a man-eater, though I think he was even more of a woman-eater; I found several bronze bangles and pieces of jewelry lodged in the old boy's intestines. Do hope to put a rhino right there over the doorway before I retire. A message to those leaving the club of the adversity that exists outside these walls. Nothing like the charge of a rhino to remind a man of his frailty."

There was nothing frail about the general. He was nearly sixty yet he had the strength of a twenty year old. He stood like a boxer throwing commands instead of punches. His big chest, big head and his big mustache made him as imposing as any rhino he would nail to a wall. "Do you hunt, Reverend Tutter?"

"Squirrels."

"Oh?"

"Yes, in Central Park. I'm quite good at it. I've gotten two with one stone on occasion. Have to use a slingshot so as to avoid notice."

"Hunting in the park? Isn't that poaching?"

"I think of it as management; there are a lot of squirrels there."

"Reverend Tutter, you can be trusted not to molest the wildlife during the expedition, can't you? The lamas are adamant about the protection of animals. A rash act would endanger the mission."

"Of course, General Bruce," I said.

"Very well." He looked around the room. Raising his voice, he said, "As we are all present, I propose a toast to our success." He raised his glass and placed his other hand on the hilt of his kukri.

"Excuse me, General Bruce, but Mr. Irvine is not here," came a voice.

"Where the devil is he?"

"I believe he is in the kitchen; seems there is a problem with the stove, and he is trying to repair it," said Mallory. "I'm afraid he'd rather mingle with machines than men."

"Rubbish! He'll mingle with the troops and on the double. Tingbo, fetch that grease monkey!"

Tingbo had Irvine in the bar in a couple of minutes, and then the general spoke.

"I must inform you that we are about to do battle with a force that knows neither fear nor fatigue nor, up until now, failure. Our enemy never sleeps and stands invincible against time and its woes, nature and her furies. Last night, as I sought to prepare a speech, I thought of Everest as an arrogant queen who casts off the petitions of yeomen with storm and avalanche, who welcomes the brave with the insidious crevasse and icefall. We march this year as conquerors, and we will return as lords of nature!"

The expedition members sang,

Hip hip hurrah! Hip hip hurrah!
We must climb for king and country
We must climb for cause that is right and true
So onward to Everest we go, lads
Till we stand, till we stand where no man has stood before!

The general wiped a tear from his eye and continued. "I shall call upon Mr. Shakespeare to speak for me."

"Once more unto the breach, dear friends, once more;...
And you, good yeoman,
Whose limbs were made in England, show us here
The mettle of your pasture; let us swear
That you are worth your breeding; which I doubt not;
For there is none of you so mean and base,
That hath not noble luster in your eyes.
I see you stand like greyhounds in the slips,
Straining upon the start. The game's afoot:
Follow your spirit, and upon this charge

Cry "God for George, England, and our bloody
feet on Everest's brow!"

"God for George, England, and our bloody feet on Everest's brow!" came the reply.

Hazard started stomping his foot and began to sing:

Take off your clothes now, my Everest queen
And lie down by my side
Now swear, now swear you, my icy bride
To take me for your king
Oh, God forbid, said the frozen maid
That ever the like betide
That ever a man that comes from Albion
Would stretch down by my side
I am that man, O frosty maid
No other than a king
I stand above you by victory made
Hail, hail your king, George Mallory!

"It is true that man has conquered nature. This mountain, this poor mountain, is the last in a figurative sense, since literally she, nature, is beaten. Her trees, her mountains, her beasts, her rivers--they may stand or wander or flow, but they are refugees. There is only one great battle left with nature. That is man against man," said a voice from behind me. I turned.

"You believe that war is the last battle with nature?" I said.

"Not exactly. You are Reverend Tutter, aren't you?"

"I am."

"Pleasure," he said as he extended his hand. "Howard Somervell. As I was saying, Reverend Tutter, man has the last battle, not literally with nature, but with the wild nature that lurks within him."

"A return to the Garden?"

"No, there is no returning. We are our own children now. The Garden is gone that ended with war and the beginning of man's greatest challenge, the conquest of human nature."

"The conquest of mankind's evil by man alone? I think not, Mr. Somervell. Man is too weak to go it alone. That is like believing one man can conquer Mount Everest," I said.

"Someday one man will conquer Everest alone, just as the good that can come from one man will inspire others. One man will climb in the footsteps of others. There is a need for God, but man is capable of moving beyond his history of tragedy."

"Is that your motive for joining the expedition, to climb the mountain alone?" I asked.

"Oh no, I'm here as a team member. When I speak of the solitary climber, I speak of mankind's journey to a world of peace, a victory that relies on the individual more than the church. I know you see a contradiction in what I'm saying, and there is one. But no doubt we will have time to discuss it, won't we, Reverend?"

"No doubt," I said as I saw Mallory climb atop a table.

He began to speak. "Gentlemen, I will not quote more words from great Englishmen, for we, too, are Englishmen, and we know what greatness lies within each of our hearts. We are Englishmen who are soon to be greater Englishmen! Suffice it to say we are here, we are ready, and today we march to conquer Everest!" he said as he raised his glass to shouts of "Everest! Everest! Everest!"

As the group quieted, Mallory looked at me. "There is another man with us, an American. He is not a climber, though from what I know of his childhood, I suspect he has a climber's grit. His congregation made a generous gift to the expedition. But I invited him not only because of the donation and his knowledge of the Tibetan language, but also because in my short time knowing him I was impressed by his empathy. It is this ability that will help the team during moments of crisis and during interactions with the Tibetans. He has offered to assist our expedition in any way he can. His only personal motive is to report to his congregation on the lives of the Tibetans he encounters in this remote wasteland in the hope that someday a mission may be established. Welcome, Reverend Tutter."

There was some clapping and there were shouts of "Welcome, Yank!" Then Hazard started singing another song:

> *If buttercups buzz'd after the bee,*
> *If boats were on land, churches on sea,*
> *If ponies rode men and if grass ate the cows,*
> *And cats should be chased into holes by the mouse,*
> *If the mamas sold their babies*
> *To the Gypsies for half a crown;*
> *If summer were spring and the other way round,*
> *And all the world would be upside down,*
> *That's the day a Yank stands on Everest's bow.*
> *Yankee Doodle, keep it up,*
> *Yankee Doodle dandy,*
> *Mind the ice and mind the snow,*
> *And with the yaks be handy.*

"Mr. Hazard, one cannot but stand in awe of your troubadour talents; we shall not want for entertainment," said General Bruce.

"Thank you, General, and my first act as official troubadour is to raise a glass to the Yank. Welcome, Reverend Doodle!" shouted Hazard to another round of cheers.

"Reverend Tutter, I know that Mr. Mallory is convinced of your capabilities. But I for one am not," said Bruce as he walked to a table in the center of the room and cleared it. "I judge a man by his arm," said Bruce as he rolled up his uniform sleeve and placed his right elbow on the table. "Come on, Reverend, let's test your mettle."

"Arm wrestling is not something one studies in seminary, sir. I am a man of subtler strengths," I felt challenged.

"Nonsense. Surely your poaching soirees have given you some conditioning."

"A poacher!" someone cried out.

"There are no poachers in America. They are woodsmen, pioneers—and individualists!" shouted someone else to a roar of laughter.

"Mr. Mallory tells me you grew up among the Tibetans; surely you didn't spend your time in prayer instead of raising a bit of hell with them?" continued General Bruce. "Up with your sleeve now."

"Here, some Scotch to thin your blood and steady your nerves, Reverend," Shebbeare said and shoved a glass in my face.

We sat at the cleared table. There was a jovial yet ruthless confidence in his eyes. The general was a warrior. I imagined him standing atop mounds of men killed in battle, noting the type and location of the guns as bullets whizzed by his head. Fear was his breakfast. If I were twelve men, he wouldn't notice. He would have walked into Khartoum alone and saved Major-General Charles George Gordon. My sweaty palms betrayed my conviction about my imminent defeat, and the Scotches from the toasts were making my head spin. I took a deep breath and set my eyes on the bar across the room to stop the spinning. Then we locked hands. His elbow was firmly on the table. I could feel his forearm and biceps tense. I moved my elbow toward him as I tried to steady myself, but my sweaty hand slid up his palm. He seemed to take no notice, perhaps thinking it yet another vanquished dervish's last wilting grasp. Then someone shouted 'Go!' I tried to move my arm, but my hand slid farther up his. For some reason, there was a pause, a stalemate. What was he doing? I suddenly felt very sick, I was going to vomit! I leaned back and turned my head. My arm followed, my torso pulling his arm toward me and at the same time turning his fingers. The general's arm must have hit the table before I fell backward onto the floor.

He actually thought I had beaten him. Maybe he was drunker than I had realized, for the next thing I knew, he was standing over me. "Why, the

Yank has some mettle. He's not just a Bible thumper after all. Give him another drink, and make it a gin and tonic; looks like the bloody heat must be affecting him, the way he fell backward."

By the time I had gotten to my feet, the general was standing at the doorway of the gymkhana. He pulled his kukri and raised it toward the Union Jack. As he stepped across the threshold, he turned to the team and shouted, "To king, to England, to Everest!" Then he was gone.

Mallory turned to me. "Seems as though the old man has taken a liking to you, Reverend. Shall we go?"

"Now?"

"We can't stay here; all the kit is well under way."

"Yes, of course. To Everest!" I shouted. Then I stepped toward the door and fell to the floor.

"Sahib need tea?"

"What?"

"Sahib need tea?"

I was in a large chair, and a grinning waiter was standing in front of me.

"Sahib was very drunk and fell. We put sahib in chair to rest. Best drink tea now."

"Ah yes. Tea, please," I said as I looked around the empty bar. The expedition had left. Looking out a window, I saw that it was dark outside. I drank the tea and stood up. I was still tipsy and had a headache, but I could walk.

"Waiter, is there a note for me from the Englishmen?"

"No, sahib, no note. They left chop-chop. General Bruce very busy, busy." So Mallory and company had left me without so much as a note or instructions. They really did dislike Americans. My equipment? Where was my equipment? Some had gone with the expedition; the rest was at the hotel. I needed a Sherpa and, now, porters, if I wanted to catch up. Catch up? I would never catch up. I was too sick to do anything except make my way back to my hotel. No, that was ridiculous. I was here to conquer Everest. I would find the help I needed and leave as soon as possible. Then I thought of Annie. I had to see Annie before I left; she would be heartbroken if I didn't say good-bye. I had to do it tonight. I wouldn't have time tomorrow. *She can't be far. Darjeeling is a small place.*

"Waiter, where is Annie's mission?"

"Annie's Mission, sahib? No Annie's Mission, sir."

"I think it is on the hill. The Baptist—"

"You are speaking of the Highroad Mission. Come, follow me. It is not far."

I followed him to the street.

"Looking up there, sir," he said, pointing to an illuminated cross. "That

47

is the mission, not far, sir. Only going straight, sir."

"Dacoits?"

"Not to worry. No dacoits, sahib," he said as he again waved his arm toward the illuminated cross. I remembered Annie saying it was on a hill overlooking the town, *The waiter must be right*, I thought. I started toward the cross. The thought of seeing Annie set my mind in motion. *Of course Annie will be happy to see me. It would make her sad if I left without saying good-bye. I mustn't let her worry about me. She is too lovely to spend her life in a wasteland. I shall ask her to marry me. Did I tell her about Sally? She can't be happy alone, helping poor people the rest of her life. I can't allow her to do that. Sally wasn't the right woman for me anyway: no sense of adventure. Dad will be upset and I'll lose out on a wealthy congregation, but it isn't love. On the other hand, I could do so much with their money and Sally is so understanding. No, I must just say good-bye to Mrs. Crowden, just good-bye.*

The road was steep and rutted and dark. I reached the top of the hill and saw the gate to the mission. I was only a few feet away and could hear women's voices coming from behind the fence. Then something caught my foot. I let out a yell as I fell to the ground. Moments later I heard Annie shouting and looked up. She was kneeling over me with her hands on my head.

"Reverend Tutter, is that you? Are you OK? And you—who are you? Get away from him! Jenny, go get Mr. Mason and Kapoor. Reverend Tutter may be injured."

"I'm OK," I said, "I must have tripped."

"Are you sure? I opened the gate and saw a body on the ground with a person—that man right there—with his hands on you. He tried to run off, but Godspeed grabbed his leg and pulled him down."

"Who is Godspeed?"

"Mr. Mason's dog."

"Oh."

Others had come out from the mission and were standing around. An Indian was speaking to the alleged assailant while Godspeed remained locked to the suspect's pants leg.

"I'm fine, Mrs. Crowden. Perhaps it was that last brandy at the gymkhana."

"Allow me to help you up, sir," came a voice as a hand was thrust into mine and pulled me to my feet. "Edward Mason, headmaster of Highroad Mission. Mrs. Crowden has spoken highly of you. But 'Let us walk honestly, as in the day; not in rioting and drunkenness,' especially when you are in a strange place."

"Mr. Mason is right, Reverend Tutter, one should not drink," chimed in Annie.

"Oh, I agree. It was the excitement of the moment. We were making predeparture toasts, and I let myself overindulge," I said.

"It is understandable, Reverend. Our Savior himself would have a difficult time refusing General Bruce, a most engaging man," said Mr. Mason as he turned his attention to the other man. "Pasang? What are you doing here? Up to your old tricks again, are you?" He left me and walked over to Pasang.

I looked at Annie.

"I have no idea who he is," she said.

Kapoor walked over to us. "That fellow is Pasang. He is a local rascal. Too much rakshi." Kapoor said. "He is a drunkard."

"So he was trying to rob me?" I asked.

"Come, let us learn, for he is telling his tale to Mr. Mason. I am sure we will find it engaging, as he is a colorful fellow," said Kapoor.

"Pasang not steal. I see gentleman in town. People say he is part of General Bruce's expedition and gentleman needs Sherpa. I follow gentleman from market to gymkhana and wait. Then I follow gentleman here. I want to talk to him, but he is busy man, so I follow, waiting and watching. I know other Sherpas also wanting work. If I am near, I have best chance to talk first. His feet not know road, not follow. Man, he fall. Road dark. I try to help him. I know he want Sherpa for Everest. Pasang need money. Pasang work. Like Englishmen say, Work, work bring money, money, Sherpa. I try to help him when dog bite me."

"Pasang, I know you have a problem with rakshi, but I have never known you to be a liar or a thief." Mason turned to me. "I think he was merely trying to help you, Reverend Tutter."

"Help me? He was trying to rob me. A thief in the night he is." I stepped toward Pasang with my arm raised; suddenly Godspeed jumped and grabbed my arm. "Stop! Get off me, you stupid dog," I said as I tried to kick him.

"Reverend Tutter, don't you dare hurt that dog," cried Annie.

"Godspeed, sit," came a command from Mason. Godspeed released me and sat.

"That dog is dangerous. He should be muzzled and on a leash," I said to Mason.

"He usually doesn't have a problem with strangers unless they try to flee, as Pasang did. Though it is odd he defended Pasang."

"I think Godspeed is a good judge of character, and you, Reverend Tutter, are a bad man. How dare you threaten Pasang when he was only trying to help you!"

"Mrs. Crowden, you believe this man's cock-and-bull story?"

"I believe him. You dog kicker!" Annie said. She turned to Jenny. "I'm sorry, Jenny, I'm too upset to go for a walk. I'm going to my room."

"I'm afraid she's right, Reverend; your behavior is not that of a Christian man, alcohol or no alcohol. There is no excuse for your actions. Good evening, Reverend Tutter," said Mason as he followed Annie and Jenny into the mission.

"Many, many poor people. You do not understand India, sir. That is a problem," said Kapoor.

"What do you mean? He tried to rob me!"

"Exactly, sir. You do not understand that this man is not a robber."

I noticed Pasang was standing a few feet away, trying to follow the conversation, nodding whenever Kapoor spoke.

"He is a robber."

"No, sir, he is only seeking employment. That is very clear."

"You said he was a drunkard, a rascal."

"This man has a hard life. That is his fate. But you can see he only wants a job."

"I see. . . Well, good night, Kapoor."

"Good night, sir."

My head was spinning. *A thief knocks me down and I am the criminal.* I needed to sleep. I took a last look at the closed gate and started down the hill to my hotel. Annie was gone, gone forever because of a Sherpa. I heard footsteps behind me. I turned. Pasang was following me.

"Trying to finish the job, are you? Well, there's no one around now to protect you!" I shouted as I took a swing at him and missed. I took a step nearer and prepared to swing again.

"Pasang Sherpa only want job."

"Job? You fool, don't you see what you've done? I've lost her because of you."

"Sahib want woman? Pasang know woman."

"No, fool, don't you know what love is? I don't want just *a* woman."

"Pasang not understand. Sahib goes to Everest but wants to stay with Christian woman. Christian woman go to Everest?"

He had a point. Maybe I was drunker than I had realized, hiking up to the mission and expecting Annie to... to be in love with me. I didn't want to stay here at the mission, saving souls. I wanted Annie to say she loved me and would sleep with me. Then I would move on. I knew it would never happen, and Pasang had actually done me a favor. "Look," I said. "Maybe I'm wrong about you. Maybe you are just looking for a job. But I can't help you. I'll only hire a guy based on a recommendation. Good night," I said, and turned toward my hotel.

6

ABANDONED

I was in a pickle. Most of my gear was with the expedition. They probably hadn't noticed my absence. Maybe when Bruce decided on a rematch, someone would take note. I could hear Bruce now as he stepped out of his tent: *Ah, the air, the mountains. Makes one burst with energy. Where is that Yank? I think a rematch is in order after breakfast. Tingbo, fetch the American. Chop-chop.* After a bit, Tingbo will say I can't be found. *What nonsense! I haven't lost a man in my thirty years of service. Fellow is probably out for some air. He'll turn up for breakfast.* Of course I wouldn't, and that would lead to speculation on my whereabouts but no thought as to why no one had noticed I had been missing for three days. *If all men count with you, but none too much...* Bruce would mumble before the inevitable, *Very well, we'll simply carry on without him.*

I had no food, tent, or map. I had to find equipment and supplies. I was going to need more than a Sherpa. I would also need porters and maybe a horse. And I would need money to pay the porters and buy supplies along the way. The money was not a problem. The problem was that the porters would know I was carrying money. Who would they tell?

I left the hotel after breakfast and headed to the marketplace. Some of the shops were like museums, with supplies and surplus objects from previous explorers and expeditions. The Raj liked to explore in style. I found the equipment I needed. The locals knew what was happening, and I soon had a following of solicitous men offering their services. It wasn't long before Pasang joined them. It was then that I realized he was the fellow that Karma Paul had pointed out in the market the day before.

"Are you Sportsman?"

"Some call me that. Where did you hear it?"

"Karma Paul told me yesterday."

"The English call me that because of a jacket I sometimes wear. Did he tell you I am drunkard?"

"He did."

"I drink but I am no drunkard. I am a Sherpa, a good Sherpa."

"Then why aren't you with the Englishmen on your way to Everest?"

"Karma Paul doesn't like me."

"Because you drink?"

"No, it is because of money."

"Did you steal?"

"No. I was Sherpa on English survey expedition. English boss like drink. Pasang like drink. One morning English boss wake up and say some money gone. Karma Paul blame me. I drink but I no steal. No matter Karma Paul blame me. I lose job."

"Is that why you were kicked out of the monastery, because you are a drunkard?"

"No. I left monastery because of woman. Nun tell Pasang sex is the only way to attain Buddhahood in one lifetime. I want to be like Buddha. I not know what sex is. Other monks talk, so Pasang must leave monastery. Pasang not mad Pasang happy, for woman better than prayer. Mr. Reverend like woman too, he follow new woman."

"I didn't follow her. I went to say good bye, whereas your expulsion and the incident with the expedition are serious issues. I need a Sherpa that is trustworthy, not a troublemaker. Sorry, but I'm not hiring you. I'll find porters and be on my way in a day or so. There are plenty of men that need the money. Good-bye Pasang," I said.

I spent the day searching for porters. Karma Paul had been right about the local Sherpas and porters. They were hopeless boozers and invalids. One fellow I interviewed for the job of porter kept his hat in his hand the entire time to hide his missing fingers. If I hired local porters, I would die. I gave up and went to find Pasang.

"Mr. Reverend can't find porters, he need Pasang's help? Pasang can help."

"It would be easier if I had an assistant, Pasang, but my reason for returning is that I want to give you a second chance. I think that there is a speck of decency in your soul and I want to give it an opportunity to grow. Mind you I won't tolerate any nonsense; no drinking and absolutely no womanizing. Is that clear?"

"Of course. Pasang top notch Sherpa. Everything go chop-chop."

"OK, Mr. Sportsman, let's go to Everest," I said.

I entrusted Pasang to find the porters while I looked for a horse. At least I could count on riding when the inevitable bouts of sickness hit. It was three days before we were ready to start. Pasang showed up on the day of departure dressed in a tweed sport coat and knickers.

"Are you intending to go to Everest dressed like that?"

"Of course, this is a proper expedition and we are gentlemen."

"Yes, I suppose we are. And these are our porters? They're all women, Pasang! What did you do? We'll be crossing the Himalayas and marching across Tibet!"

"They are Sherpa women, very strong, no drink, no fight, just carry and cook."

What could I do? I had tried and failed and, if nothing else, a couple of them were even attractive. Though after Annie and Godspeed showed up at the last minute so that she could give Pasang a package of sweets, I had the feeling that the women were more than porters. My God, had he seduced Annie too? I thought a good-bye was in order, so I approached Annie as she stood talking to Pasang.

"Mrs. Crowden, I wish you the best in your work at the mission," I said.

"Thank you, Reverend Tutter. I hope your endeavor is successful. I am glad to see there is some element of God's love still in you. You have recognized that Pasang is a good man. I hope that Pasang can forgive you."

"Oh yes, Reverend, I forgive me," chimed in Pasang.

"Considering the circumstances, I think I was reasonable to suspect Pasang."

"Reverend Tutter, you are as far from a Christian as Kansas is from Cuba. How do you live with yourself?" She turned back to Pasang.

I reached out to touch her arm and started to speak, Godspeed jumped between us, grabbed my sleeve, and pulled me off balance. I stumbled and fell against Pasang as the porters watched and laughed. Annie never looked at me. I had just lost all authority in their eyes. I glanced at Pasang. He was expressionless, but I knew that from now until I caught up with Mallory and company I needed to be in control.

"Come, Godspeed, come," was all Annie said.

"Annie not like Reverend Tutter. Reverend Tutter not to worry. Sherpa women different from American women. Reverend Tutter is sahib."

"Of course Mrs. Crowden likes me. It is only that she is away from home for the first time in a foreign land, a widow, and idealistic. I do my best to help her, but she is very insecure."

"Woman without man is monsoon, endless misery. Mrs. Crowden comes to help but brings misery."

"You may have a point, Pasang."

I looked over the porters and zeroed in on the smallest one. "Pasang, are you sure she is fit to carry a load?" I was a foot and a half taller than her. I hoped that my size conveyed a sense of authority. I grabbed her basket and gave it a shake; she nearly fell over. I walked among them, shaking the loads by slightly lifting and then twisting before releasing. I was able to make even the strongest look overloaded. I frowned to show Pasang that I knew what I was doing and that I was in control. He was unfazed. I studied the features of the porters. One had her missing left hand hidden under her right; another had a constant cough. The strongest looking of the lot had cataracts and wouldn't be able to tell a snowfield from a bale of cotton. When I held my hand in front of her face, Pasang stepped forward and offered excuses and apologies.

"Enough of your excuses, Pasang! Do you really think that these women can make it to Everest? I don't think they can make it to Gangtok. I've entrusted you with my life, and this is what you do? How can a blind woman be a porter?" He was silent. He had lost some face, but I knew he needed the money so he would stay. In truth, the porters would all be fine, except the one who coughed.

"Pasang, have you heard her coughing? I think she has TB. The work would kill her."

"She is poor, Reverend Tutter. A widow. I only wanted to help her."

"Killing her is not helping her. I'm dismissing her. And I'm deducting part of your pay and giving it to her. I won't tolerate exploiting the sick. Do you understand?" I placed some money in her hands and then placed my hands over hers for a moment. Turning back to the Sherpa, I said, "Pasang, you must find someone else—quickly now! I want to be on the trail in an hour."

He returned in short order with another woman. She was younger than the rest and very beautiful. Her name was Chhamzi. I had five porters plus Pasang. We were as ready as we'd ever be.

7

THE MISSION

It took a month to get to Tingri. Conditions were terrible: lots of rain and then snow on the high trails and passes. I was wet, cold, and miserable yet Pasang and the porters seemed to take no notice of the conditions. I had expected a rebellion or at least a demand for more money, but there was never a complaint. Pasang did a good job. My suspicions were unfounded. Three days before Tingri, my horse was swept away during a stream crossing. Riding had made me soft. In spite of carrying just a knapsack, I could not keep up with the porters. By the end of the second day, I was exhausted.

"Pasang I'm worried, you are driving these women too hard. I'm a fast hiker, but I stay in the rear to slow the pace. It can't be good for them. Tomorrow we will go at a slower pace even if it takes an extra day to reach the mission."

"Women not have problem. I chose good Sherpa women. I think sahib is tired. Tomorrow I wait for sahib with chai while porters go ahead."

"Nonsense, I'm not tired I'm worried about the women. Tomorrow we will walk at a normal speed. Do you understand?"

"Yes, sahib."

The next day was no different. Within twenty minutes of starting, the porters were out of sight.

"Pasang, why didn't you tell them to slow down," I shouted as he waited for me at the top of a hill with a thermos of chai.

"They are going slow, sahib. Sahib tired, sahib very slow."

"Nonsense, now leave me the thermos and you go find them. Have them wait until I arrive. That's an order."

"Pasang can't do."

"What?"

"Sherpa women are waiting now. Reverend Tutter, look mission over there."

He was right. The mission was just across the valley. The porters were already there. An hour later I was at the Gangtok mission run by Dr. Joyell and his daughters.

Dr. Joyell had been married to an American, and he had a fondness for them. He was more than happy to have me as a guest. He would even loan me a horse. I accepted his offer to stay in Gangtok for a few days, and sent Pasang and company ahead. The doctor had built a small hospital. His daughters were the nurses, administrators, and fundraisers. The doctor cared little for accolades. He was there to provide medical care. He would have worked under the shade of a neem tree or in the most modern hospital. His only interest was in helping patients. It was the same with his daughter Eliza. Like her father, she saw her work as a moral obligation to help those in need. Her sister, Stella, saw it a different way. She wanted out and money was the doorway. One morning after breakfast, Dr. Joyell gave me a tour of the hospital.

"And this is the ward for the terminally ill."

"This is the nicest place in the hospital," I said.

"Yes. One mustn't give up hope."

"But you said these are the terminally ill. There is no hope."

"That is true for them but not for me. I cannot give up hope. I come here every day."

"But why? Your time would be better spent with the patients that you can help."

"Because if I stopped believing in miracles, my world would end. If I ceased caring about a patient, then I would lose everything."

"Father is right. We cannot stop caring, ever," said Eliza.

"We are trapped by our guilt, our selfish guilt, and nothing more," said Stella.

"Nonsense, Stella."

"No, Father, it isn't. Money helps more than guilt. Reverend Tutter is proof of that. He is here and not stuck in some desolate American village preaching to ignorant farmers. Money, not guilt or faith, makes that possible."

"I don't think it is that simple, Miss Joyell."

"It is that simple, Reverend Tutter. Money moves more rocks than faith. Mr. Mallory and company are obsessive lunatics, and were it not for the money given them, they would be climbing the walls of an asylum."

"Stella, please. Reverend Tutter is our guest," said Dr. Joyell.

"He is an opportunist. How can you ignore the fact that your faith is a ball and chain. At least dying patients have the hope that they will escape this prison," said Stella as she looked me up and down. Then she walked away.

"I'm sorry, Reverend Tutter. Stella has never fit in here. Any visitor's presence upsets her. She longs to be somewhere else, yet deep inside she does care for others."

"I understand."

After lunch, Dr. Joyell and Eliza returned to the hospital. I decided to take the mare for a ride, as I would be riding her for a few days until I caught up with Pasang and the porters. I headed up a trail that Joyell recommended for its views of the Himalayas. Crossing one of its innumerable streams, I glanced downstream at a large pool. Stella sat by the water in a patch of sunlight. I tied up the mare and walked over.

"Miss Joyell, no hard feelings. I can understand a person's frustration at living in an isolated place, especially if that individual is ambitious and intelligent."

"Aren't you going to add 'beautiful and lonely'? Aren't you going to offer me a way out of here? You think that my comments are the result of my being frustrated?"

"It seems that way to me. I lived in a mission in China. I couldn't wait to get out."

Stella was beautiful and her coolness made her even more attractive. Were her angry words a type of foreplay? I went over and sat beside her.

"Do you mind?"

"Do I mind if you try to seduce me?"

I had never met a woman so blunt. I tried to kiss her. She pulled away.

"Surely you don't think I'm in love with you?"

"Well, I think two people can meet and feel something that can only be described as love."

"Perhaps, Miss Joyell, I succumbed to lust just now, in part because the feeling seemed to be mutual."

"No, it is not, but we do have something in common; You're part of an expedition and I want to join it. You are an American, and you want to climb Everest with a party of Englishmen. That is simply not possible. This expedition is for the glory of England. One only need look at how Mr. Finch, the Australian, was treated to know that you are tolerated because of your money. You'll be lucky to reach the base camp. The expedition has passed through here twice before. I know how they think."

"You seem certain that I want to reach the summit."

Stella rose and looked toward the surrounding peaks. "*Beloved congregation, as I stood on the step that is highest and closest to the Lord and looked down upon his creation...*"

I smiled.

She continued: "Or will it be, '*Beloved congregation, I could only dream of stepping closer to our Lord as I looked up...*'"

My smile faded.

"Or worse yet, '*Dear members of the congregation: As I sit in camp waiting for the climbers to reach the summit of the world's highest peak, I too wonder what it might be like to stand and…*'"

I frowned. She had a point. But what influence did she have with the expedition?

"Most men would do anything to be part of the first scenario, but I'm afraid that without my help you'll be sitting in camp writing."

"Help me, how can you help me?"

"I'm a beautiful woman."

"I joined this expedition as an observer. Of course, the idea of standing on the summit intrigues me. But although you are an attractive woman, I think you are mistaken if you think you can charm your way into getting whatever you want. By the way, what do you want?"

"I get you to the summit and you take me to America and provide me with a few introductions. That's it."

"Providing for you on the expedition would be no easy task. First of all, most of my supplies are with the expedition. I was lucky to find some replacements in Darjeeling. Now I'm about to enter Tibet, and you know as well as I how marginal life is there."

"You have money."

"Money won't do anything if there is nothing to buy. Have you ever left the mission?"

"Of course I've left the mission."

"Then you know that you can't waltz across Tibet even if you have a pocket full of money."

"It has never been a problem. Father has maintained the mission by buying from the local farmers."

"It is not the same. The Tibetans are serfs, living hand to mouth. They might not have an egg to sell. Mallory and company are prepared. Why do you think they have all those porters carrying supplies? I have Pasang and the porters to support me until I catch up with them. Besides, I'm married. I can't simply take you home with me."

"So your answer is no?"

"It's no."

"I'm disappointed in you. Actually, I'm disappointed in myself, for what I assumed was ruthless opportunism on your part is actually an uncanny ability to find stupid or lazy victims."

So how much did the summit mean to me? Stella's proposition was a face slap. Somehow I had taken my position for granted, when in reality it was as she had described. Why else had I been left at the gymkhana. I was a barely tolerated tagalong who was helping to pay for the expedition. And what about her? Why didn't she just leave? She wasn't some peasant who had never been on the other side of the riverbank. No husband. No kids.

She had another motive.

"You've got what you need to leave, upstairs and downstairs. Why come with me?" I asked. "And who is it that you're in love with? Mallory? Irvine? Or is it the general?"

"General Bruce? Certainly not! In fact, I haven't the least interest in any of them."

"Just a lady out for a hike, eh?"

"I'm not fond of hiking. The truth is, I want to make Eliza jealous."

"You want to go to the middle of nowhere just to make your sister unhappy?"

"Yes."

"You'd cut off your nose to spite your face?"

"I want her to be miserable, and you offer the perfect opportunity for me to make her unhappy. Leaving with you would present me with so many possibilities that it would frustrate her for a long, long time."

"I don't understand."

"My sister is living a lie. I have tried to help her, but she rebuffs me. She hates it here. She stays only out of guilt and pity. If I left for England, she would tell herself that I'm not cut out for this type of life. But if I ran off with you, it would slowly poison her, in a good way of course—or at least I hope so. She relies on emotion, not rationality, to make sense of her world, so the only way for her to see herself is to push her to the emotional edge."

It was the most convoluted logic I had ever heard. Either she loved her father and sister or she didn't, and if she didn't she should leave. Why make it complicated. She was a nut case. If I took her along with me, I'd regret it.

"What will it be, Reverend?"

"Your place is here with your family. I can't allow myself to be used to hurt someone else."

"Very well, Reverend. I understand."

She got up and started back to the road. As she passed I waited for a knife in the back, but it never came. I had been honest with her, and I hadn't been honest in a long, long time. It was an odd feeling.

I continued with my ride. Joyell had loaned me a great horse. Endswell handled the mud with ease, crossed a bridge without hesitation, had a good pace, and waited patiently. I had a great horse I thought to myself when she suddenly stopped. I gave her a squeeze, but she stood still, so I gave her another—nothing. I looked up. I had been lost in my thoughts. There was Kanchenjunga. I had never before ridden a horse who appreciated a view.

"Beautiful, eh, Endswell? I can see why Crowley regretted giving up," I said.

Her ears shot back and she reared up as if she were fighting for her life.

"Easy, Endswell, Are you the rebirth of a mountaineer?"

She pawed the ground with her right hoof, and her head reared back.

Then she continued on the trail, seeming to never take her eyes off the mountain. I would have to ask Joyell about the horse.

Seeing Kanchenjunga inspired me. I did want to reach the summit of Everest. Stella was right about me being a tagalong, but she was wrong about her ability to get me on the team. At least she was wrong in her approach to getting me on the team. She was no vamp, but she could turn heads, especially if all the heads belonged to lonely mountaineers. Having Stella along might create enough dissent to create an opening for me. I would just need to make sure she turned the right heads at the right time.

It was getting late, so I turned around. "OK, Endswell, are you ready for Everest?" I should have thought before I spoke. As she reared up, I nearly fell.

That evening at dinner, I asked about the horse. "Where did you get that amazing horse, Endswell, Dr. Joyell? Judging by her actions, I'd say she was a mountaineer."

"Interesting story. She was found near Timigela, a village south of Kanchenjunga, after Timigela had been destroyed by a freak mudslide. One of my men, Kumar, had a brother there, and after he heard what had happened, he went to Timigela. Endswell was the only survivor alive. That was back in 1908, I believe. Kumar brought her to the mission, and my wife, Edith, fell in love with her."

"Were I not a rational man, I would venture to say that Endswell was a reincarnated mountaineer, perhaps someone from Crowley's Kanchenjunga expedition."

"The thought has entered my mind too, Reverend Tutter, for every time an expedition passes through, Endswell has to be restrained from following it."

"Would you be averse to selling her?"

"I could never sell her. She was my wife's horse. She saved her life once, as a matter of fact. Edith was sitting in the garden taking in the sun. I had taken her there before I went up to the hospital. She was weak, but able to be left unattended for an hour or two. Do you know what the most dangerous creature in Sikkim is, Reverend Tutter?"

"A cobra."

"No, it's a tiger, an old, starving, nearly blind tiger whose only prey are the weak or injured. He was working his way up to Edith from behind. We don't know how Endswell knew, for you can't see the garden from the stable. Yet she came charging into the garden and kicked the beast to death when he was no more than a yard from her. Edith had heard an agitated tailorbird's call just before Endswell arrived and I can't think of another explanation. You can see the smashed skull, his hide is under this table."

"Amazing."

"But the idea of her going to Everest is intriguing. Why don't you borrow her?"

"There is the risk of injury or loss. I will be passing through bandit territory."

"I'm aware of the risk, and I can accept it. But selling her would be like selling my memory of Edith. Take Endswell—she has been waiting for you! I only wish you would reconsider letting Stella join you."

"Excuse me?"

"I know Stella wants to go. She asks everyone who passes through to help her leave, so I'm sure she has approached you as well."

"She did and I declined."

"I know you did. I saw it in her eyes. I realize that the mission is not the right place for Stella, but I've never felt that there was a way for her to leave until you arrived, Reverend."

"But why Tibet? Why not England?"

"Were she to go to England, she might never return. It is her life, of course. But I fear she would fall in with a bad crowd—Bolsheviks and artist types and such. I see the expedition as an opportunity for her to take a few deep breaths. She would be with a group of adventurers, fellows with a goal, who wouldn't be wasting time moaning about the world's injustices. Tibet is a big, open-to-the-skies place where she can find her place in the world."

"Then why didn't you let her go with the expedition?"

"Because of Mr. Mallory. He is a naturist and a Bloomsbury Bolshevik."

"A naturist?"

"Yes, I witnessed it myself on two occasions, and the subject came up repeatedly in the presence of my daughters."

"But surely he isn't a communist; why, he was a valiant soldier."

"I have a copy of the *London Times*, Reverend, and there is an article about the Bloomsbury Group in which Mr. Mallory is mentioned several times. Do you know what they stand for?"

"Aren't they intellectuals?"

"Do you know what their idea of intellectualism is? According to Mr. G. E. Moore, it is 'love, the creation and enjoyment of aesthetic experience, and the pursuit of knowledge.'"

"Shocking! I can understand why his naturism is a concern. But why do you want Stella to go?"

"Because I have no choice. I can't build a fence high enough around Stella any longer. If I don't let her go, then she'll leave for London and all hope will be lost. I've given Stella the best life I can. But it is her life, and she has her own path ahead of her. There is one thing though that remains."

"Dr. Joyell, your daughter is safe with me."

"I have no doubts regarding your morals. The fact that you have already left two letters to be sent to your wife is more than enough proof of your moral fiber. No, it's this: I want you to say a few words tomorrow, Sunday. Would you do that for me?"

"Certainly. But why? I don't think there is anything that I can say that can improve life here at the mission."

"The Bible is the word of God, but each man hears a different song. You are a new voice, a different musician. Sound the trumpet, my good fellow! Shake their souls! Let them know God is everywhere, not just in church."

"A revival! Is that what you want?"

"Yes, bring a bit of excitement to this outpost of hope. Brilliant idea."

On Sunday I gave them a revival.

"Let us break the ice we stand upon, so we know who is to sink and who is to swim into the arms of God. Let those who won't swim drown, swept away with the currents of darkness!" I shouted as I leaned forward and stared into every pair of eyes that dared to meet mine. "Upon that water shines the light of our Savior; below is the devil's mud of decay, which drags us down ever deeper. Those of you here are on ice. The frozen words of great men—the disciples—you hear their words, but those words are two thousand years old. They are good words, but they are not in your soul, for I can see it, I can hear it, and I can smell it on your breath! Liars! How dare you speak the Lord's words like a machine, like a phonograph! Stand, each and every one of you, and jump, jump, jump for joy! For we are going to break the ice in our souls! Now follow me, Brothers and Sisters, to the river. For I tell you that the river down there is frozen, and we shall walk upon it because we have frozen souls, and we shall jump with our arms raised to God as we ask ourselves, *Do I believe, do I believe, do I trust in God?* And then we shall break the ice! And then through God's almighty grace we will, one and all, swim to shore. Amen."

"Reverend, surely you aren't going to the river," said Joyell as we left the chapel.

"Without faith, God's word is nothing better than the sole of a sandal, there for comfort."

Of course the river wasn't frozen; most didn't even know what ice was. But it didn't matter, for they believed as we stood ankle-deep in the water. "Do you feel it? Do you feel the ice beneath your feet?"

"We do!"

"Do you want to join Jesus in the mighty river of life? Do you want to break the ice?"

"Yes, we do!"

"Then reach out to our Lord and Savior!" I cried out as I turned toward the deeper water. "Cry out his name and jump!"

"Jump! Jump! Jump!" shouted the congregation as they all turned to face the center of the river and jumped toward it.

I had chosen a spot where the channel had cut a steep drop-off, so that when I jumped forward I landed in waist-deep water, which began to carry me downstream. "Feel the power of the Lord, for I have joined his ever-present spirit!" I shouted as I floated down the river.

"Feel the power!" replied the floating chorus.

"Stop, Reverend, stop! They can't swim. They'll drown!"

I turned and saw Joyell and Eliza frantically dragging people from the river. "Fear not, God will not abandon them," I replied as I floated downstream with the remaining believers. And God didn't abandon them, for in a few hundred feet the river widened and we walked ashore.

I said, "Dr. Joyell, did the Lord enter your soul, did you feel the Spirit? I must say I truly felt the Spirit, and I am so touched to see all of these souls here in the sunshine."

Joyell was silent and then smiled slightly. "Reverend, I put on my best shoes today, and I fear they are now ruined. Maybe that is a good thing, for I have never seen the word of God so enthusiastically received. It is as if God has actually entered each and every soul."

"As if? He *has*."

Joyell sighed as he wiped mud from his shoelaces. "Perhaps I am the one in need of a revival, a revival of priorities," he said. He took off the shoes, threw them into the river, and then grasped my hands with his. "Reverend, you must stop here on your return. Will you promise me?"

"Of course."

8

TIBET

Stella and I left the next morning. We caught up with Pasang and the porters in a couple of days. Two mules had fallen off cliffs and food had been stolen during my absence, but Pasang was in good spirits. He was still wearing the cast-off European clothing; no doubt he intended to impress upon anyone he encountered on the trail that he was in charge. We soon crossed into Tibet. The rain was gone, but the cold and wind were brutal replacements.

"You don't seem to be in any great hurry to catch up with the expedition, Reverend Tutter," said Stella.

"Missing teatime and conversation? I'm not one to abuse porters. It's safer to go slow and steady than to rush and injure one of them," I said. In truth I had decided to keep my distance until no longer possible.

Stella got her tea when we arrived at Tinru, an English outpost that was an island of tidiness surrounded by woolly yaks and Tibetan dwellings that at first glance were hard to distinguish from rubble. That island was the home of Captain and Mrs. Hennessy.

"It looks so English," said Stella.

And it was. We were welcomed by Mrs. Hennessy, and after tea she was more than happy to show us around.

"This is my herb and vegetable garden," Mrs. Hennessy said, leading Stella through their tiny oasis on the moon. "I'll be serving potatoes and cabbage from here in tonight's dinner. The dry climate does wonders for the pest problem."

"That is an amazing cabbage; it must weigh six pounds." I stepped over to get a closer look.

"Reverend, you must not do that," said Mrs. Hennessy.

Just at that moment there was growl, and I found myself knocked to the ground with a 130-pound mastiff standing on me.

"Get off me!" I cried as I tried to get up.

"Perhaps a moment of prayer is in order," said Stella.

"Hercules! Off!" said Mrs. Hennessy.

"He doesn't seem to be listening. Is he trained to catch thieves in the garden?" asked Stella.

"It would be bare and full of yaks if it weren't for Hercules. I can't understand why he won't release Reverend Tutter. Off, Hercules! Reverend Tutter is not a thief."

I tried to roll. Hercules growled. Mrs. Hennessy ordered Hercules again.

"I suspect Hercules knows something we don't," said Stella.

Mrs. Hennessy began to pull the dog by his collar, but to no avail.

"I've never seen him act this way before; it is as if he has gone mad. He has been an outstanding dog in every respect."

"Do you think he has rabies?" I asked.

"His mouth does seem a bit frothy," said Stella.

"I don't want to die! Do something!"

"Hercules, you simply must get up this very instant. Hercules, do you hear me?" Though the dog failed to obey he did have rhythm, for I noticed his tail thumped the ground in time with Mrs. Hennessy's singsong command.

"Hercules, stand down!" called a thundering voice. The dog was gone. I looked in the direction of the voice. It was Captain Hennessy and there was Hercules, sitting proudly at his side.

"You must be Reverend Tutter. General Bruce said he thought you had grit and to not be surprised if you showed up," said Captain Hennessy. "You must excuse Hercules. He is a good soldier, never one to shirk his duty. I remember the time he caught a bandit in the stable stealing a horse. Hercules got the fellow by his ankle as he was riding off, and he refused to let go. We followed the skidding marks from his paws for two miles until the bandit's foot had relinquished its ties to the chap's body. He could have ripped the fellow to shreds, but after his ankle was severed and he fell from the horse, Hercules simply laid down on him until we arrived."

"Mrs. Hennessy thought he was acting a bit unusual, and there is a bit of foam on his mouth. Do you think he has rabies?" I asked.

"Rabies? Nonsense, why he has probably just…" Captain Hennessy turned to Hercules, took his head, and opened his mouth. Face-to-face with the dog, he peered into his mouth and took a long sniff. "Ha, I thought so. *Chhaang!* I say, Edith, I think Hercules has been in the barracks again and taken a nip." The captain stood up and said, "Attention."

Hercules got up, moved to the captain's side, and sat.

"Hercules, you are confined to quarters until further notice," said Captain Hennessy. He took a whistle from his pocket and blew it. Then he yelled, "Sergeant Battis!"

Moments later a Gurkha came running.

"Sir."

"Sergeant Battis, you are to escort Hercules to his quarters. He is to remain there until further notice. He is intoxicated. Furthermore, the cause of his intoxication is chhaang. You are to search the barracks and destroy any chhaang that you find. Dismissed."

"Yes, sir. Hercules, attention. March, chop-chop!" snapped Sergeant Battis.

"Quarters?" Asked Stella.

"The doghouse," whispered Mrs. Hennessy.

"I'd say tea is in order now," said the captain as he led us to the house.

"Sugar, Reverend Tutter?"

"Yes, thank you."

"So you see, Reverend Tutter, even though the populace has been stable since Lieutenant Colonel Sir Francis Younghusband's diplomatic endeavor, we must remain diligent, for the northern threat persists."

"What threat is that?"

"The Russians. I simply don't understand how America is willing to forget what the Great War was about and let the world return to the Dark Ages. America is part of Western civilization, perhaps a rather poor part, but still a candle in the midst of darkness. Regretfully, the responsibility has fallen upon England's shoulders, but England will stand, even if alone, and hold the light, forever if need be."

"Captain Hennessy, Reverend Tutter is a guest, and I'm sure he must be very tired after crossing the pass," said Mrs. Hennessy.

"Ah, excuse me, Reverend. America is not all bad. I have half a dozen indigent relatives living there, and that's not counting Mrs. Hennessy's side of the family. If it weren't for America, I daresay they would be here in Tinru. A wretched thought. We could put them in the monasteries, I suppose. Best not to think about it. You made quite an impression on General Bruce. He said you were a minister with a bit of the soldier in you. Have you ever been put to the test?"

"What test?"

"Action. Put one's foot across the threshold of mediocrity. Have greatness thrust upon you!"

"No, I've never been a soldier."

"Pity. There are no other endeavors that reveal the inner man."

"America has tried to remain a neutral country, as you have observed. Of course, as the recent past has shown, it isn't always possible. The army is not a popular career. Business is where we field our warriors."

"Rubbish, you're comparing starving rats to a lion. The true test of character can come only under fire."

"You wouldn't call that pluck when Reverend Tutter defended himself against Hercules?" asked Stella.

"No, I'm afraid I wouldn't, Miss Joyell. What I am speaking of must be experienced in a life-and-death situation where the dark angel awaits the vanquished. There is no substitute! Money, commerce, ha! Isn't that right, Agamemnon?" said Captain Hennessy as he looked up at the stuffed boar's head mounted on the wall. "I say, it's not war, but it's a jolly good test of man, and I'm sure General Bruce would enjoy hearing of your bout. Are you game, Reverend?"

"Game for what?"

"I'm talking about a bit of pig sticking. Surely you've heard of the Kadir Cup?"

My pulse jumped. "No."

"Horse, lance, hog, and glory, I like to say," said Captain Hennessy. "Of course, this is not the Kadir Cup here in Tinru. We call it the Varson Cup after one of Tom Longstaff's men. He actually took a wild boar and spear with him during the expedition just to stay in form."

"Are you talking about catching a greased pig in a pen?"

"My god, man, don't you understand? I'm not speaking about a bowlegged ham sandwich. I'm speaking of the porcus indomitus, the wild boar!"

"There are no wild boars in Tibet; it's too dry and barren."

"Of course not. I have a private herd. Agamemnon there is the sire of some of the most indomitable boar on the continent. Come with me."

We left the house and hiked for a few minutes to the top of a hill behind Captain Hennessy's home.

"Do you see that lake over there and the gully that empties into it?"

"Yes."

"I call it Swinegri-La. I daresay there must be at least forty boar there."

"Do you hunt them in the pen?" I asked.

"No! They are released down in the marshy area by Lake Mampo, where there is brush and cover for them and turf for the horses. Are you game, sir? I can have a hunt prepared for tomorrow. I haven't put Triumph in action for a while, but it will be good sport if nothing else. I'll have Sergeant Battis move some boar out to the lake and put some beaters at the outlet, just so it won't take all day to find one of them. What say you to that?"

"I need to keep moving. My sirdar and porters are a lot slower than I had planned."

"Just send them ahead. Miss Joyell can watch over them. This is friendly territory; there is absolutely no danger from bandits. I'll go over the route with her myself."

"Well, if you think she'll be safe. I promised her father I would take care of her."

"It's completely safe and with your horse you can do in a day what they do in three. Now I'll take you over to the stable and have Private Burke set you up with a spear and whatever else you need. I'll speak to Miss Joyell while you are preparing."

I went over to the stable and began to test the feel of the various spears. Private Burke suggested I test the spear while mounted and standing in the stirrups, which meant I would need my boots.

"A man's balance is not the same when he is in stirrups as when he is standing on the ground. It's best to be up and active if you want the best from a spear," said Burke.

"I'll get my boots and be right back."

"As you like, sir."

As I passed the garden gate, I saw Captain Hennessy and Stella together. The wind and sun were such that I could hear and see them while being unnoticed. I stopped and listened.

"So you see, Miss Joyell, the situation in Tibet is far from stable. Although the British government seeks opportunities for trade with the Tibetans, the isolationist policy of the Tibetan government rebuffs the interests of the competing powers."

"The Russians?"

"The Russians and other interests. His Majesty's interest is dual: increasing our influence while restricting the influence of the opposing powers. It is a most delicate situation. Frankly, it is not a job for a soldier, but I have decided to make the best of it."

"What does this have to do with my journey to Everest?"

"Everything. There are two opposing religious factions in this country, plus the Dalai Lama. One group opposes opening the country, and the other group encourages it. Right now, those that encourage interaction have the Dalai Lama's ear."

"Isn't that good?"

"Yes and no, for the isolationists claim that the Everest expeditions are the cause of recent natural disasters and other problems. Climbing that mountain is an assault on many of their sacred beliefs. If the expedition succeeds and anything unusual happens—and I mean *anything*, such as a bird dying in the Dalai Lama's garden—it will be used to bring the isolationists back to power. Miss Joyell, you are in a perfect position to make sure the Everest expedition fails."

"If they fail, others will return."

"True, but with each passing year, the isolationists will lose more power. We need only a few more years to cement the stability of the reformists," the captain said.

"What right has England to control Tibet?"

"What right has darkness to smother a candle? You know the work your father has done. Do you want to see what life is like without that candle? Shall we take a tour? Shall we step outside of Pax Britannica and see the filth, disease, and brutality that are the norm in this feudal society? Miss Joyell, you are a product of the Enlightenment, as am I and as is England. Had Jane Austen been born Tibetan, she would have been tied to a plow and would have never known pen and paper. Shakespeare making prayer flags? Really, have you no appreciation for England's gifts to the world? In the name of king and country, I ask you to make this expedition fail."

"Very well, I will. But I must remind you of what Oscar Wilde said," replied Stella.

"Wilde? That wretched fellow."

"He said, 'In this world there are only two tragedies. One is not getting what one wants, and the other is getting it.' It is my opinion that the British government lacks experience with the second."

"But you will help?"

"For king and country? I will."

"Excellent. My suggestion is that you attach your affections to Mr. Mallory; he is the key climber and motivating force behind the expedition. If he falters, then the expedition falters. Mind you, he is a married man, and in no way do I condone adultery."

"Shall I bring you his head or only his locks?"

"Just bring me failure," said Captain Hennessy. "As for compensation, I cannot offer you anything. But should you decide to go to England, the government has advised me that a fund to assist you in your relocation will be provided."

"And what about the reverend? Is he to slide into a crevasse, be buried under an avalanche, or fall off a cliff?"

"Actually, I agree with General Bruce. Reverend Tutter is a gentleman and a man of the highest moral caliber."

Stella cleared her throat.

The captain continued: "When Mr. Mallory was here, he became agitated when the reverend's name was mentioned. Before I met Reverend Tutter, I assumed Mr. Mallory was concerned that the reverend had fallen behind or worse at the start of the march and that his actions might compromise the expedition in some way. It was Mr. Mallory who pushed for his being allowed to tag along, owing to his financial contribution. And Mr. Mallory is a gentleman and takes his agreements seriously; furthermore, I'm told he is not one to abandon a fellow. After I spoke with Colonel Norton, it became clear that Mr. Mallory's unease was due to Mr. Hinks's and the Royal Geographical Society's extreme reluctance to have non-British on the expedition."

"Captain Hennessy, the reverend is a womanizer and a liar," said Stella.

"If that is the case, I find it most interesting that you as a single woman would elect to accompany him to the ends of the earth."

"He provided me with an opportunity."

"No doubt he has, and you choose to repay it with slander. Miss Joyell, I am a cavalry officer, and one thing I know is that a man's true character is never clearer than when he is on horseback. I watched the reverend with Endswell, and I've never seen a finer team; that teamwork can come only from mutual trust and respect. Miss Joyell, I hope that your comments about Reverend Tutter are based on your inexperience and immaturity. Now Miss Joyell, if you would come with me, I have one more thing to show you."

"And that is?"

"The proper use of a pistol."

"Surely I won't need that. Are you concerned about Reverend Tutter?"

"The reverend? No. I just told you that the reverend is a most honorable man. You will be without the reverend for a few days until he catches up with you. I have suspicions about Pasang. Have you noticed how he dresses in European clothes? Strikes me as a bit of a womanizer, he does. Miss Joyell, you are an Englishwoman in Tibet, a rose among thorns. Never forget that." Hennessy motioned her toward the gate. I went to my room, got the boots, and returned to the stable.

"Right you are, sir. I got Endswell all ready for you. She's a good horse, I can tell you that. She's not one to hesitate or flinch. This horse, Endswell, she's got something."

"What's that?"

"When I brought her in here and she saw the spears on the wall, her ears shot straight up and she took to snorting and stomping her feet like she couldn't wait to get started. I've never seen a horse do that before. She'll take care of you, sir. Leg up, sir, leg up," said Private Burke.

As I took the spear from Burke, Endswell reared up and snorted.

"Take her over there, sir, by the trees, and do some turns to see how the spear feels. I'll bring others over for you to try. Remember, sir, keep your heels down. Go for the pig's vitals, and never let him get under your horse. Go round that tree and have a go at those piles of straw."

After a few trials, I had the knack of it. I heard pistol shots and rode over to where they came from.

"Does the captain think you are not safe in my company?" I asked Stella.

"Frankly, he doesn't think you are much of a danger to anyone except perhaps yourself," said Stella as she glanced at Captain Hennessy. He was silent for a moment and then took her hand.

"Remember, don't hold and fire. Bring the pistol up slowly to aim and then fire, like this."

The gun fired and a bottle shattered.

"Excellent," said the captain. "I think you've got it. And how about you, Reverend Tutter. Are you ready?"

"That I am."

9

THE HUNT

The next morning Stella, Pasang, and company resumed the march to Everest. It took longer than expected to arrange the hunt. The pigs had been overfed and were so lethargic that a man riding a tortoise could have killed one.

"Sorry, we will have to postpone. No sport, no glory. They'll come around in a couple of days. I remember in Afghanistan, the Pasha Khan would put his men on half rations for a couple of days before a battle. Rascals fought like hornets."

A couple of days later, Sergeant Battis reported that the pigs were very animated and that a half dozen had been selected. After breakfast on the day of the hunt, we rode to Lake Mampo. We paused on a small hill overlooking the lake and valley.

"Remember, Tutter, let your horse follow the pig, and let your lance follow your eye on the pig. Triumph is a master at anticipating the swine's tactics. From the looks of Endswell, I'd say she's all-out if she puts her mind to it. Fine day for a hunt—cool, no wind. Sergeant Battis has released six boar, and the beaters have driven them down toward the lake. The pigs won't go past the end of the lake, where there is a canyon. They don't like canyons; too confining for them, I suspect. You would do well to stay clear of the canyon also. They'll either stand and fight or run back up through the marsh to this end of the lake if you end up down there," said Captain Hennessy.

"I see."

"Ready?"

"Yes," I said.

"Very well. Best of luck to you. Sergeant Battis, sound the charge!"

At the sound of the bugle, Endswell reared, snorted, and then leaped forward and charged toward the lake. I was knocked off balance and only stayed on by grabbing her mane.

"No prisoners!" I heard Captain Hennessy shout as I hung on.

I had no sooner recovered my balance than Endswell turned to the left and leaped over several boulders. Had she gone mad? I hadn't seen a pig or heard a sound. She landed and stood motionless for a moment in a small clearing, then suddenly spun around and headed for a gap between two large boulders. As she did, I saw a boar bolt ahead of us. The boar was cornered. We blocked his only escape. I raised my lance, but the boar faced us head-on, so there was no clear shot at his vitals.

"Back, Endswell, give him room. Let him come around to the right."

The boar saw an escape to his left and went for it. As he passed, I threw my lance. It landed between the boar's front legs, and as the boar rolled, the lance flew into the air, hit a rock, and then hit me in the head. I fell to the ground as Endswell turned to pursue the boar.

"Endswell, wait!" I cried. To my amazement, she stopped.

"Did your horse stumble? That was a fantastic cornering maneuver, Reverend Tutter, worthy of the 36th Jacob's Horse regiment."

"Endswell is a fine horse, but she is a novice when it comes to boar. When the boar turned on us, Endswell panicked and stumbled as she tried to back up. It was all I could do to keep her from running off," I said.

"One does see this quite often with a novice horse. Why don't you take Triumph and I'll take Endswell, as Triumph is a made pony and I have a lot of experience on green horses. I wouldn't want you to miss another opportunity because of a skittish pony."

"Oh no, I couldn't."

"Really, it's no bother. I insist. When I saw you charge off as the bugle sounded, I thought, *if the chap only had a made pony, there'd be no swine left in all of India.*"

"I'm sorry. I must decline."

"Why the devil would you decline?"

"I suppose it's an American thing. Once we latch onto someone, we like to see them through it. It's faith, really: Americans believe anyone can achieve anything, and in this case, the anyone is Endswell."

"It's a most peculiar notion. To hear you tell it, one day America may have a horse for a president. But if that is your decision, then let's get on with the hunt. I suggest we head down near the outlet, as the pigs like the marsh. I'll swing wide to the east and drive them across to you. Then as they come up the hill, you will have the high ground and a clear shot. It will give Endswell a leg up also, as this is all new to her."

It went as planned. Two hogs came charging from the marsh and up the hill via a gully. This time, I was ready. I nudged Endswell, but she stood firm. I squeezed my calves again, but she stood still. The hogs were nearly underfoot.

"Forward, Endswell—charge!"

It was useless; she ignored me. The pigs ran past us. Luckily, the captain was chasing a boar along the edge of the marsh and did not see what was going on. I tried to turn and pursue the two pigs, yet Endswell refused to budge. I gave her a couple of heels, but still she stood motionless. And then I saw him. It was the largest boar I had ever seen, with monstrous tusks and a woolly coat that rivaled that of the hairiest yak. The boar was so confident that he moved not in a scurrying, nose-scraping manner like the others, but with a self-assured trot, his head aloft. Endswell snorted and reared. Now I understood. She had been waiting for the king of the porkers and a real fight. The boar heard Endswell's snort. He stopped and leaned back to stretch his front legs while kicking large rocks down the gully with his rear legs. Raising his head, he rolled his snout and sounded a loud, trumpeting grunt. With head lowered, ears forward, and hackles raised, he charged. Endswell leaped forward. I thought the boar was stupid for attempting an uphill charge until I tried a thrust with my lance. I was riding downhill and was off balance. If I tried to throw, then I would fall. The hog knew this! He had led Endswell into the steepest part of the gulley. Our momentum was such that we could not stop. Suddenly, the pig stopped and dropped to the ground. As Endswell passed over him, the hog jumped, turned, and tried to gore the horse. Endswell stumbled and fell, taking me with her as I attempted a last defensive thrust with my spear. As I got to my feet, I saw the hog charging at me. I ran for some rocks and climbed them, I knew no pig could climb boulders, but the boar followed and continued to follow as I moved toward the rugged protection of the canyon walls. I saw Endswell rearing up, with her front legs frantically clawing at the rocks. She was unable to follow me on the steep cliff where I had sought sanctuary. I stopped and threw a large rock at the boar, but with one swipe of his snout he batted it back toward me. No matter where I climbed, he followed. He acted more like a goat than a pig.

Then I found myself with nowhere to go. I stood on a narrow ledge on the canyon wall above the raging torrent that flowed from the lake. His snout moved slowly back and forth, as if he were contemplating the most painful torture that his tusks could deliver. He grunted as his head jutted forward several times, testing to see how much room I had. Then he snorted and lowered his head. He was going to rip me from toe to belly in one long swoop. From below I heard the captain yell.

"My God, man! You've taken on Tiberius. He's no boar—he's a demon. I haven't seen him since he killed three beaters a couple of years ago. One can only marvel at his grit; he is a true warrior."

"He's going to kill me!"

"Ah yes, he does seem intent on that, now that you mention it."

"Help me now! Use your lance."

"Sorry, old boy, I've got a bad knee and can't climb. Not to worry though. I'll send Sergeant Battis for a rifle. It'll be a clean shot from here."

"God help me!" I cried as Tiberius lifted my leg from the ground.

I remember flying into the air, falling a long way, and then hitting the river.

10

THE CONVENT

Om ... mani ... padme ... hum ... . Om ... mani ... padme ... hum ... . Om mani padme hum ... . Om mani padme hum ... . Om mani padme hum!

"Stop, stop. I can't breathe. Stop! Where am I?"

The chanting stopped. I opened my eyes, but it was dark. There was a dim yellow light near my feet. I moved my toes. I felt my legs and there were no gouges on them. But the boar had thrown me from the cliff.

"Where am I?" I shouted.

I shouted again and then I started coughing. It was hard to breathe because of all the smoke. I thought I was suffocating. I got up and tried to flee but blacked out and fell to the floor.

Om mani padme hum....Om mani padme hum....Om mani padme hum!

I heard the chanting again and opened my eyes. This time there was another light and beside it was a face. She had a halo, but it was a black halo. Her face was smeared in soot; her clothes were dirty and ragged. She held a cup of hot liquid to my mouth.

"Drink."

I tried to drink but gagged. It was rancid butter tea. I had all but forgotten how bad it tasted.

"You must drink. You are weak. You have slept for two days since Ani Pema and I found you in the river. We brought you here."

"Where is here?"

"You are in the Gampopa nunnery, and I am Ani Dawa."

"I need to get back to Tinru."

"That will be difficult. Tinru is far away."

"How many days away?"

"I don't know. I have never been. I have only heard of Tinru because it is the birthplace of the Abbess Notgob."

"Then I must speak to her."

"You cannot do that. The abbess is in seclusion for a month. She can't be disturbed. If you want her blessing, then you will have to wait."

"I don't want her blessing. I just want directions to Tinru. Isn't there anyone else here who knows?"

"No. We are nuns and were brought here when we were very young. Most of us do not know where we are from or by what route we arrived. In my case, I only remember riding on a pony for many weeks."

"Then I will go and find Tinru."

I got up and tried to walk. My right knee was very stiff, and as I put on my boots I noticed the top of the right boot was ripped. Tiberius's tusk must have caught the boot instead of my leg when he threw me from the cliff.

"How do I get out of here?"

"I will show you," said Ani Dawa.

She led me through a door, down a hall, and through another door to the outside. I was on one of a series of roofs.

"You can go down this ladder."

I looked out onto a desolate place. The monastery was perched on the edge of a vertical canyon wall, and in every other direction there was nothing but an endless vista of large boulders. Crossing them, I would be like an ant in a bowl of marbles. Escape would be impossible unless I knew the way.

"If I follow the river downstream, where will I end up?"

"I don't know; only the abbess knows."

"Then I must see her."

"You can't. She is in seclusion, meditating, as I have told you."

"Can you give her a note?"

"It is not permitted."

"What about when she eats? I could talk to her then."

"We do not know when she eats. We just place food in her chamber every evening."

"OK."

"So you will leave now?"

"No, I must rest my knee for a day or so before I can go. Ani Dawa, how did you get me here? It looks impossible to get to the river."

"There are steps carved into the canyon wall. They were made by the hermits who came here long, long ago, before the monastery existed. We carried you up them."

"So if I go to the river, then I can cross it and follow the trail."

"I do not know if there is a trail on the other side."

"Then how do people come and go?"

"No one really comes and goes. Sometimes monks come for festivals, and once a year the abbess goes to the monastery at Shekar Dzong. We grow our food and pray. I must go now."

Ani Dawa left me. I could walk but had a bad limp. I needed a horse. I wandered around the monastery, trying to find the abbess's cell. Eventually I found a door with a small bowl of food sitting in front of it. I tried to open the door, but a voice called from down the hall.

"You must leave. Go away."

"Oh, I'm sorry. I was looking for Ani Dawa."

I turned and saw an old woman moving toward me.

"Go away. Get out."

The old nun's hairstyle was even more elaborate than Ani Dawa's. It consisted of three hair halos with mirrors in between them. She had prayer wheels in each hand but could barely manage to spin them because of her age and frailty. She kept telling me to leave, but it was in the cadence of prayers. I don't think she had uttered any words other than prayers for most of her life.

I left and went to the courtyard to plan my next move. The monastery was a charming but ramshackle accumulation of stone, mud, yak hair, sticks, and dung. There was no rhyme or reason to the construction. I realized that my cell was directly below the abbess's cell and that all I had to do was crawl out of my cell window, climb up, and crawl into hers. I would do it tonight, after her meal had been delivered and the nuns had gone to bed.

I opened my window and stuck my torso out. There was no balcony to stand on, but there were several beams sticking out of the wall above the window. I had made loops from fabric, and I used them as stirrups. I tossed one over a beam, put my foot into it, and raised myself. I was now halfway to her window I hooked a beam over the upper window with another piece of fabric and pulled myself up. I crouched on the window ledge. I paused and listened; her room was silent. I pulled on the window and it opened. I climbed inside. Once again I was overwhelmed by a suffocating cloud of incense and the smell of rancid butter; it took all my energy to keep from gagging. There was a faint glow of a candle coming from across the room, and as my eyes adjusted to the darkness I saw the silhouette of a figure seated on the floor. I entered the room and crept toward the figure, which remained motionless. It was a woman and she was chanting. I gently touched her shoulder. No response I touched it again. Still no response but the chanting continued. *Perhaps she is so old that she is senile.* I moved around to the front of the abbess. I touched her again and spoke.

"Your Holiness, I must speak to you. I am sorry to bother you, but I have to get back to my people, and you are the only one who can help me. I fell into the river. Ani Dawa found me and brought me here. But I can't stay. I have to leave," I said.

The chanting had stopped.

"I know who you are, Mr. Tutter. You do not need to tell me." As she spoke, she turned and looked at me. The light from the candle brought her face into view. She was young and beautiful. *How can she be so young?* I thought.

"Mr. Tutter, you are a man of God, yet you fear for what you do not have."

"No, I'm not afraid. I just have to get back to the expedition."

"Desire is not fear?"

What have I gotten myself into? I thought. *I just want directions.*

"Your Holiness, I can never hope to be graced by your wisdom. Your words are like rain upon the frozen ground; better that you share them in the spring with the warmth of the coming sun."

"Your leaving is not a problem; it has never been a problem. You are free to leave at any time."

"I know that but I don't know the way."

"Nor do I."

"But you travel once a year to Shekar Dzong."

"I do."

"Then you must know the way," I said.

"The way is not important, nor is the destination; only the journey matters."

I was becoming frustrated but spoke calmly. "Your Holiness, the monastery is surrounded by a wasteland on three sides and an impassable gorge on the fourth. Without directions, it is impossible to leave here—not to mention, my leg is injured."

"Yes, your leg is injured. Have you been to the springs?"

"What springs?"

"Tanggomu, "tears of the repentant demons." Come, follow me."

She stood up, grabbed the candle, and stepped behind a curtain. I followed. Behind the curtain was a shaft with a ladder descending into darkness. I followed her down. At the bottom of the shaft was a door that opened into a gap between large boulders that lay against the monastery wall. She grabbed my hand and led me through a maze of boulders, and in a few minutes we were in a clearing with several small pools of steaming water. She let go of my hand, walked to the uppermost pool, removed her robe, and got in. I started to follow.

"No, Mr. Tutter, this is the curative spring for overwhelming desire. You must go over there to the spring of restorative graces. Each spring has a special power, which comes from the tears of the demons that wept when the great monk Milarepa recited the Nine Blossom Sutra before them. Now go and soak."

I asked what the other springs cured, but she did not respond. I could hear her faint chanting. There was enough moonlight to make out the basics of the springs. I counted six springs; each had a small sign that both promoted the benefits of the spring and downplayed the virtues of the neighboring springs. Some of the springs were surrounded by boulders with paintings on them. My spring had paintings of a crippled person being led into the water by a flying Milarepa and emerging healed. What with the warm water and the lack of pain, I nodded off. For a few minutes, I understood why the demons had wept at the monk's words. I understood that the giant boulders surrounding the monastery were the false tears of the unrepentant demons, and when these tears covered the earth all of humanity would be trapped in chaos. I understood the meaning of compassion. I saw the boulders melting into water. I saw a thousand million points of light floating in the pools; the essences of every living thing in the universe. Then the abbess kicked me in the head.

"Come, we must go."

We went back to her chamber, back to the darkness, smoke, and isolation.

"How is your leg?"

"Much better, thank you. I was dreaming when you kicked me. I saw the boulders turn to water and points of light floating in the pools."

"That was no dream, Mr. Tutter. You only opened your eyes to the light of truth. Would you like tea?"

"Yes, please."

She turned and placed a pot on a small charcoal stove, and then she moved the candle to a shelf to find the tea. When she did, the candle lit the wall above it. It was an erotic painting. She saw me take note of it.

"Do you like my painting?"

"Well...yes, it's very nice."

"You seem hesitant."

"I am. It's not what I expected to see in an abbess's cell."

"Am I not young and am I not beautiful?"

"You are."

"And are those not illusions?"

"Well, not for me. You, me, this floor, your beauty are real, not illusions."

"And the unhappiness that springs from your reality—that is also real?"

"Of course. 'That's life,' as we say."

"This painting is to remind me of the fatal path of desire and the suffering that comes from desire."

"You follow the path of righteousness."

"I follow the path of light, but I still stumble in darkness," she said.

She turned and removed the pot from the stove. Then she faced me and dropped her robe. "I need to know if desire is truly suffering," she said as she took my hand....

The first light of dawn entered her window as she lifted her head from my chest and kissed me.

"You must go. Everyone will soon be up."

"But you are in retreat. Who will know?"

"They will know. Go now, please."

"And the directions—will you help me get back to the expedition?"

"I will."

"Today?"

"No, not today but soon," she replied.

I dressed and went to the window. As I climbed out, I turned and said, "I don't know your first name."

"Chesa."

I made it back to my room without anyone seeming to notice. I saw Chesa again the next night and the following. I had no intention of falling in love with her, but she was falling in love with me.

"I think love is more powerful than prayer. When I am with you, I see a light greater than the love of a million yogis."

"And when I leave, where will your light go?" I said as I looked at the painting.

"You can't leave; I won't let you. You love me, don't you?"

"Of course I love you, and I speak of leaving only because I want to protect you. Don't you see that we are putting our lives in danger. We will be punished if we are found out. You could be expelled. I don't know what would happen to me."

"No one will find out."

"But they will."

She turned away and said, "Then go!"

As I dropped from the window, I felt a tear hit my cheek.

Things seemed normal around the monastery. I didn't detect any stares or attempts to avoid me. I helped with chores as a form of gratitude but also because it gave me access to food and supplies. I decided to leave. I would hike down to the river and try to follow what looked like a very faint path up the other side. I didn't know if it was the best way to go, but it was in the right direction—or at least I hoped it was.

I climbed up to the window one last time, but it was locked. I knocked, but there was no response. I went back to my cell and waited for dawn and breakfast. I sat at the long table with the nuns, having a breakfast of tea and tsamba. Suddenly there was noise and screaming in the courtyard. The door flew open and a woman carrying a rifle and dressed in a lambskin coat and felt boots stepped in. She was dragging a crying Chesa by her hair.

"So your abbess is the whore who dares to hide the foreigner from me!"

She let go of Chesa's hair and jumped up on the table. Chesa fell to the floor. Several more men and women, also carrying rifles and dressed in thick lambskin coats and felt boots, had come into the room.

"Who dares to defile the sister of Nima, the bandit queen of Buddha's blessings!" she screamed. She didn't have to look far to find the answer. I started to get up, hoping to run for the other door, when I felt a knife against my side. It was Ani Dawa; so she too was a member of the bandits and had told Nima about me and my affair with the abbess. I sat back down. Nima stood next to me and placed the tip of her sword under my chin. She lifted my head until our eyes met.

"You are not as ugly as I thought you would be, but you are still ugly," she said. Then she turned to Chesa and said, "For this pig you have blackened our family's name. This is how you shame me after my many gifts to you, the abbess." Addressing her companions, she said, "Take her robe and give her filthy rags to match the darkness of her soul. Then cut her hair, give a bowl, and send this whore to Phari."

A couple of the bandits grabbed Chesa.

"No, sister, please! Tutter, help me! Please help me!" she cried.

"Chesa is a good woman. Please be compassionate. If she erred, it is because of youth," I said.

"And she did not err because of you? The foreigner who entered her cell, violating the rules of the monastery? You deny seducing her?"

"Of course I deny it. I entered her cell because I wanted to leave here. I was told that only the abbess—"

"She is no longer the abbess! She is a nothing!"

"I was told that Chesa was the only one who knew the way out. Chesa refused to help me unless I slept with her."

"The words of a whore," cried Nima.

"No, sister, please listen to me. I erred because I stepped onto the left-hand path. I felt desire, but I felt only love in that desire. Surely Lord Buddha knows that it is better to learn to swim in order to cross the river rather than to just contemplate the life on the other side."

"You quote the scriptures to your liking, not to their intent. I will not hear more of your lies."

Chesa must have realized at that moment that arguing virtue with a bandit was useless.

"Tutter is a liar! He climbed into my room and raped me. I speak the truth now. I lied before because I thought in compassion all would rise to the light like the lotus. He said if I told anyone, he would kill me."

Nima's sword returned to my neck. "So the ugly dog lies."

"I do not lie. Go to the cell of Chesa and look at the painting. See the soul of this woman. See her map to power using the union of male and female. Ask her to recite the tantric verses she spoke as she swelled from the male energy she took." Words rolled off my tongue as I created scene after lurid scene worthy of Dante. Chesa tried to speak, but Nima ordered her gagged. Finally I put my hands together in prayer and placed my head upon them. "May God have mercy on her soul," I said.

Nima dropped to her knees and placed her hand on my head.

"I am a lowly bandit who sought favor by giving money to the holy ones. But never until this moment have I felt the presence of one who is truly touched by God. Come, Mr. Tutter, I will take you to your people."

11

THE BANDIT QUEEN

We left the monastery and took the path to the river, where the rest of Nima's band and their horses were waiting. I looked back and saw Chesa, head shaved and in rags, heading down the path to the river.

"Get on. You will ride with me until we get another horse," said Nima.

"Is it far?"

"Two nights of cold and then a day of wind," she said.

"Chesa has no food. How will she survive?"

"Let her tears grow food."

Nima and I were the last to cross the river. We traveled for two days through the maze of boulders. On the third night, Nima ordered the bandits to set up her tent. There was a bit of a ruckus until she threatened to castrate one of them.

"They are like dogs; they think that by running ahead, they are leading. I should kill them."

"Kill them? They are members of your band. Don't you trust and depend on them?"

"No. I rule by fear. They hate me, but they hate each other more than me. They know that if I die, then one of them will take over and that he or she will kill his or her enemies. If they leave me then they will die, for they are criminals. They are in hell and Nima is their master. Look, do you see how they sit around the fire, sharing the food but counting the grains of barley in their bowls. Theirs is an uneasy peace. That is how I sleep, Tutter. Nima is their goddess of life. Come."

We went into her tent and she made tea. She handed me a cup, which I took without looking at until I started to drink from it. I dropped it.

"It's a skull!" I cried.

"Yes," she said as she refilled it and gave it to me again.

"I thought only lamas had these cups."

"I killed a lama and now his cup is mine."

"You killed a lama? Why?"

"He promised me a thousand blossoms of gold and silk shoes. He said that I had been sent by Pe-har to bring forth a million points of light. When I asked when the blossoms would arrive, he said, 'Soon.' He always said, 'Soon.'"

She pulled her hair back on the right side of her head. Her ear was missing. "'Here is your blossom, leper,' he told me as he cut off my ear,'" she said. "Then he brought me before the other monks and said that I was a leper. Everyone believed him. I had nothing. I became an outcast, and my only friends were beggars and thieves because they could afford to know the truth. One night I went to the altar of Chakrasamvara; the next day I found boots and a coat. I prayed again and a wild horse came to my cave. I went to the altar a third time, and on my return to the cave the rock I had used to close it had been split by a sword.

"When I told the others what had happened, they said the goddess had given me the tools for revenge. I said I would kill the lama. They were frightened because they knew that the goddess had given me the power and that I would use it. Chakrasamvara told me to build an alliance to destroy the power of the Red Hats. My sister was to be abbess of Gampopa and let Ani Dawa build an army of invincible nuns under the banner of the Seven Diamond virtues. But you corrupted her and so my plan has been corrupted."

"And for that she must die?"

Nima laughed. "She will not die; she is with my brothers in Lhating. I humiliated her only so that the Red Hat spies would believe that I truly had made her abbess to show my devotion to the universal compassion of Lord Buddha. Now sleep. Tomorrow we will get food and horses."

The next morning there was a different attitude among the bandits. Instead of the moody shuffling about, there was an air of excitement. The horses were groomed, and bells and ribbons were tied to them. Some of the bandits even used their filthy fingers to scrub their teeth.

"Fat lambs and fresh tsamba tonight!" shouted Nima as she fired a shot into the air. "Get on, Tutter."

"I'll wait here."

She pointed her pistol at my groin. "You will ride because you must pick a horse."

"Surely you are safer with just one rider on your horse. You can choose one for me."

A shot went between my legs. "Only the dead stay behind; there are no cowards among us."

We rode down from the hills and into a wide valley. From the hills we had seen that the shepherds were still in their tents. I had assumed that Nima was trying to surprise them, but to my shock she fired a few rounds in the air. The herdsmen began to sally forth from the tents.

"What are you doing? We could have surprised them. Now they are going fight us."

"Of course they will fight. Do you think I would steal from a sleeping man? Do you think I am a coward because I am a woman? Hang on; if you fall, then you will die. These nomads are from the northern lands and know nothing but sheep, horses, and revenge. If they catch you, then they will turn your skull into a cup, for they are kin of the dead lama."

We were charging full-on into a group of them with harquebuses aimed at us. Others ran to their horses and sheep. Nima took her harquebus from its scabbard and handed it to me.

"I prefer a sword. Kill the ugly ones first. I want to save the handsome ones till last."

I looked over her shoulder. We were no more than thirty feet away from two nomads and their guns. "By the power of the goddess Chakrasamvara, I banish you to the Nine Infinite Hells of Ice!" she shouted before putting the reins in her mouth. She had a pistol in one hand and her sword in the other. Both nomads had their harquebuses trained on her, which meant they were basically trained on me as well. I panicked; I was going to die! Nima was a lunatic. I started to drop the harquebus when she raised her arm and sword, jolting me back. I pulled the trigger, the gun fired, and a nomad fell.

Seeing the other harquebus trained on her, Nima rolled and dropped to the right side of her horse for cover. I didn't know what she was doing, so I tried to compensate by leaning the other way and was thrown onto the other nomad as he fired. His shot ricocheted off my harquebus, causing it to spin around. As I landed at his feet, the stock hit him in the head, knocking him out cold.

"You are a fearless man, Tutter. Leave the harquebus and take his sword; we don't have time to reload the gun," said Nima. "Now get on. We have to hurry. They are trying to drive their horses and sheep off in order to save them."

It turned out that the two nomads with the harquebuses were the only ones armed with guns. Some had been pointing bone trumpets, hoping to frighten us. The others, who had gone to release the horses and sheep, had only knives. We rode back and forth through their hopeless defensive gestures until they either ran off or were knocked to the ground.

"Tutter, go find a horse worthy of your courage," said Nima, as she dismounted and began to walk among the injured nomads.

I went over to where the horses were tied up. I tried to mount a mare, but she bit me. Another kicked me after throwing me off. Finally, I settled on an indifferent stallion. As I rode back toward the bandits, I noticed that Nima was still inspecting the vanquished nomad men. I rode over to her.

"He is a fine-looking horse, Tutter. I can see you know many things. Perhaps you are actually Tibetan. Do you not want a woman?"

I looked at her questioningly.

"These nomad women are famous for their passion. It is said they can melt the ice of hell with only their eyes!" she said, looking around at the other bandits as they nodded in agreement.

"No, I don't want a woman," I said.

"As you like."

Then she pointed to a nomad sitting on the ground and said, "Norbu, Pemba, bring him." The bandits grabbed the man, tied his hands, and put him on a horse.

12

SONAM

That night I noticed Nima's tent was decorated with lanterns and banners. Nima was absent from the campfire and meal. I was sitting with the bandits, drinking looted chhaang and listening to their increasingly preposterous tales of bravery, when Nima shouted from the tent, "Rabten, bring him."

"Our queen awaits you; do not disappoint her and you may live," Rabten said as he grabbed the nomad by his tied hands and led him to her tent.

Pemba looked at me, brushed a lock of hair from her eyes, and said, "Like the others here, I rob to live. But our queen robs for pleasure."

"No, Pemba, she robs for revenge. Though her flesh seeks treasure, her heart longs for the warmth that can only be found in those whose lives have not been cursed," said Tashi, another woman bandit.

I saw the others nod as she spoke.

"That is why you are not in her tent, Tutter. Because you slept with Chesa, she knows that she cannot find the Golden Jewel of Refuge through you," said Tashi.

The hum of a repetitive chanting came from the tent.

"She is invoking the goddess Chakrasamvara," said Pemba.

A few minutes later the candles dimmed, and moans of passion filled the camp. The bandits looked uneasy; their devil-may-care attitude was replaced by nervous glances. One by one they moved away from the fire and went to sleep among the rocks and bushes until I was left alone with Pemba.

"Come with me," she said.

We walked to the edge of the camp, where the mountainside fell away to the distant valley.

"Out there to the north, on the other side of this valley, that is where you will find your people. Rabten met them just before we got to the convent. He was disguised as a wandering monk. After giving the expedition his blessing, he told them he would send other monks to help with the climb, as he had had a dream that the climbers would find a sacred treasure hidden by the great monk Milarepa. That treasure will summon a thousand chanting Buddhas, who will build a great monastery on the island in the center of Lake Pomotangprea. He told them that the monastery will be a great blessing for the people, and that was why he and other monks wanted to help. Tell me, Tutter, is that why the strangers climb Chomolungma, to find treasure?"

"No."

"Then why do the foreigners go to the icy home of demons?"

"For us, it is not hell, but rather a challenge. We are like Nima, who robbed the nomads but only after she knew they were waiting for her. She wanted the challenge, the sport. We go because we are warriors without a war and our bellies are full."

"If my belly were always full, then I would be happy to grow old and idle," she said. After a pause she asked, "So there is no treasure on Chomolungma?"

"No."

"So that means she has only you."

"What?"

"Do you understand why Nima did not kill you? She plans to take you to the mountaineers to gain their favor, and then she will steal the treasure. But once she knows there is no treasure, then the only thing of value is your life."

"The expedition won't pay a ransom for me. They don't have any money and I'm not a member."

"Then she will kill you because her plan has failed. She doesn't like being wrong."

"Then I'll go. I'll leave tonight."

"If I let you go, then Nima will kill me."

"Come with me."

"No, I stay with Nima."

I had to call Pemba's bluff. I turned and walked away.

I woke up when I felt dirt hitting my face. I was lying on the ground and tied to a stake, next to the nomad Nima had kidnapped.

"Are we both to die?" he asked.

"Of course not. Nima does this only to intimidate her followers. After a bit of bluster, she'll release us."

Suddenly there was a boot on my head. Nima.

"So you would leave Nima?"

"After Pemba told me where the group was, I thought it was best if I just left. I didn't see any reason to bother you about it. Besides, if you took me to the group, you might encounter the authorities."

"You think that I am a coward? That I am afraid of Tibetan soldiers?"

"No."

"Then you would deny me treasure?"

"There is no treasure. Besides, you are a great warrior. Why would you care for treasure?"

"You see that Nima is great. You see that she cares little for money. Do you not also see that those who protect their wealth make the best adversaries?"

"Mountaineers will not make great adversaries. They come to climb. This is the third expedition. Have you ever heard of them finding treasure?"

"That is why they return."

"No, they return because they failed before. They are driven by excitement and adventure, like when you robbed the nomads."

She started to kick me when the sound of a rider approaching caused her to turn around. The rider got off his horse and spoke animatedly. The look on Nima's face indicated something important was going on. When the rider finished, she turned back to me.

"You are blessed, Tutter. Rabten, untie him. Your friends have received the blessing and protection of the lama of Shekar Dzong. I am bound to honor the lama's commands because the monastery is sacred to the goddess Chakrasamvara. You may leave anytime you want. Rabten will get your horse and give you food."

"Are you going to free the nomad?" I asked.

"No."

"Why not?"

"Because I love him," said Nima as she walked over and gently rubbed the side of her boot against his cheek.

Nima knew I had to cross nomad territory to reach the expedition. They would recognize me and their horse.

"I need a different horse."

"No."

"If I try to cross nomad territory with this horse, I will die."

"Yes."

"What about the lama's orders?"

"I'm setting you free."

"You're sending me to my death."

I looked at the other bandits. They looked at me with what I thought were stupid smiles. But maybe they weren't stupid. Maybe they were smiles of respect, for I had been blessed by the lama. Nima had not killed me. That had to count for something. I needed a miracle, so I decided to make one.

"No, I will take another horse, and I will take the nomad with me. He will ride the horse I took from the nomads."

I dropped to my knees to untie the nomad. Nima put her sword to my neck. I continued to untie him as she moved the blade across my throat; a few drops of blood fell on the nomad's face. He was trembling. I finished untying his hands and placed his left hand on his chest with the right hand on top of it. Then I moved to untie his feet; all the while, Nima kept her sword to my neck. Thousands of images of my death passed through my mind. I took a deep breath, and as I exhaled I could see Nima, the bandits, the nomad, and myself below me. I was a lotus about to burst to the surface. There was a light coming from my hands as the ropes fell away from the nomad's feet. As I finished untying him, I saw the light move to the nomad's face. His look of terror had turned to serenity. I grabbed his hands and we stood up together. Nima dropped her sword and took several steps backward as she saw our horses come trotting over and lower their heads before us. We mounted the horses and rode through the bandits, who made way for us. Then my vision evaporated. I was on horseback, riding next to the nomad. We were both covered in sweat, and my neck was bleeding. I dared not look back.

From a distance the nomads recognized their stolen horse. We soon were surrounded by howls of joy and looks of amazement.

"Wangdue!" said the nomad as he jumped from his horse and led me through the crowd of nomads.

"Wangdue has saved Sonam from the bandit queen!" he cried out again and again.

He had named me Wangdue, the conqueror. Even the two nomads whom I had injured during the attack were celebrating.

"Wangdue will stay with my people," Sonam said.

"No, Sonam, I must get back to my friends."

"Then Sonam will take you to your friends."

We feasted that night. There were countless toasts to my heroism and even a reenactment of my charge by several drunken nomads. The next morning, Sonam and I set off for Shekar Dzong.

13

SHEKAR DZONG

When we arrived at Shekar Dzong, I learned that the expedition had left for Rongbuk two weeks earlier. I also learned from traders that Pasang and Stella were only a day or two away from Shekar Dzong. Once I was reunited with Pasang and the porters, I had no need for Sonam. I said good-bye to him, but he refused to go.

"I cannot let you travel alone, Tutter. I will help you in your quest."

"I appreciate that, Sonam, but where I am going requires experience and skills that you do not have. Nor do I have equipment for you."

"Then I will go as far as I can with what I have, and I will wait there until you return."

I tried to dissuade him but failed. So in the end, I sent him to the market to find what he could buy to make his journey as comfortable as possible.

The next day I went to see the lama Dargye. He was busy creating a thangka while the other monks in the room were quietly chanting. I thought he was unaware of my presence at first. When he stepped back from his painting, his lantern illuminated a grotesque scene: long-nosed Caucasian men lay on the ground, being torn apart by demons, while Mount Everest stood defiantly in the background. I was stunned. This was the lama whose blessing had saved my life; now he was painting a picture foretelling the expedition's doom.

He laid down his brush and turned to me. As my eyes adjusted to the dim light, I tried to resolve the contradiction between the violent painting and his kind face and gentle demeanor.

"The painting is derived from meditation. The goddess of Chomolungma will never submit to a white man."

"But Your Holiness gave your blessing to our expedition; in fact, your blessing saved me from the bandit queen Nima. Why do you paint a mural like this?"

"I can ask the goddess for compassion, but I cannot change her mind. Her world of spirits and demons is especially turbulent, for Chomolungma is a unique place. The goddess never expected men to go there. To go there is to challenge her, and to challenge the goddess is to bring chaos. The Dalai Lama ordered that all the monasteries offer help and blessings to the expedition, but he lives far from here. Though he is of the Gelug school— the Yellow Hats—and we are of the Nyingma school—the Red Hats—we follow his orders because he is the Dalai Lama."

So Captain Hennessy's recruitment of Stella was no idle fantasy by a bored frontier officer after all. The Red Hats were a reactionary sect that hated foreigners. Captain Hennessy and the British government did fear that the conquest of Everest could lead to a backlash against outsiders. I didn't believe his mumbo jumbo about the goddess and demons, but I knew Pasang and the porters did. I needed the lama's personal blessing. I had planned for Stella to present a gift to the lama, but my separation from the expedition had left me with only the clothes on my back. I could ask for another audience with the lama, but after seeing the painting, that didn't seem like a good idea. The lama had returned to his painting. I stood behind him, and the lantern illuminated him and his work while his body cast a shadow over me. As he painted, he was repeating prayers.

"Your Holiness, may I ask for a personal blessing? Not a blessing to climb the mountain, but a blessing that opens my eyes so that I may teach the other climbers of the dangers of angering the spirits that live on Chomolungma."

He did not respond. I moved beside him to ask again. As I did, the light from his lantern hit my belt buckle and sparkled. The lama turned his head to look at the belt buckle, a gold-plated relief of my father-in-law's church with tiny rhinestones on the cross atop the steeple.

"What is that?" he asked.

"It is a picture of my father-in-law's church. He commissioned these belts as a way to earn money for his church when he traveled the American West several years ago. He gave me one. Do you like it?"

He smiled. "Your father-in-law has a church? He is like a lama, with a monastery and monks?"

"It is not the same as here. No one lives at the church; people mostly come on Sundays. Some are there on other days, when they work on programs, such as helping the poor."

"The prayer wheels stop?"

"We don't have prayer wheels."

"Then the demons and spirits must be upset that they are ignored."

The lama had plenty of time to think about such things and enjoyed inquiring about them. But I didn't want to explain the differences between

93

our beliefs. I just wanted a few prayer flags to show Pasang and the porters.

"Well, actually, that is what the diamonds are for," I said as I removed my belt. "The diamonds on the steeple emit a light that reminds the demons of the eternal brilliance of God, day and night. So we don't have to use prayer wheels."

"Amazing."

I removed the buckle from the belt and gave it to the lama. He held it to the light of the lantern and watched the rays of light move around the room.

"This steeple is like a stupa with diamonds?"

"Yes, Your Holiness."

"Your monastery is very wealthy to have so many diamonds."

"We have many generous members. Please keep the buckle. It is my gift."

The lama held the buckle to his forehead and called to the monks present in the room. They came over and sat in front of the lama.

"This man has given a gift to the monastery," he said as he moved the buckle around so that they could see the sparkling rhinestones. "See how the divine light of wisdom cuts through the darkness. The foreigners are very rich. They have a chorten that is one thousand feet tall, with diamonds as big as yak eyes. He has given us this power bolt, which he wears around his waist to protect him from spirits and demons, so that we can copy it. When every monk has one, we will use our powers to summon the demons that live below the rocks. The demons will bring us diamonds as big as yak eyes, and we will build a thousand-foot-tall chorten whose brilliance will banish darkness. We will have the greatest monastery in the world."

The word of the buckle had spread throughout the monastery, and the chamber quickly became packed. The lama was lifted up and walked on the shoulders and heads of the enthralled monks to make his way across the room to the statue of the Buddha. For a few moments he appeared to be floating, rather than stepping on the monks. When he reached the statue, he leaped to the floor, took a bunch of masks from the wall behind the Buddha, and threw them to the monks. The monks with masks started dancing as they moved in a counterclockwise direction around the outer edges of the chamber. The lama stood in front of the statue, which was lit up by lanterns on each side of it. Between the sparkling rhinestones and his shadows, it was a dramatic sight.

He held the buckle in his right hand. His left hand was under his right elbow and his left foot hooked behind his right calf. He started chanting ecstatically and then would thrust his hand toward a masked monk, who would then fall to the floor. One after another, the masked monks were symbolically vanquished, to the cheers of the other monks. When the last masked monk fell, the lama turned to sit at the foot of the Buddha statue, placing the buckle at its feet.

His meditative posture must have been a signal to the monks, for as soon as he was seated, they all left the room. I was alone with him. I approached the lama and spoke: "Your Holiness, I am honored that my gift will help the monastery. Can you give me a blessing that I may present to my Sherpa and my porters? I'm sure that you know how much it would mean to them."

He did not respond; as a matter of fact, he acted like he didn't hear me. I repeated my request. Again no response. I touched his shoulder. Still no response. I put my face to his and again asked for a blessing while shaking his shoulder. He did not respond. I had to have something from the lama if I wanted to remain in control of Pasang and the porters on the mountain. I looked around. The room was full of artifacts, everything from small golden Buddha statues to pendants and drums.

I thought of taking a Buddha statue but realized that it would be hard to convince the porters that the statue carried a specific blessing for them. A prayer flag hanging above the statue had an inscription about crossing snow in bad weather. It was probably used for monks when they were crossing passes. That would work! I climbed up the statue and stood on its shoulders while I ripped the flag down and shoved it in my pocket. I looked down, the lama was still meditating, so I grabbed a couple more flags to sell or trade to locals in case I needed a favor. I climbed down and left the monastery. Sonam was waiting for me at the top of the stairs, just outside the doors.

"Wangdue, you have been with the lama a long time. He must have liked you."

"He did, Sonam," I said as we walked away from the monastery. "He was delighted to give his blessing to our group, and he gave me a prayer flag dedicated especially to us."

"If he made a flag for you, that explains why you were there for so long."

"Yes, he was very impressed with our expedition."

That evening Pasang and Stella arrived at Shekar Dzong and set up camp outside the village. My presence took them by surprise, as they had assumed that I was behind them.

"Tutter! Tutter!" shouted Pasang as I walked into the camp. "Where have you been? There were many times I wanted to turn back to find you, but I knew that you expected me to continue with Stella to the English at Chomolungma."

I had no way of knowing if he was telling the truth. In fact, I was surprised to see him. I had feared he would take everything and head to Lhasa. I don't think Stella would have noticed until she saw the Potala

Palace.

"You have done an excellent job, Pasang. How are the porters?"

"They are nervous because they are far from home. They have heard stories of the dangers that live on Chomolungma."

"I have just received the blessing of the lama of Shekar Dzong. I'll go and show it to them."

The porters were gathered around a fire and cooking when I approached them. I greeted them, but they remained seated, staring at the fire.

"Pasang tells me that you are all well and that your spirits are high. I know that one reason you are excited is that the lama of Shekar Dzong is a famous and powerful lama and that you hope to receive his blessing for our expedition. Unfortunately, the lama is in seclusion and cannot be disturbed." There was a mumbling and head turning when I mentioned the lama was in seclusion, and one of the women stood up. It was Chhamzi. I hadn't taken much note of her when she was hired back in Darjeeling but had started to notice that she was not the average Sherpa woman as the march progressed. I realized now that she was too intelligent be content with a porter's life.

"We can't go farther unless we meet the lama. It is too dangerous," she said as she pointed to the monastery. The others nodded in agreement.

"I know that. I am sorry that he is unavailable, but I did meet him just before he went into seclusion and he gave his blessing for the expedition."

"How do we know that?" asked Chhamzi.

"Because he gave me this prayer flag to take with us." I removed the flag from my pocket and held it up for them to see. I looked around for Pasang. I knew he could read, and I didn't want him looking over my shoulder and asking questions. He had gotten distracted by a local selling eggs and was not paying attention to me. There was murmuring and then nodding and smiles among the porters as I walked around and let the women touch the flag. They bowed their heads and put their hands together in thanks. When I got to Chhamzi, she took the prayer flag in her hands and carefully smoothed it out so as to read it. I could see her lips move as she scrutinized each word. It dawned on me that she might be literate as well as intelligent, something I would never want in a porter.

"'*Om mani padme hum...*'" Then she stopped, looked at me, and said, "Where does it say Chomolungma? I don't see it."

I started to take the flag away from her but stopped. I didn't want to give her any encouragement. Besides, maybe she recognized only a few words. I decided to call her bluff.

I leaned toward her and said, "I'm very impressed, but you need to read more of it to find the lama's blessing."

Her lips began to move and then stopped. They started again but she did not speak.

"Let's read it together for the others," I said as I took the flag from her hands and held it up for the others to see: "'From the unreal lead me to the real, from the dark lead me to the light, from death lead me to immortality.'"

She knew the mantra and started reciting it as soon as I started reading. I knew now that she had just recognized one or two phrases but could not read. In reciting with me, she had relinquished her bid to challenge my authority. The porters were excited and for a moment I thought about my sermons at home and how rarely they were listened to with such intentness. Most of the congregation saw them as credits toward a ticket to heaven. I felt inspired. A few minutes ago, the women had been on the verge of rebellion; now they were willing to march into what they considered the depths of hell. I needed to forge more prayers as soon as possible. I decided to steal a prayer wheel from the chorten on the way to Rongbuk, so that I would have a supply of mantras.

"You are a virtuous man, Wangdue," said Sonam. He had been standing behind me, listening. "You use the lama's blessing to lead the porters. There are many men, even among my people, who use the words of the holy men to cheat and harm others."

"Wangdue? What, pray tell, is a wangdue?" asked Stella, who had followed me.

"It means 'conqueror.' He is a nomad; I saved his life."

"And where on earth did you find a pulpit from which to do that noble deed?"

"You're in great form, Miss Joyell. I had worried that you might not be up to the march," I said. "As for Sonam, I saved him from a murderous bandit, not the devil. He feels indebted and insisted on accompanying me."

Sonam piped up: "Wangdue is great man. I owe my life to him."

"What did he say?"

"He said he owes his life to me."

Stella was unmoved. "I expect you'll see your debt is more costly than you ever realized."

"What does she say, Wangdue?"

"She says it is true, Wangdue is a great man."

"What did you tell him?" asked Stella.

"I said that you agreed."

"I never said that."

"I know. But that is what he wants to hear."

"He wants to hear lies?" Said Stella surrounded by a barren, windswept landscape. She stared at me while one lock of hair kept flopping in her face.

A grinning Sonam stood beside me. He looked at me and then he looked at Stella.

"There is a time for everything, and right now our goal is to join the expedition and help it succeed and not judge each other."

"Perhaps in some ways I have misjudged you. I haven't exactly lived a cosmopolitan life," she said.

I turned to the porters and said, "This is Sonam. He will be joining us, so make him welcome."

Stella and I joined Pasang for dinner. I told them of my encounter with Nima. Pasang said that surely I was protected by the most powerful spirits and gods, for the only captives that he knew of who had survived Nima's wrath were amputees who had been freed as warnings to others. Stella's eyes widened; I could see that she was impressed. The next morning we set off for Rongbuk.

14

RONGBUK

What a contrast they were: Mount Everest, the top of the world, only fifteen miles away, and the low, flat buildings of the Rongbuk monastery. Only the chorten beacon for the Buddha's wisdom dared to rise above what was needed for human habitation. Pasang had gone ahead of us and spoken to the lamas at Rongbuk. He met us just outside the monastery.

"The abbot of Rongbuk, Nogmo, has just finished six months of living in isolation in a local cave and is very weak. Nevertheless, we are welcome to visit, and he will give us his blessing. The lamas told me that the foreign men and Sherpas came down from the mountain a few days ago to receive his blessing, as things have not been going well. He gave them his blessing but warned them, 'Chomolungma, the goddess mother, will never allow a white man to reach the summit.' They then returned to base camp and the climb while Mr. Mallory has stayed behind with altitude sickness. He hopes that a dry room and rest will get him back in shape."

"Mr. Mallory is here?" said an excited Stella.

"Yes, as I said, he is ill and resting," said Pasang.

We set up camp outside the monastery and then prepared for an audience with the abbot. George Mallory heard that we had arrived and came out to the camp.

"Reverend, I thought that I would never see you again after that mix-up in Darjeeling. General Bruce is quite the disciplined chap, and once he set his plan in motion, it was all fall in and march off after we left the gymkhana. Do you know it was several days before he noticed you were missing?

"I'm not surprised."

Mallory laughed. "Yes, it was one morning at breakfast when the subject of strength and endurance came up, and he decided it was time for another bout of arm wrestling. He called your name, and when you didn't answer he sent one of his boys round the camp; of course they reported you were nowhere to be found."

"No one else noticed I was missing either?"

"We did. It was Shebby who mentioned it first. But you must understand that we were on the march, and many things needed to be sorted out, it's like in a war, one can take account of a situation only when one's nerves can relax."

Stella spoke up: "The English mind can be overly focused at times, Reverend Tutter; I'm afraid they just forgot about you. One need only read the papers and see the postings of parents inquiring as to their lost progeny, of whom their last recollection was seeing them off to boarding school. It was nothing personal, was it, Mr. Mallory," said Stella.

Mallory was freed from the quagmire of searching for excuses as he took notice of Stella.

"Yes, that's it. We English tend toward self-absorption. I remember how strange America was. One was expected to participate in any number of activities simultaneously. The important thing, Reverend, is that you have caught up with us. You have more grit than I imagined, following us across this barren wasteland with its barbarian inhabitants."

Mallory turned his attention to Stella. "Miss Joyell, I am shocked to see you here. Surely you haven't been kidnapped by the reverend as barter for some brigand," he said as he gave her a flirtatious smile. "I'm surprised your father let you leave."

"Actually, Father encouraged it. You see, I had been thinking of leaving for England, and he was in a bother about the influence of the Bolsheviks there."

"No mention of that radical Bloomsbury Group?" asked Mallory.

"They are suspect too. Reverend Tutter, on the other hand, made quite a positive impression on Father. He felt that a man of his character would be an ideal guide for me when I tested life's waters. Father decided that he would rather see me wander across a windblown wasteland and eat supper cooked over a yak dung fire than flirt with musicians and such at piano recitals in London."

"If you continue to base camp, then you'll have your fill of windblown wasteland and smoke."

"Of course I am continuing to base camp."

"We can't offer you much there: We are at war with a relentless adversary, Mount Everest. Though she lacks trenches and barbed wire, she has crevasses and icefalls. Her artillery is avalanches and her storms humble the Haber-Bosch gas attacks. We are fighting humanity's last great war with nature."

Mallory's eyes sparkled as he spoke to Stella, and she stared at him, biting her lower lip. Was she smitten? Or just going to work? I couldn't tell.

Despite his obvious attraction to Stella, I knew that Mallory loved his wife. While in New York, he told me he had written her daily, and I remembered him sending a boy to the post office with a letter to her and his children when I was in Darjeeling. Could Stella seduce him? She had grown up on a remote mission in India. She was smart, but was she worldly? I had to wait and see.

Pasang and the porters were excited about the audience with the abbot. They rummaged through their meager belongings for the white scarves they had brought to offer as gifts to him. Most of the porters had only the clothes on their backs to wear, so all they could do was dust off and mend their clothes. Pasang, however, had a clean shirt and an odd-looking feather-filled coat.

"Pasang, where did you get that coat?"

"It is a gift from Mr. Finch. When he left Darjeeling, he gave it to me for helping him recover many of his things stolen by the porters on his return from Chomolungma. I spent several days searching the markets and homes of the porters for the missing things, and he gave me this coat as a reward. He said he wouldn't need it any longer."

"The abbot may be impressed, but I hope you are not going to take that silly thing on the mountain. You look like an old lady wearing a feed sack," I said. "It's so long that it will get in your way when you have to climb."

"I will take it, sahib; it is very warm."

The next day Mallory had planned to head back to base camp. But Stella asked him to stay and explain the ritual involved in the meeting with the abbot. Unfortunately, Mallory's only knowledge of Tibet, despite two previous expeditions, was a 200-word Tibetan dictionary and his maps. In spite of his Cambridge days and intelligence, he was not curious. He considered Tibet a horrible place full of mean people. He was a singularly dedicated man. Unlike Somervell, with his watercolors and ear for Tibetan music, or Noel, with his incredible imagination and cinematic genius, Mallory had but one interest as a mountaineer: the summit of Mount Everest.

We gathered in the courtyard in front of the monastery entrance. The porters sat at the foot of the steps leading into the monastery to ensure they heard his every word. The abbot was dressed in brightly colored robes and seated on a large chair. The light was brighter on his upper body and head, making him appear otherworldly, while the surrounding monks were barely visible. The abbot accepted the scarves from the porters and then offered prayers and a blessing. After I gave the abbot a scarf, I nudged Stella, who seemed hesitant to approach him.

"Go on, he won't bite," said Mallory, who was standing beside her.

She approached the abbot and held out the scarf, and he graciously accepted it. As she turned to walk away, the abbot spoke to her. She realized he was speaking to her but could not understand what he was saying. I motioned for her to turn and face the abbot, and I translated his words.

"You are the white woman called Stella from the land of Dorje. Two nights ago I had a dream in which you were surrounded by Cham dancers. I was awakened by a howling dog before the dream was complete. It is rare to dream of the Cham dance. In fact, I have never heard of a lama having dreamed of it. When the real dance is performed, no one leaves before it has ended, for to do so is to leave your life in the throat of the devil. I think it must be the same with this dream. Will you stay and watch as my monks complete the dance in your presence?"

I caught a glimpse of Mallory; he was shaking his head, seemingly in disbelief, as Stella turned and looked at us.

"What is the Cham dance?" asked Stella.

"We know it as the devil dance," I said.

"Devil dance? A devout Anglican girl surrounded by dancing devils! Has Aleister Crowley been here recently? What am I to do? I've never been in such a situation."

Mallory said, "Superstitious rubbish. The only reason to be here is that the porters believe in it, and that keeps them on the mountain; as for you, Miss Joyell, your time would be better spent getting under way."

"Reverend, speaking their language must give you a certain insight into the lama's mind. What do you think?"

I knew Pasang was listening and that the porters counted on him to keep them informed about what the foreigners were saying. Whether he told the truth was another story. The porters would take a refusal as a slight to the abbot and a negation of his blessing. Politically, it made sense to honor the abbot's request, and on a personal level I was curious.

"I think it's an honor to have the abbot ask you. The devil dance is a rare and unique performance. Their costumes are probably hundreds of years old."

"No doubt full of hundreds of years of fleas also. Miss Joyell, the porters have their blessing. Let's move on before these characters come up with another scheme to ask for something. Their entire lives are nothing but exercises in self-absorption. The abbot is engaging in hocus-pocus to impress his minions," said Mallory.

"Cham dhee tho-tshey. Joyell ga-tshey rey," said Sonam, with clasped hands. He bowed repeatedly, first toward the abbot and then toward Stella, to the obvious pleasure of the porters.

"What is he saying?"

"'Cham very important. Miss Joyell important.' You can see it means a lot to them," I said.

"Oh, very well. I can't see any harm coming from it. Please tell the abbot I'm honored to watch it."

I relayed the message, and within seconds the low rumbling of trumpets was audible from the interior of the monastery. Dark-robed monks in crested caps stepped from the shadows and entered the courtyard to form a perimeter. The monks stood with the ends of their long bronze horns resting on the ground of the dusty courtyard. Then two monks stepped to either side of the monastery doorway and sounded their instruments, decorated conch shells. Masked figures charged from the building swinging swords and staffs as they engaged in a mock battle. The masks were anthropomorphized animals or combinations of animal heads. Some had horns; others had large pointed ears and long fangs; and one had a trunk and deerlike horns.

I had expected to see a drama between good and evil, but what I saw looked like senseless fighting. An angelic figure with a painted face and wearing a long gown slowly descended from the balcony and hung suspended above the animal demons. I assumed the bleached blonde yak-hair wig indicated that the figure was meant to be Stella. I gave her a nudge and said, "Good job with the hair," but she shook her head and remained silent, fixated on the dance. The animal figures took notice of the celestial figure and stopped fighting; suddenly the scene was pastoral.

The Stella apparition began to chant, and as she did, the creatures formed a circle and danced around and under her in simple but clumsy steps. This went on for a while until six of the animals ripped off their animal masks to reveal huge, grotesque humanlike heads. These dancers attacked the others with their swords. The recently pacified animals did not defend themselves and fell to the ground. The human heads' dance became frantic as they celebrated the demise of the animal heads. The frightened yak-wigged angel attempted to flee. The demons leaped at her, but she remained out of their reach. Then they formed a pyramid of bodies to try to reach her. The ugliest one, his face covered with oozing pustules, made his way to the top.

Just as he got there, another figure entered the courtyard. The large-headed figure represented a European and was dressed as a mountain climber; it looked like Mallory and even had a crude ice ax. How could a group of monks in a remote Tibetan monastery make such a convincing mask? The mountaineer demon danced as he circled the demons in the pyramid, who tried to kick him away. Suddenly he leaped onto the pyramid and scrambled toward the top, where the uppermost demon was attacking the angel. The lower demons used their large heads as battering rams against the climber, but he was too agile and quick. In a few moments, he was locked in struggle with the uppermost demon.

The mountaineer demon, though smaller than the demon with pustules, gave a mighty swing of his head and knocked the first demon to the ground. He then stood on top of the other demons and joined his palms with the yak-wigged angel above him as she turned to face him. She started to smile when suddenly the demons in the pyramid released their grips on each other and allowed the pyramid to open. The mountaineer fell, and the demons closed in upon him with swords and clubs.

Stella grabbed my arm. I expected the angel figure to react with shock, but she ripped the wig from her head and then the flowing gown from her body to reveal a bloodstained skull with glowing eyes and a skeleton figure. Stella raised her hands to her face and screamed, throwing herself onto Mallory. It was a confusing story. Even though as a child I had listened to dozens of Buddhist and Tibetan folktales, I had nothing to compare it to. I looked around. Pasang had gone from smiling to sullen. The porters were obviously distressed. Sonam stared at me in disbelief, as if I had suddenly betrayed him.

The abbot was clever. His "dream" was actually a well-planned scheme to frighten the porters and the members of the monastery. He had given his blessing, as ordered by the Dalai Lama, but he knew that it was worthless, for the superstitious minds of the Tibetans were convinced that his dream was reality. Except for Stella's sobbing and Mallory's gentle pats on her back, the onlookers were silent. As the dancers returned to the monastery, the abbot began to chant. The chant was answered in a call-and-response style by the monks who were standing around him.

"What is he saying? I fear he is about to sic more of the horrible men on us," said Stella.

I listened for a few moments. "He is invoking the goddess of Mount Everest, Chomolungma. He says that now he understands the dream and that his prayers are for the foreigners, that they may understand that the goddess is all-powerful. That she is the loving, peace-bestowing goddess of the world, yet she is also the fearless destroyer of those who challenge her, be they demons or men. The monks are responding by saying that they respect the goddess and thank her for her wisdom and justice."

"George, it's a curse. The abbot has put a curse on you. It was not a dream. He planned the whole thing," said Stella, her left hand clutching his jacket sleeve.

"I didn't think these people had it in them to put on a show like this. They have more imagination than I had thought possible," said Mallory as he stepped back from Stella and looked at me. "I can see that the fairy tale has made Miss Joyell distraught. Thankfully, Somervell wasn't witness to this. He'd be going on for weeks about the connections to Celtic runes or Stonehenge or some other rot. But it's nothing more than a Brothers Grimm tale in a foreign land."

"I think it is more complicated than that, Mr. Mallory," I said.

"Complicated? Or rubbish with an exotic cast? I didn't come halfway round the world to contemplate rubbish. I came here to climb a mountain. As a matter of record, I've come here three times with one purpose: to climb that mountain," said Mallory as he pointed to the south. "I expect I'll see you and your party in base camp shortly. Good day."

He turned and, being a fast walker, was out of sight in a few minutes.

"I can't believe he is ignoring the dream," said Stella.

"He is a driven man. He knows that this is his last chance. I don't think anything but the mountain itself will stop him," I said.

"But he can't ignore the wisdom of the lamas. They have meditated and prayed for centuries; one can't simply dismiss it. They have powers that we Europeans will never understand. By ignoring them, he is creating anarchy. Suppose Mr. Mallory succeeds in his endeavor. The lamas will lose control, and Tibet will be turned topsy-turvy."

"You sound as if you care more for the status quo than for Mr. Mallory's welfare, Miss Joyell," I said.

"I am concerned for Mr. Mallory. But having lived most of my life as an Englishwoman among the native people at the mission, I can say that many foreigners have little regard for other cultures. To dismiss these people, as Mr. Mallory has, is not only rude but could invite the more unsavory and reactionary elements in Tibetan society to engage in behavior that would endanger the Western presence here. And the West has much to offer Tibet."

"Life is not static. As an American, I can testify to that."

"Anarchy and reactionary behavior are best not encouraged. It took years of diplomacy before an Englishman could openly set foot in Tibet. I don't think that Mr. Mallory or his colleagues appreciate that fact."

It was obvious that Stella was in Hennessy's camp. But how far would she go to disrupt the expedition? I had assumed she would rely on her beauty as her primary method of disruption. I was wrong. She was more than a coquette.

"Do you really believe the abbot had that dream?" I asked.

"Yes. Why shouldn't I?"

"I thought it was very well organized, considering we arrived the day before. Do you really think blondes are part of Buddhist mythology? "

"Considering your background, Reverend, you are in a better position than I am to answer that. But a culture that has made meditation and self-knowledge a cornerstone of its society probably understands what we take for the occult or unknowable. And I cannot believe the performance is a plot to disrupt the expedition. Is that what you are saying?"

"It did enter my mind, in part because I think the time spent in meditation is not always spent thinking about the intangibles of life."

"Are you referring to politics?"

"Yes. The abbot is playing a political game, and I am on the short end of the stick. We gave him gifts and got a blessing. Then he turned around and used a so-called dream to negate everything by frightening the porters. It is going to take a real effort and money to get them to continue."

"Why would the abbot go to so much trouble when he could have been unavailable for the blessing? And why didn't Mr. Mallory mention a problem with the expedition when they were here and received a blessing?"

Maybe she was right, I thought. Maybe the abbot did have a dream. I could not believe that Stella had planned the dream-play. She wouldn't have had the time or knowledge, plus she had been truly frightened by it. Hennessy hadn't done it: He was too interested in his pigs to write a play whose dramatics were worthy of Shakespeare. That left the abbot; his world was changing and he probably didn't like it. He had the time and people to do it. No doubt his spies had given him information on Stella. By giving his blessing, he followed the Dalai Lama's orders. By performing the dream-play, he took away the blessing. Stella had used the drama as a chance to woo Mallory, but he was indifferent. So she let him return to the mountain without shedding a tear. She was shrewd and able to think on her feet. It would be difficult to manipulate her. Stella could derail the entire expedition because she didn't need a plan, only the right opportunity. But if I didn't make it to base camp, it wouldn't matter to me what she did. I went back to our camp to talk to Pasang and the porters.

The lama's dream-play had left them terrified. No amount of talking or money motivated them. The only exception was Sonam. He seemed to believe that I could challenge even the deities. I finally threatened to fire them all and withhold the money owed them, saying I would continue alone if they refused my last offer. I pretended to be indifferent to their pleas and excuses. Forsaking my equipment, my Sherpa, and my porters and going to base camp would leave me in a vulnerable position, for I would have no idea if my equipment had been brought along, abandoned, given away, or stolen. The same was true for my food rations. Asking Mallory had been useless: His mind went blank when he was asked the slightest logistical or technical question. Trying to convince Pasang and the porters to accompany me to the base camp had given me a headache. I told them I would go for a hike and climb as high as possible to see how powerful the goddess was. If she was as powerful as the abbot had implied, I would not return. They began chanting.

I turned my back to their pleas and headed toward a nearby peak, with Sonam following me. We headed up the trail that led toward the base camp, and then we turned off onto a ridge, which led to a small peak that was clearly visible from our camp. In three hours Sonam and I were on the summit. I waved my arms, shouted, and even rolled a few boulders down the mountain to make sure the goddess knew I was there. Sonam was cautious and avoided what he thought might offend the goddess but nevertheless laughed as the boulders rolled down the mountain.

"You see, Sonam, there is no goddess," I said.

He smiled. I hoped Pasang and the porters had seen us and that my bravado trumped the abbot's dream. We had just enough daylight to make it back to camp. As we started back down, I noticed clouds in what had been a clear sky. Within twenty minutes we were enveloped in a dense fog. I thought if we kept to the ridge, it would be a straightforward descent. We would pop out of the fog at a lower elevation. But the fog did not clear, and somewhere on the ridge we unwittingly took a spur. We had walked for nearly three hours, and it was nearly dark. We were lost. I turned to Sonam and said, "I'm afraid we'll have to spend the night here. Let's find a rock and wait till dawn."

"Her wrath is sometimes like a poison," he said.

I stared at him questioningly.

"The goddess is going to kill us because you angered her. This is not fog. It is the breath of vengeance, and we will die when we fall asleep."

"Nonsense. This is fog. It happens all the time. If I had been paying attention and not been so upset with Pasang and the porters, I would have waited until tomorrow morning to climb. This fog will clear late tonight. We will find a rock, get under it, and leave in the morning."

At that moment, there was a sudden wind and a pelting of hail. Sonam dropped to his knees and began to mumble a prayer.

"It's only the wind. Get up! If we don't get out of this weather, we will be soaked in no time." I grabbed him by his collar and started to drag him when I heard the clatter of ricocheting rocks above. "Move now!" I cried as I pulled. He was a bag of sand, but somehow I moved him a few feet. Moments later, a mass of rocks landed where he had knelt.

"You insulted the goddess. We will die!" He screamed.

"It is just evening rockfall due to the temperature change."

He wasn't listening to me. He was in a stupor, mumbling gibberish. It was useless to talk to him. I went and sat under a rock to wait for dawn. I thought about how everything had gone wrong, and instead of encouraging Pasang and the porters, I had confirmed their fears. I had underestimated Tibet. In my long absence, I had forgotten that only one thing mattered here: maintaining the truce between man and spirit. I had broken the truce. I had angered the spirits of the mountains; any Tibetan could see that. Today I had played the madman, and they had all seen it. I had been defeated by superstition. Everything that happened in Tibet was the result of powers that were usually tolerant but never indifferent. In the morning I would go on alone to the base camp with what I could carry and take my chances. With luck, word of what had happened would not reach there for a while. I nodded off.

I awoke to the light of dawn. Sonam was curled up on the ground, fast asleep. We were still enveloped in fog. There was no sense in going anywhere until we knew where we were. I let Sonam sleep and walked as far as I could without losing sight of him. We were in a small depression on a ridge. As I hiked up and out of it to the crest of the ridge, there was a slight breeze. I stopped and listened, hoping it might carry the sound of water running nearby. What I heard wasn't water: It was chanting. For a moment I thought it might be the sounds of Rongbuk. Maybe we had ended up near the monastery. I stood still and listened. The fog was so thick I couldn't see for more than one hundred feet. The chanting continued; it was only one voice, a man's. Suddenly the breeze cut a path through the fog. I saw him, a monk sitting on the ground in front of a cave. He was a hermit in tattered robes with long, matted hair, and in front of him stood an emaciated yak. I went and woke Sonam. "It's time to go. I found a hermit monk; he can tell us where we are. Come on."

He was silent but got up and followed. He didn't seem any the worse for wear for having lain on the ground all night. We made our way through the fog to the hermit. The monk took no notice of us as we approached. He ignored us for quite a while as he sat facing the yak and chanting. Finally he turned to a small fire and began to brew tea.

Sonam whispered to me, "He is a very holy man. Look at his skin. It is green; he is living on nettles."

Sonam was right. He was brewing nettle tea, though I wasn't sure that was why his skin was green. After he filled the pot, he went into his cave and returned with two cups. He filled the cups with tea and turned to us.

"Welcome to the abode of plenty.
Where endless bounty is measured in a spoon and
fame is humbled by the setting sun.
All glory is prey to the ants as
flesh is cleansed of suffering and grows a universe minuscule new.
All diversions in a breath dissolve
while solitude illuminates the infinite."

Sonam dropped to his knees and crawled toward the hermit until the hermit touched Sonam's head and bade him to stand. The monk again offered the tea and we accepted, then he turned his attention back to the yak. He offered the yak tea, but it refused. The yak was definitely ill. His eyes were dull and his breathing heavy. Plus, as woolly as he was, I saw that he was very skinny. I went over and put my hand on him. The poor guy didn't even react. It looked like he was starving to death.

The hermit said a few more prayers and then poured the bowl of tea he had made for the yak back into his pot.

"When he came here, he was healthy. He stood outside my cave every morning, waiting for me to emerge. He listened patiently to my prayers and then he went off and grazed. Only a very special yak would do that. Look at his horns; see how they are curved inward. He is a reincarnated monk, but somehow a demon has taken control of him, no doubt because the demon realized that the yak is aware of his former life."

"Demons can do that?" I asked.

"It is one of their favorite things to do, because by doing so they feast on the sacred wisdom that was passed on at rebirth. That is why the yak is so skinny. Normally my prayers can drive the demon out, but this demon is very powerful. I think he comes from high in the mountains, in the ice caves."

"How does a demon enter the soul of a yak?"

"It is hard, for the yak is not like a man and tempted by a beautiful woman or like a woman and tempted by silk and gold. A yak is a humble but proud animal who follows the middle path and seldom wanders. You see that bowl by the cave? It was full of tsamba, a gift from the farmers of Shekar Dzong, so that I might make chhaang. I think the ice demon became the water in the stream that I added to the tsamba, for one day after gathering nettles I found that the bowl was empty and the yak was standing nearby with grains of tsamba on his lips. 'Oh yak,' I said to him, 'for a former monk you are most impatient and have eaten what was to be my chhaang. Perhaps you are not the virtuous monk I thought you were.' As I said that, there came a hideous and vile green belched gas, which swirled around my body as it formed wisps of serpents that tried to enter my ears and nose and mouth. Only by reciting the sutras of blessed faith did I foil the demon."

The hermit knew his stuff. He recognized a demon when he saw one. I had spent time with my uncle on his farm, and I remembered some of his cows getting something he called the twisted stomach, eating a bunch of oats after I left the feed bin open. I was pretty certain that the yak had the same thing. The yak was suffering, and no amount of prayers or nettle tea was going to help. I knew what to do, and I saw an opportunity to undo my foolish actions.

"The abbot of Rongbuk says the goddess of Chomolungma is angry because foreigners like me have come to climb the goddess's home. Are you sure the yak is not possessed by her or one of her demons? Maybe this yak was used by the foreigners and is being punished," I said. I glanced at Sonam. He was nodding. The theory made complete sense to him.

The hermit chuckled. "So the abbot had a dream about the goddess and she is angry."

"Why, yes," I said. "How did you know?"

"I was in the monastery with Nogmo when I first became a monk. He always wanted to stay in Lhasa and be a politician. He hates Rongbuk and the isolation. Anytime there is a problem, he says the goddess is angry. If strangers pass through, she is angry. If no one visits the monastery, she is angry because she is neglected. He wants to close the monastery and uses the goddess as the excuse. I have lived here for eleven years, since the year of the Tiger. He arrived at Rongbuk a year later and visited me one time. Visitors speak of him when they come, so I know that he has not changed. Living here I have never seen the goddess angry. The foreigners have come here and placed their tools and nests on her. She is not angered because she sees all as temporal. When the ice falls, that is the shedding of the self. When the wind and snow swirl, those are errant spirits seeking her comfort. Chomolungma is not angry. There is anger," he said, pointing to the yak.

"Last night the goddess tried to kill us with falling rocks," said Sonam.

"You were on the ridge at sunset?"

"Yes," said Sonam.

"That was only a yaksha that was preparing for sleep, and you were stepping on his spine," the hermit explained.

The hermit was just the man to motivate my Sherpas, and if I could ingratiate myself with him, he might go out of his way to help me.

"Your Holiness, in my homeland we have different kinds of yaks. We call them cows. They are sometimes seized by demons. As a minister, I was trained to exorcise them. May I try to rid the yak of his demon?"

"Winds carry the seed of evil around the world, and so too the path of dharma weaves vines of evil that creep unnoticed. To end the suffering of but one creature is to light a lamp brighter than a million suns."

I took that to mean yes. I needed a rope but the only thing available was a series of cords that the hermit used to suspend prayer flags around the entrance to his cave.

"Great teacher, may I use the cords and prayer flags to subdue the demon?" I asked. He nodded and I took down the cords. I tied one end around the yak's neck and then fed the other end under the yak between his legs.

"Sonam, take the end of the cord that is near the back legs, and pull when I tell you," I said as I took the end of the cord that was near the head. "Be careful of his legs." But the yak had already kicked him in the shoulder and knocked him to the ground. The monk laughed and recited a few prayers to motivate Sonam, who did not want to get up.

"I thought you were a nomad, but you look more like a fisherman by the way you act around this yak," I said. "Now get the rope and pull when I say." Even half starved, the yak was a tough character, but after several tries we knocked him over and had his legs facing straight up in the air. The yak made some muted snorts, which the hermit interpreted as curses, and responded to by thrusting a spinning prayer wheel toward the offending yak lips. I grabbed the legs, one at a time, and wiggled the yak. Then I went to his right side and punched him, but before I did, I made a few theatrical gestures and cried out, "Lord above, free this humble beast of the evil that lurks within him! Do not let the devil remain in this enchanted land of peace, but drive him back to hell!" I knelt beside the yak and placed my head and hands against his stomach.

Then I raised my head toward heaven, lifted my hands, put them together, and gave the yak a massive punch in the stomach. "Out, out, doer of harm! Pillager of peace!" I cried. The yak shook as I saw his stomach move into place. He snorted and then stood up. He was motionless for a few moments, and then a massive belch of green gas came forth, followed by frothy green saliva. The wind was such that the belched gas appeared to be pulsating around the head of the yak.

I saw the hermit carefully watching, as if it were a battle and the demon were trying to reenter the yak. He spun his prayer wheel and shouted at the green cloud. Suddenly a gust of wind roared down the mountain and blew the cloud away. The yak yawned, shook his tail, walked to the stream and drank. Then he started grazing, as if nothing had ever happened. The hermit was all smiles.

"Wangdue, you drove the demon from the yak. Only the holiest of men can do such things!" said Sonam.

I had regained Sonam's loyalty, but he had no influence over Pasang and the porters. I needed the hermit for that. The hermit had collected his prayer flags and cord and was in the process of putting them back when Sonam approached him. Sonam went on and on about how great I was to the hermit, who remained silent. I was puzzled, for earlier he had been so animated. By saving the yak, had I actually turned him against me? Was I a threat? If so, then I was no better off than before. After they had rehung the prayer flags, the lama again made tea for us. Then he went and sat on a boulder facing the sun and spoke.

"Wangdue," he said. "That is a good name but not just for your actions. It is also a name for your spirit because you have embraced the Noble Eightfold Path. In my years of meditation, never—not even in the light of a million, million glowing diamonds—could I see the path through the belch of a yak. I sought to banish the demon, but I did not have the right action. I am a hermit, renouncing all, so that I may know the Four Noble Truths. Yet I take the path of the arrogant doctor who sees all suffering as distraction; he is critical of the patient and tolerant of the disease. I hold my hands in prayer but shun the grip of courage. I walk a path but praise the clouds and sky, not my feet. When I arrived, my head was shorn and my will resolute; now my hair reaches the ground, and inner strength is like the grass of the meadows, yielding to the winds regardless of their direction."

The monk turned to me. "Do you have a knife?"

"I do."

"Cut my hair."

"My knife is not very sharp."

"No matter. Cut my hair, that I may open my heart to the path of selflessness."

I cut his hair and he seemed to take great pleasure in rubbing his palms across the stubble. "Thank you," he muttered.

Just then, the sun broke through the clouds. The hermit stood and pointed to a valley below.

"At the end of that valley is Rongbuk. It is an easy walk from here."

After all of the monk's praise, I didn't know how to ask him for a blessing. I was going to have to rely on Sonam to win over the others. I stood in the warm sunlight looking down the mountain towards Rongbuk. Snow dusted ridges ran like exposed roots to the valleys below. Thin green bands marked where the ridges ended and streams began. Most continued on to the sea, but the stream below me ended in a lake—a lake that ebbed and flowed with the seasons but never let its gift of life extend beyond its shores, like the meditating hermit. Only the Lord could create beauty in such a barren landscape I thought as I sat for a moment of reflection. Before I knew it, the warm sunlight put me to sleep. When I awoke a couple of hours later, the hermit was tying something to the yak. It was an amulet made of his hair. Where each end of the dorje met the circle, he had used a small piece of thread (no doubt from his robe) to join them.

"This will protect the yak. Do you see the dorje, symbol of indestructability and irresistible force in the center of the circle?" he said as he presented me with a handful of identical amulets.

"Wangdue, please take these amulets and the prayers and blessings they contain as my offering for the success of your journey. I prayed to the goddess that she will know you and protect you, your Sherpas, and your porters. Tell the Sherpas and porters that each hair contains a thousand blessings by the stumbling hermit Marepa."

"Marepa!" shouted Sonam. He placed his hands together over his heart and bowed his head. Several moments later he looked up and said, "Wangdue, this is the Rinpoche Marepa. He is the wisest lama in all of Tibet, and he has given us amulets. With his blessing, we have nothing to fear."

Sonam took the amulets and carefully wrapped them in his silk scarf. I thanked Marepa for the amulets; short of his coming down to Rongbuk, they were the perfect antidote to the abbot's dream. I gave him my pocketknife and offered to have a runner bring up a small mirror. He accepted the knife but refused the mirror, saying that he preferred to use his hands to guide the knife because the mirror was just one more illusion. We said good-bye and hiked down the mountain to Rongbuk.

When we arrived at the monastery, there were a lot of surprised looks but no signs of relief. It took a bit of effort to convince Pasang that I was not a ghost. There had been no thought of going to look for us; the only issues were when to return to Darjeeling and the pay owed to them. My kit and the supplies had already been distributed in lieu of back pay. And why not? Our deaths had been expected, especially after my cavalier actions on the summit the day before.

"Reverend Tutter, I can't imagine why, but it appears you have a guardian angel," said Stella. "Nevertheless I am not continuing to base camp and I think it best that Pasang and the others also not continue."

I didn't want to say much about the incident with Marepa, as I thought it better to have Sonam relate the incident. "Oh, it wasn't more than a bit of roughing it and waking up to find an eccentric hermit living behind the rock you slept under," I said. "The fellow, Marepa, says he survives on nettle tea alone. He made quite an impression on Sonam, who says the monk is famous. Marepa gave Sonam those amulets that the porters are all excited about. They're made from his hair, which I cut for him."

"You cut his hair? He must be a sight."

"Well, the yak was the only other creature around, and he didn't seem to mind."

"But a handful of knotted and filthy hair won't change anyone's mind about going on."

"If Sonam is any indication, Marepa is considered an important holy man, maybe even more important than the abbot. The solitary hermit is held in great respect in Tibet."

"Tutter, sahib," said Pasang as he approached with the other porters. "Sahib did not tell me that he met Marepa. It is auspicious that you have met him. It was not an accident. Sonam has given us his amulets." Pasang had tied a string around his neck and fastened his amulet to it. He touched it as he said, "This is not a dream, this is real. Tutter is welcome on Chomolungma, and we are friends of Tutter's. We will go with you."

Stella spoke up. "Pasang, these amulets won't protect you. The only way to be safe is not to go. Even if the abbot's dream was just a dream, it was still based on the fact that the mountain is dangerous."

Why was Stella so intent on stopping my porters? She had billed herself as the one who was going to have me accepted as a member of the expedition.

"Even if they mutiny, I will continue. Mallory said most of my original kit was still with the expedition."

"I don't care about you, Reverend. And anyway, your presence is probably a greater hindrance to the climb that anything I can do."

"Are you saying you want to stop the climb?"

"No." She paused. "I'm saying that after hiking across Tibet, I realize what an overwhelming undertaking the climb is."

"I see," I said. "So you are thinking only of the safety of Pasang and the porters?"

"I am."

"They freely accepted the job and knew the risks."

"They are desperately poor people, and you are a desperate charlatan."

"You wanted to come along. You offered to help me."

"At the time, I had no idea of your true nature."

It was pointless to argue. I had let her good looks cloud my judgment. I decided to go on up and play it by ear. I turned to Pasang.

"Are we ready to go?"

"Yes, sahib."

We left Rongbuk and Stella.

15

BASE CAMP

Base camp looked more like a stockyard than the headquarters of the British Everest Expedition. Dozens of yaks and ponies were wandering around the camp, which was in a flat boulder free spot at the end of a large moraine. Tents were in two groups, one for the English and the other for the porters. The yaks however took no notice of that.

"Bloody beast get away from here before I put you on a spit," cried Dr. Hingston, stepping out of one of the larger tents to chase a yak away from a case of tea.

I called out to the doctor.

"Well, Reverend Tutter, what a surprise. I was just checking on Manbahadur. Poor fellow froze his feet, and I'm afraid he is going to lose them. We have another fellow that lost a toe and one that is snow-blind. Mr. Beetham has dysentery but is improving. Other than these fellows, I'd say were a rather fit lot considering the conditions. You look quite fit. I gather you had a pleasant journey."

"Oh, a few detours here and there, but nothing serious," I said.

Hingston filled me in on what had happened since the expedition had established the base camp, though he had only recently returned from Gangtok, after having taken General Bruce there.

"Malaria. No doubt he picked it up on that tiger hunt in Nepal. Lucky he didn't die here, what with the altitude. At first, I thought he would be marching right back as soon as he was feeling better—not that I wanted that. Actually, I think it's because he is a soldier that he turned it over to Colonel Norton. 'Best to step aside and let the strong carry on. No sense in fighting two wars,' was what he told me. Knows we are going to make it; ordered his whiskey sent up here."

"But I am dwelling in the past, for the current situation is not a positive one. It seems that Hazard took twelve porters to supply camp IV. They were to spend the night and then return to camp III, but bad weather set in. Bruce and Odell were due up with porters the next day. They were to spend the night in camp IV and then go on to establish camp V, but the weather kept them in camp III. Hazard and the porters stayed a second night. On the third day, he evacuated, leaving the cook, because he thought Bruce and Odell were on their way. But they had turned back, defeated by deep snow. When Hazard arrived at camp III, he was shocked to find that there were only eight porters. The others had turned back in fear. When Colonel Norton discovered this, he was outraged, and said that saving the porters was more important than the summit, knowing that it might take what little reserve of time and energy they had left. So he took Odell and Somervell and went up and got them. They were successful, but it has taken a terrible toll on us. Well beyond the healing powers of tea and whiskey, I'd say."

Hingston was a practical man.

"Norton has ordered a council of war. I think you should go up to camp I. You're fit and can no doubt handle a rope. How are your porters—do they have any mountain experience?"

"Yes. As a matter of fact, we spent time practicing on a couple of passes on our way here and Pasang, my sirdar, has climbed with Dr. Kellas," I said.

"Really?" He arched an eyebrow.

"Yes. I was skeptical at first, but I made inquiries and verified it. I must warn you, though, that asking Pasang about Dr. Kellas will lead to nothing. He is reluctant to speak of him. It seems his brother died on one of the climbs under odd circumstances. I found out about it in the most roundabout way. Most of the time he will deny it and act as if he doesn't know what you are talking about."

"Won't talk, eh?" he said, staring at Pasang as he supervised the setting up of our tents. "Perhaps I should go and…"

I froze. I'd made up the Kellas story on the spot. If Hingston questioned him I'd be in trouble.

Hingston shook his head. "No. I'll leave him be. It's a form of shock, and I saw a lot of it in the war. I'll let him set his own pace. I'll warn the mountaineers and keep an eye on the Sherpas, as they can be petty at times, thinking that humiliating each other in front of a sahib is the way to recognition. Who is that other fellow? He doesn't look like a Sherpa to me."

"That is Sonam, a Tibetan nomad captured by bandits. He was a slave when I rescued him."

"Bandits? I've not heard of bandits. Where on earth did you encounter them?"

"I took a detour through a small valley in order to drop off food and basics to a colony of lepers, something my church congregation feels strongly about. I never mentioned it before because I knew the expedition would worry about delays and the prejudices of the porters. The lepers are poor but have a small mine that they work to earn their keep. The bandits were taking the lion's share and using Sonam to carry the silver, as they were afraid of contracting leprosy. I'm a man of God, but sometimes a gun is more powerful than prayer. I shot a couple of them, and thankfully that was all it took for them to run and leave the kid behind."

"I had no idea such behavior existed here. I admire your courage."

"Dr. Hingston!" came a shout from the distance.

It was Stella. Somehow she had gotten some monks to carry her gear. I also recognized one of the abbot's assistants with her.

"Miss Joyell! What in heaven's name are you doing here?"

"I thought I might be of assistance, and Reverend Tutter was kind enough to allow me to accompany him."

"I see," said Hingston.

"Her father ensured we had the provisions to take care of her so that she wouldn't be a drain on the expedition." Stella must have realized the monastery was not the paradise she had thought it was and cajoled her way up here. "I thought you were planning on staying on as the abbot's guest for a while?" I said.

"He has gone into seclusion, partially because he wants to meditate on his dream about the expedition. But before he did, he told me not to be afraid to come here and share the dream with everyone. That is why Nigma is here: He is going to tell the story to the porters. Luckily, I can speak to him in Hindi."

I had assumed Stella would be hamstrung by the language barrier, but Nigma's mother was from Gangtok and so he spoke Hindi. Stella was not giving up on her mission.

"This comes at an inopportune time. As I was explaining to the reverend, we've had bad luck up there. Major Norton has called for a council of war."

"George—Mr. Mallory—isn't in trouble, is he?" said Stella.

"Quite the opposite. He's gone up to help out with the stranded porters."

"Stranded porters! As in the dream," said Stella. She turned to Nigma and, speaking in Hindi, repeated the news. Nigma closed his eyes and began to spin his prayer wheel. His fellow monks started chanting. After a while the porters in base camp came over to find out what was going on. It wouldn't take long before the dream story spread to all the Sherpas and porters. I glanced at Pasang and my porters. The yak charms were working, for they had not the least interest in Nigma's prayers. I had to keep Stella off the mountain. With her good looks and drama, she might be able to sway the expedition, especially if there was a crisis.

"Miss Joyell is just the person to care for Mandurbar and Beetham in your absence," I said to Hingston.

"Why, you're quite right, Reverend. She's worked in her father's hospital."

I smiled.

Hingston turned to the lady in question. "Miss Joyell, your arrival is a godsend." He called to a servant, "Lopsang, see that the lady sahib has her own tent. If necessary, she can take mine and I'll share another tent." Addressing Stella again, he said, "Come with me and I'll go over what needs to be done." Hingston put his hand on her back and steered her to Mandurbar before she seemed able to utter a word. Over his shoulder he addressed me: "I'll be right back, Reverend; we must be off if we are to get to camp I before dark. Bring your cold-weather gear. If you are lacking, check with Lopsang; we have most of your original kit in the supply tent. Best bring a couple of your men too, though I see that your porters are all women. Why the devil did you. . . I digress. Come along, Miss Joyell."

Stella wasn't going to stay behind if she could help it. "Mr. Hingston, I must go with you. Just because my father is a doctor doesn't mean that I am qualified."

"I haven't time to debate, Miss Joyell, and I'm afraid I must order you to stay here or leave immediately by the way you arrived. We have no quarters for stragglers. This is an expedition. We are here to conquer this mountain and we shall, but only if we are resolute in our struggle, only if we defeat adversity, whether it be the mightiest avalanche or the cries of an injured comrade. Do you need an escort back to that mud hole of meditation? Or do you stay and fight?"

"I'll stay. Just tell me what to do."

"Very well. Come with me," Hingston said. As he entered the hospital tent, he turned and spoke to me: "Reverend Tutter, we'll leave in fifteen minutes."

Stella was out of the way, at least for now. I went to get what I needed to spend the night at camp I. Luckily, Karma Paul was up on the mountain, so I had time to brief Pasang on what he should and shouldn't say.

"Sahib knows that Pasang is fearless."

"Yes, but the English do not know that. That is why I told them you have a lot of experience. They know you are a Sherpa and that Sherpa people are natural mountaineers. That is why they always choose the Sherpa people for climbing porters. But the English do not know you. Remember that the Englishman who is brave never speaks of it. You must be like the Englishman in that way: show them that you are a Sirdar, do not tell them you are a sirdar. They will be watching you and they will see. Karma Paul will say bad things about you because he knows you are a great sirdar. That is why he kept you away from the English. Now you have a chance to show the English that you are great. But you must not argue with him."

"I will not. Marepa has blessed me."

"Good. Now get what we need for camp I. Sonam is coming with me. While I am away, teach our porters what it's like to be on the mountain. Also, instruct our porters to flirt with the expedition's Sherpas, so that if Karma Paul tries to stop us, his Sherpas will complain.

16

NORTON'S PLAN

The gray sky and the snow-covered ground merged into one disorienting world. I only knew the ground was below me because that was where my boots were. Hingston led the way, following the rapidly disappearing path to Camp I as snow, heavy wet snow fell and I followed his blurred silhouette, hoping that his comment that the monsoon had arrived was wrong. In spite of the conditions, we made it to camp I. The men had gathered in Irvine's tent and were having tea when we arrived. Hingston entered first and sat at the table without announcing my presence. When I entered the tent, they were shocked.

"It's the Yank!" said Bruce. "What the devil are you doing here?"

I hesitated, hoping that Mallory would speak and break the ice. But he didn't, and apparently he hadn't even mentioned that he had seen me at Rongbuk.

"Well, you know I got a late start, and one thing led to another."

"By 'another,' he means Dr. Joyell's daughter Stella," said Mallory.

"Stella?" said Norton. "See here, Reverend Tutter, if you intend to turn this expedition into a luncheon on the grass, it will not be tolerated. Is she here now?"

"She is in base camp, tending to Mandurbar and Beetham," said Hingston.

"A nurse, is she? Well, see that she stays there. I'll have more to say about this later," said Norton. "Don't stand in the door, Tutter. Come in and sit down. Any man who can make his way across Tibet with a thrown-together expedition team must have some sort of talent. Maybe you can be of help."

"Point well made," said Bruce.

"Tea, Reverend Tutter?" asked Somervell.

"For the benefit of you and Hingston, I will go over the situation as I see it. Then we'll resume the discussion and decide on a plan," said Colonel Norton.

Norton saw the weather as the most important element in the equation. Being a soldier, he could muster the men. But against a monsoon, he knew he was helpless. Against Mallory's wishes and Irvine's assurances that the system worked, he also decided to forgo the use of oxygen.

"Mr. Irvine is a brilliant mechanic. But the record of the oxygen apparatus is poor, and I cannot allow its use, especially considering the extra weight the climber must carry if it is used."

"But the weight is more than offset by the faster climbing," said Irvine.

"Nonsense. Too heavy, too unreliable. I wouldn't send a man to war with such equipment, and I daresay we are at war," said Norton.

Mallory started to respond but then lowered his head and stared at the floor. My mind flashed back to the monastery and the dream; maybe it had affected him. That evening in the tent, other changes occurred. The plans for well-established advance camps were abandoned. The new plan was more of a charge on the summit by pairs of climbers. There would be advance camps, but supplies would be minimal and each team would have just one shot at the summit. Mallory had enough experience and respect from the other men to challenge Norton, but he didn't.

"How are you feeling, Reverend? Has the altitude affected you?" asked Norton.

"No, I don't think it has."

"Good. I want you and the Sherpas to pitch in. You understand that we're short of men, what with injury and sickness. Do you think your men are up to it?"

"I say, is there actually a need for more men?" said Hingston.

"Of course there is. We're down to fifteen reliable men. That won't do. You know that, Hingston. What the devil are you getting at?"

"Reverend Tutter's team—with the exception of Pasang and the herdsman, Sonam—is composed of women."

"Tutter! You marched across Tibet with a band of women?"

My path to the summit was evaporating.

"Don't dismiss them out of hand, Colonel. They could be Amazons," said Bruce.

"Have you gone mad, Major Bruce?" said the colonel.

"I think the major was trying to inject some humor into the situation," said Mallory.

"Are you suggesting that we lack motivation and that a native derriere can lead us where English pride and determination can't?"

"Wouldn't be the first time, I suspect. I'm speaking as a physician," said Hingston.

Norton laughed. "Touché, Doctor."

Norton's laughter had changed everyone's mood, and within moments a couple of bottles had appeared.

"Mr. Irvine, I'd like to raise a couple of toasts before we retire for the night," said Norton as he stood with a glass in his hand.

"Please do."

"My first toast is to our success: Long shall the English shadow fall on foreign lands when the Union Jack waves from that summit where now only God and the sun look down upon it. Let all men know that if there they go, here first stood an Englishman."

"Bravo! Bravo!" shouted Somervell, as he suddenly came to life. "The sun shall never set upon colors that touch the stars."

"Right you are, old man," said Norton.

Then Mallory stood, looked around the tent at each face, and said, "I think Kipling said it best: 'We have forty million reasons for failure, but not a single excuse.'"

That struck a chord with everyone and led to another round of cheers.

Colonel Norton resumed his speech. "My second toast is to the Yank, a chap who has shown remarkable courage and grit, the proof of which is his presence at this table. Most of us here were soldiers, and we know 'forward courage,' the courage of the moment to see your way through a sudden crisis. But what we seldom see is 'humble courage,' or selflessness. By continuing on alone in order to stand by, he has shown selfless dedication. Reverend Tutter, I drink to you."

Everyone stood again and toasted me.

"Thank you, Colonel Norton," I said. "It is an honor and a privilege to be part of this team," I said, raising my glass.

"One last thing," said Norton. "Odell, Shebbeare, and Noel are coming down tomorrow. When they get here, we will sort out the final logistics. Good night."

After that, everyone headed back to their tents except Mallory. I had a hunch he wanted to speak in confidence to Irvine. I left and headed to my tent. But I stopped midway and crept back on the downwind side and sat on a rock, pretending to tie my boot.

"We might make it without a camp VII, but we'll never make it without the oxygen, Sandy. All this council of war and military jargon is rubbish. Norton's stuck on the notion that an Englishman won't use oxygen because it's not cricket, and it's going to cost us this mountain. This is my last chance. I have to use whatever tools I can. Will the oxygen equipment work?"

"Certainly. There is no doubt in my mind."

"Can *I* make it work? I'm a bumbler when it comes to technical things."

"It will work even for you, George," said Irvine.

"It's our only chance; are you with me?"

"I'm with you, George, but there are others who are better climbers. What about Odell?"

"It has to be you, Sandy, because of the kit. You're the only one who can keep it working. And besides, you're strong. Alpine pedigrees are a lot of bollocks invented by the Royal Geographical Society to keep the common folk off the mountain. How many bottles will it take to get us to the top? I reckon we won't need any to get us down, as we'll be full of pride."

There was a long pause. Irvine, I was to learn, never guessed.

"We can do it with three apiece."

"If that's what it takes, then it means we'll need to have it already on the mountain."

"How? The old man's plan won't allow time for extra supply trips."

"That's where the American comes in. Norton's over the moon about him. Thinks he's a hero because he found his way across Tibet, I suppose, though the old man knows the Yank has porters with all their fingers and toes and we need them."

"You must have some faith in him. It was your endorsement that allowed him to join us."

"True, I endorsed him. And publicly I said that I did so because he had lived here and spoke the language. The real reason of course was the money he contributed. He's a typical American: He won't give a halfpenny unless he gets something in return. Frankly, I never thought he'd follow through, as they're usually all talk and little action. The old man is going to ask the reverend to turn his porters over to us and then return to base camp with a nonsense task and the title to go with it. When Norton proposes this, I'm going to insist the reverend, along with a few of his best porters and his Sherpa as aides and possible backups, stay on the mountain because of his language skills. I'll also toss in something about Karma Paul and the lack of enthusiasm among our own porters, contrasting them with the reverend's porters, who must be incredibly loyal to him or they would not have marched across Tibet. You remember all the work stoppages and other acts of nonsense we put up with on our way here. In summary, while Norton is loading up 'the reverend's porters,' we'll ensure they're carrying the extra oxygen for us. Are you with me?"

"Just the two of us? Isn't that underhanded? After all, the goal is to put as many on the summit as possible, and there are enough bottles for two teams."

"No, there aren't."

"But there are. I did an inventory a few days ago, and there are definitely enough bottles for four climbers."

"You're mistaken, Sandy. There are enough bottles for only two climbers because of the leaks."

"I don't follow you, George."

"With Norton's plan, no one is going to make the summit because it can't be done without oxygen. If there are only six bottles left, then even if the idea comes up it will be dismissed because of the lack of supply. That's what I want, because I want a plan from Norton to get us up the hill as fast as possible. More bottles mean more porters and more time—and we don't have time. And anyway, if I promote the use of oxygen, he'll knock me off the roster

"The old man would never do that."

"He's the Royal Military Academy, Woolwich, you know. 'The men fit the plan, not the other way round.'"

There was a long silence.

"Well, I don't want to go against the colonel, but no man is going to get to the top of this mountain without oxygen. I'm with you, George."

"Good, Sandy. We're going to make it. Good night."

I had just enough time to get behind a rock before Mallory left the tent. His tent was up the hill, so when his back was to me I got up and carefully worked my way down to my tent, where Sonam was already asleep. As I lay in my sleeping bag, I thought about Mallory's plan. He knew his weaknesses. That was why he wanted Irvine. But he also had no doubts about his abilities. Mallory was a born mountaineer. He had every pitch on the mountain memorized and was able to predict the snow and ice conditions from a distance by watching how the wind and spindrift moved across the slopes.

Having failed twice, Mallory saw what Norton and the others refused to see. It wasn't the invincible Englishman, climbing ever upward regardless of the conditions, who would conquer Everest. It was the innovative and opportunistic climber who would. Finch had not been popular with the 1922 expedition members, including Mallory, who thought him too focused on his science. But Mallory, unlike most of the others, recognized Finch's achievement in his use of oxygen. He was not going to fail a third time.

17

STELLA

The next morning, Norton laid out his plan. Sure enough, he asked that I loan my porters to the effort.

"With your abilities, if you were to return to base camp, we could put you to your highest and best use there, Reverend. Besides, our rations are already stretched," said Norton.

"I'd be of better use if I stayed on the mountain, Colonel."

"No, I'm afraid not, Reverend."

Right on cue, Mallory spoke up: "Actually, Colonel, besides yourself he is the only white man who speaks Tibetan. If things get dicey, it might be good to have him around."

"I suppose that is a possibility. I can't be everywhere on the mountain."

Mallory went on with his script and, as he had predicted, Norton agreed. It was decided that I would return to base camp to pick my best porters and return as soon as possible. I went to get Sonam, who was in the tent.

We had barely stepped out of the tent when there was a bang. Something hit my head, and I fell to the ground. I must have been out for a few moments, for the next thing I remember was Sonam screaming, "Wangdue! Wangdue!" Then I heard more shouting. It was Stella.

"You bastard, you evil bastard! I'll never let you spread your tainted words and send these men to their deaths. Don't move."

I heard the revolver's hammer click again. I remembered Hennessy giving her shooting instructions, and I remembered the target. I was a dead man. Sonam jumped up and charged, she fired, and he fell to the ground. She stood above me with a foot on my neck. The climbers had crowded around us but had not touched her.

"I simply cannot let you go on. That is why I have to stop Reverend Tutter. It is not only me. The abbot of Rongbuk also says you must stop. That is why he sent his assistant and monks with me. If you continue, you will die. George, you saw the dream-play. You know what will happen. You can't go on."

"Mr. Mallory, what is she talking about?" asked Norton.

Mallory responded, "When I was at Rongbuk recuperating, the abbot said he had a dream about a disaster on the mountain. He insisted on making a drama of it. It was rather poor, but nonetheless effective on the natives. I actually think he had planned the thing for some time. I suppose Miss Joyell was a catalyst of sorts. But if one stopped to consider superstition in Tibet, well, we'd still be at the border. I never mentioned it because I assumed any educated person saw it was nonsense."

"I see," said Norton.

There was silence. *What about me. Isn't anyone going to help me?* I thought. I heard Noel complaining that he hadn't had his camera ready.

"Classic, simply classic. If I'd had my camera out, the scene would have turned my documentary into an epic."

"See here, Miss Joyell. We had an agreement that you were to mind Mandurbar. In his condition, he must not be left alone," said Hingston.

"Mandurbar is dead."

"Dead? Did you follow my instructions?"

"Please shut up, Dr. Hingston," said Stella.

My head was still flat against the ground, limiting my view, but I saw Norton's boots as he inched toward Stella.

"Miss Joyell, this camp—actually, Tibet—is no place for an Englishwoman. No doubt your adventures have left you fatigued. Why don't you give me the gun and have some tea."

"Tea? I came here to save your life, and you want to offer me tea!"

At that moment the monks began chanting, drowning out Norton's voice. They did not let up until Stella spoke.

"Colonel Norton, the fact that I'm here says all that need be said about my abilities. If you wish to discuss abilities, perhaps you, sir, should pay a visit to base camp and consider the lives there—or should I say, what remains of the lives there—which you have destroyed by offending the goddess of Chomolungma."

Once again, the chanting started up.

Norton's boots turned in the gravel. I cleared my throat, hoping that Norton, whose left boot was nearly on my nose, would notice me.

He shouted to be heard above the chanting. "Perhaps someday you and I can take time to discuss duty, adversity, and sacrifice, but now I must ask you to give me the revolver."

"Not until Mr. Mallory quits the expedition."

"I'm not going to quit, Miss Joyell. Stop this nonsense," said Mallory, who was standing behind Norton.

"Then I will stop you."

I heard Mallory shout, "No, stop!" There was a shifting of feet and then a scuffle. A shot was fired and then there was a loud roar and a crashing. The Sherpas were screaming. One shouted, "English air! English air!" Stella fell backward. I turned my head and saw that Hingston and Noel had grabbed her. I wiggled my fingers and my toes. Then I felt my chest and legs. I didn't seem to have been hit by a bullet after all. Perhaps it had been a rock kicked up by the bullet. I got up and looked around.

Stella was lying on the ground, staring up at Mallory and Norton. She had shot an oxygen tank and hit the valve, which had sent the cylinder flying over the heads of the monks. The oxygen had caused their incense to burst into flames. The monks were awestruck. When the Sherpas told the monks that the tanks contained English air, they forgot Stella and went over to the stack of cylinders and asked for more magic. Hingston was kneeling over Sonam.

"He isn't dead, is he?" I said.

"Lucky fellow. The bullet grazed his temple, causing him to fall, which knocked him out. I think he'll be fine. I saw a number of these during the war. No way to explain it except luck. One chap gets a bullet and walks away. Another, tucked away in a trench, gets a fragment and dies. As a matter of fact, why don't we use a bit of that English air on him."

Irvine brought over a tank, and Hingston held the mask to Sonam's face. Within seconds he was moving. The monks had followed Irvine, and when they saw Sonam's reaction to the oxygen, it was clear that the English air was powerful, even magical.

Noel had his camera out. "Epic, epic," he said as he filmed Sonam rise from the dead with the awestruck monks watching.

"Karma Paul!" shouted Norton.

"Yes, sahib."

"Escort Miss Joyell to the monastery, and make an offering of coin to the abbot, so that Miss Joyell may spend a month at the monastery in peaceful meditation."

"Yes, sahib."

"You can't just lock me away in a monastery. You have no authority. I'm not some peasant. I'm English!"

"That you are, but unfortunately your emotions seem to have gotten the better of you, and I won't have you interfering with us again," said Norton as he motioned to Karma Paul.

Stella started to struggle with the Sherpas, but soon gave up. My plan no longer needed Stella, and it was obvious that she was no longer welcome in the expedition. I wanted to destroy any credibility she had with the monks, so I followed up on Norton's orders by addressing the monks: "You see, English air can bring life to the dead. The English do not need dreams or magic because they know how to capture life and use it when they need it.

Because of this, they will conquer Chomolungma. Because of this, they are the strongest people in the world. Some English don't believe in English air but instead think that by following the advice of demons they can achieve power. This woman is such an English person. She made a pact with a demon. She seeks to control others through lies and death. But this is not the way of the good English. And it is not the way of the good English to harm the bad English. Their way is to help them, and they will help this woman by sending her back to the monastery and then to her land, where she may breathe English air until all the blackness of the demon is gone from her lungs."

"This isn't Sunday school, Reverend. We're here to climb a mountain, not start a bloody cult. I'd appreciate your staying off the pulpit. Not that you aren't effective. But it's against everything I stand for as an officer. I've always dealt with the facts when confronting a problem, for when the hill of rubbish you've made collapses, you'll have nothing but muck to stand in."

I had forgotten that Norton spoke Tibetan.

I apologized, but I had accomplished what I wanted to do.

"Do you really believe all that, Reverend?" said Mallory after Karma Paul had translated my Tibetan. "Because if you do, I daresay all we'll need is a few more of your sermons to get us to the top."

That brought a laugh from the others.

Karma Paul set off immediately with Stella for the monastery while Sonam and I returned to base camp.

Pasang had done a great job preparing for the climb. He had selected the best-looking porters and had made sure the expedition's Sherpas had gotten to know them. The fraternizing had worked better than I had expected, for the Sherpas had given my porters advice and instructions on climbing. By the time Karma Paul returned to base camp from the monastery, I had most of the loose ends tied up.

"I'll take charge of your porters, Reverend Tutter," said Karma Paul. "From here on it is dangerous, and my experience is necessary for their safety."

"Reverend Tutter has climbed mountains before. He is a good leader," said Pasang.

"What do you know? You are a drunkard," snapped Karma Paul.

"I won't tolerate that slander, Karma Paul," I said.

"I speak the truth."

"You speak only what the English want to hear. You are not a true Sherpa."

I looked for the source of the voice. It was Chhamzi.

"Shut up, woman," said Karma Paul.

Chhamzi stepped forward and slapped Karma Paul. He started to grab her, but as he did the other Sherpas, who had been listening, moved in and grabbed him.

"Let me go! I'm the sirdar," he shouted.

They didn't and as he struggled, several of the expedition Sherpas berated him.

"You are a bad sirdar. Many are injured. Ang Tshiri has lost his toes, Tenzing has lost his fingers, and Phurba is blind, yet you want us to keep climbing. You care only for gold."

Then Chhamzi said, "While you were on the mountain, your Sherpas taught us about the world of ice but warned us that if we fell behind or made a mistake you would leave us as you had left others."

"I didn't leave them."

"Yes, you did! You want to be with the English, and now you return only because you need us," they shouted as they crowded around and started to shove him to and fro.

"That's enough," I said. "Let him go." I explained that although the Sherpas were right, Karma Paul was a good mountaineer and an asset to the expedition. On the other hand, his leadership skills were not enough to make him a great leader. I looked around; the Sherpas were nodding. I would not put my porters under his control. If it were up to me, I would make Pasang the sirdar. But as I was a guest of the English, I could not do that. I said that I hoped he had learned there was more to being a sirdar than ordering men and women about. That got a lot of nods. Karma Paul gave me a long cold stare, then he walked away. A few minutes later, he returned with Bently Beetham. Beetham had not left his tent when I first arrived. Now I saw why; dysentery had reduced him to skin and bones.

"What the devil is going on here? Mr. Tutter," he said. "I hear you are fomenting more problems. It seems like there has been a lot of chaos since your arrival." He turned to Karma Paul, who was standing behind him. "Karma Paul says you are taking over. Is that so?"

Karma Paul chimed in: "The reverend doesn't want me to take control of his porters. He wants to take over."

"Is that so, Mr. Tutter? Surely you don't think you are capable of that?"

"I'm only following Norton's orders, which are to go to base camp and return with my best porters as soon as possible. Norton never mentioned Karma Paul to me, probably because Karma Paul already had a task: take Miss Joyell to the monastery and then return. Norton never told me that Karma Paul was to take up my porters."

"I can't see any harm in Karma Paul doing his job, so why don't we let him take up these porters and sort it out later, it's only fair."

I wasn't in the mood to hear a lecture on English fairness and knew that Mallory and Norton couldn't care less about who was in charge of my porters. They just wanted the workers.

"Well, that sounds reasonable—"

"Excellent."

"Except my porters won't go."

"What?"

"They don't like him. They say he is responsible for the injured Sherpas."

"Surely you don't believe that."

"It isn't my place to judge. I just want to help out, and I don't want to get involved in personality issues."

"Rubbish! This has nothing to do with personalities. It's about following orders." He turned to Karma Paul and said, "Now tell them the Englishman is in charge and that he says they are to obey you, not the reverend."

Karma Paul smiled and translated what Beetham had just said.

Chhamzi smiled and said, "Never!" She turned and walked away, followed by my porters and then the expedition Sherpas.

"See," said Beetham. "I just needed to crack the whip."

"You misunderstood. She said, 'Never.' They're not preparing to leave. They're going to make tea," I said.

"Mr. Paul, you will repeat my order!"

Karma Paul repeated Beetham's order, but nothing happened. An hour went by, with Beetham issuing more orders. Then pleas. Then orders. "Mr. Tutter, you must talk to them. This can't go on."

"I don't know what to say to them. I can't tell them to follow your order."

"Why not?"

"Because they'll think that I've deceived them. They know that we have been blessed by the monk Marepa and that the blessing was given by him to me to give to them. If I told them to follow Karma Paul, I would be breaking a sacred tradition. Basically, I would be saying that anyone can take a blessing and then transfer it to someone else. They would find that sacrilegious."

"You speak of avoiding personality issues, yet you stand here and go on about some troglodyte miracle worker. You had more in mind than serving the Lord when you donned the cloth, Reverend."

"Nothing could be further from the truth, Mr. Beetham. I take my vows very seriously."

"Well, then you take your pilgrims and Godspeed."

He turned to Karma Paul: "I'm afraid I must give up, Karma Paul. The reverend is a cagey fellow, let him have his way. You head back up and report to the colonel. I'll speak to Norton when I see him."

I didn't think that Beetham was fit enough to go back up, but if he did I still had Mallory to intercede for me. I decided not to worry about him.

Most of the supplies were already at camp II, so I was able to hide a couple of oxygen bottles in the upward-bound loads. I found another oxygen bottle in the medical tent and switched it with empties that had been tossed. I cracked the valves to make it look like they were empty because of leaking. With these and the ones I had found at camp, I had as many as Irvine's plan called for.

We arrived at camp I and picked up loads for camp II.

Norton said, "Good job, Reverend. You've got eight porters. Excellent. No need to worry about the North Col holding your men and women back. Bruce and Irvine have installed a rope ladder on the ice wall. I reckon a blind horse could climb it now. Now the plan is to have three teams of two, and twelve Sherpas, or tigers, as I like to call them, to assist. Go see Mr. Shebbeare about what needs to be taken up to camp III, and we'll see you there," said Norton.

"Colonel Norton, I must speak to you."

It was Beetham.

"Colonel, I must object in the strongest terms to the inclusion of the American, for I feel he hasn't been forthright with us."

"I see," said Norton as he turned from Beetham and stared at me. "Is there any merit to Mr. Beetham's charge, Reverend?"

"Of course not. I have no idea what Mr. Beetham is referring to."

"I'm referring to the Sherpa rebellion!" said Beetham.

I spoke before Beetham could continue. "Rebellion? Hardly. Karma Paul is romantically interested in Chhamzi, and I thought it best to keep them separated until they finish the jobs they were hired to do."

Beetham began to cough and gasp for air. He lost his balance and grabbed Norton's arm. After a moment's rest he managed to say, "That's nonsense you liar. It has nothing to do with a woman, it's about a coup d'état."

"Coup d'état?" Norton repeated. "A coup d'état on Mount Everest led by a minister and a Tibetan Amazon? Have you gone mad, Mr. Beetham? What pray tell is the objective?"

"The objective is to put an American flag on top of this mountain," sputtered Beetham.

Norton turned to me and asked, "Reverend are you a mutineer?"

"Of course not," I said.

"I didn't think you were. However you will remind your 'Amazon' that the task at hand is portage, not romance." He turned back to Beetham and said, "Mr. Beetham, return to base camp at once before your condition causes further damage to your health and inconvenience to the expedition."

18

GENTLEMEN'S AGREEMENT

We moved our loads up to camp III, and on Saturday carried more loads to camp IV, also known as the North Col, to support Mallory, Bruce, Irvine, and Odell. Norton and Somervell had stayed behind in camp III, preparing for the second attempt after Mallory and Bruce's. The plan was that on Sunday Mallory and Bruce would take eight porters and establish camp V. On Monday they would establish the highest camp, camp VI. I had returned to camp III with my porters, but not before I had hidden the pilfered oxygen tanks above camp IV. I had no reason to think that Mallory and Bruce would fail. It was windy, very windy, but if they could get to the northeast ridge as planned and stay just below it, there was a good chance that the wind would be minimal. Mallory wasn't going to return to Everest for a fourth time, so it would take more than wind to stop him.

"A fine Sunday, Reverend. Any plans for a service?" asked Hingston.

"I haven't thought about that in a long time," I said as I looked at the weathered, sunburned face of the good doctor. "Are you serious?"

"Actually, I'm not sure. . . Well, look here at this insect. It's a black Attid."

"A what?"

"A spider. He's crawling around, as if on a Sunday stroll, surrounded by ice and rock. Not a plant or living thing in sight except for us, and here he is at twenty-one thousand feet, acting as if everything were normal."

"I suspect he hasn't the intelligence to know he is in trouble; once he wanders into the shade, he'll freeze."

"That is a distinct possibility. I am disposed to anthropomorphizing and found myself thinking of our undertaking and what it means to be human. Supposing this little fellow had been blown to the top of this mountain instead of here. Unlike ourselves, he'd have no concept of what he had done. Yet how many of us are like this insect: achieving greatness without knowing it? That I think was what inspired me to think of a sermon."

"How could you achieve greatness without knowing it?"

"Why through selfless love, of course."

Hingston had gone native! Maybe it was the altitude or the nettle tea, but he had changed for sure. He had spoken of meeting a hermit a few days earlier; maybe that was it.

"Are you telling me that some bug that lands on top of Everest because of a hurricane is great?" I asked.

"You are missing the point, Reverend. Don't you see that our very act of thinking leads to prioritizing, or desire, which in turn leads to conflict and unhappiness. The insect, by virtue of its lack of ego, can achieve what the angry man cannot."

"If it has no ego, then it hasn't achieved anything, because it doesn't understand its own actions."

"That is my point. We look at life through the eyes and the ego. Yet ultimately that is useless."

"Well, I don't think that I can deliver a sermon on that."

Hingston smiled at me, walked over to a sunny rock, and let the spider go. He recited what sounded like a Tibetan prayer and then looked toward the summit.

When I thought of a Sunday sermon, I thought of people living in relative comfort, but with inner doubts and problems, who turned to me for the solace and advice that only God can provide. What need for that was there here with these veterans of the Great War? What could I or even God say to them? How could they have doubts about their lives? They could only have doubts about humanity. Maybe that was what Hingston was trying to say. I stood with my eyes closed in the silence of the high and empty place. With the sun on my shoulders, everything seemed perfect. Then a cloud passed under the sun, and Norton's voice called out to me.

"Reverend Tutter, keep your porters here in camp III as a reserve while Somervell and I take six Sherpas and move up to camp V. As long as Mr. Irvine's ice ladder in the Col hasn't been ripped off the mountain, we will be at camp IV tonight and at V tomorrow. I will send word down if we need any porters. Is that clear?"

"Understood. They'll be here if you need them. Good luck."

"Let's hope I have the strength to use the luck. Cheerio."

My opportunity was gone. The upper camps were in good shape, and Odell, fitter than any Sherpa or porter, was in camp IV, ready to help if needed. He might call for a couple of Sherpas, but with Norton up there, a Tibetan speaker was not needed. A few more clouds came in, and the wind picked up. I wondered how the spider felt now.

Irvine called from his tent, "I say, Reverend, would you give me a hand with this oxygen cylinder? I'm trying to fit a new hose on it, and with the cold it is going to take an extra hand."

"Sure, but I'm no mechanic."

"I daresay there is not a mechanic on this mountain except for me. Not something expected from a gentleman or an officer."

"Why are you working on the oxygen? I thought the colonel was set against it," I asked.

"It's something Mallory wants, just in case. He knows we have little time left, as the monsoon season is rapidly approaching. The advance camps will be little more than a tent for the night. There is no time for a long siege. The only chance will be if we are high enough and the weather is cooperative."

"I see."

Later that day, it became clear how frail the best of plans are on the tallest mountain in the world when Mallory and Bruce unexpectedly walked into camp III.

"Mr. Irvine, are you fit enough to climb?" Mallory asked as he stepped into the tent and took off his goggles. There was a determination in his eyes that I hadn't seen since divinity school. I knew he had only two options: success or death.

"I'm a bit burned and blistered but otherwise quite functional."

"Very well. We've got a day to prepare."

"Prepare for what?" asked Irvine.

"The top."

"I'm sorry, but I thought the plan was to supply the upper camps. You must have talked to Colonel Norton and Somervell on their way up."

"They're flogging a dead horse."

"What?"

"Four porters dropped their loads and refused to go on. Bruce and I struggled on for another three hundred feet with the four other porters and managed to scrape out a spot for the night. I sent the four and Dawa, who was sick, down to the North Col. We planned to move up the next morning and make a higher camp, but the three remaining porters refused to go, so I came back down. I spoke to Odell at the North Col, and I think he understands."

"Understands what?" asked Irvine.

"He understands the only way is to use the oxygen and go fast and light. We must forget the Sherpas. We can't rely on them. That's the problem with the current plan. We're slow as snails in the park in August, and if we continue like this, we'll be up to our necks in monsoon snow with nowhere to go except to our frozen graves."

"But Norton and Somervell are on the way up. Norton is keen on the possibility of going below the ridge and then up. I'm sure he is right about it being a possible route," said Irvine.

Mallory said, "I daresay it won't be any different with Norton and Somervell. As a matter of fact, Somervell was doting on one of his porters when we passed them on their way up. Look, we need the porters, but we can't depend on them. I've got Bruce trying to find who's fit, and God only knows if I should even hope for dependable. We'll use them as best we can, but there'll be no depending on them. It's a bloody mess, but it's the only way we have a chance. My hope is that he'll find some, and that you and I can be off on Wednesday morning to camp IV."

Just then Bruce came into the tent. "We've got a rebellion on our hands; seems like frostbite and a demon have made them reluctant to go anywhere but down," said Bruce.

"Who?"

"The four you sent down."

"Those lazy reprobates."

"Well they lost no time getting here, and Gambo—"

"Which one is he?"

"The tall one who wears the ascot. He's complaining about a frostbitten thumb."

"We've all got frostbite," snapped Mallory.

"Agreed," said Bruce, "but he said the frostbite was not from the cold but from a demon, and that his injury was a warning to stay away from the summit."

"Rubbish. He only needs to wear his gloves."

"He was right about the demon," I said.

For a moment Mallory forgot where he was, and his schoolmaster persona appeared. "Would the reverend like to explain to the class how the demon injured Gambo's thumb?"

"Their version of hell is not one of fire and brimstone but one of a frozen wasteland inhabited by demons. You are leading them into hell, and it is only reasonable that any problems they encounter will be seen to be a result of that."

"That's absurd. How could hell be frozen?" said Mallory.

"Actually, Somervell said something about that to me a while back. He wondered how many of us would defy our deepest religious convictions or fears for a few shillings," said Bruce.

"So it's not a lot of rubbish?" asked Mallory.

"I'm afraid not," said Bruce.

"So you tried more money."

"Yes, and they're not interested. Pity there are no bullets."

Mallory looked at him quizzically.

Bruce explained, "During the War, one had a fear of the unknown, but that usually played second fiddle to the bullets whizzing past."

"Motivation. We lack a means of motivation, and without that we're helpless," said Mallory.

"My porters will go," I said.

"And why will your porters go when our Sherpas won't?" asked Mallory.

"They've been blessed."

"Blessed? Do your porters have magic charms?"

"Yes. Exactly."

"Reverend, I'm stuck on the world's tallest mountain. This is no time for a joke."

"I'm not joking. Pasang!" Moments later, Pasang came into the tent. "Pasang can explain the importance of the charms to you in English, although he wasn't there when I met the monk who gave them to me and the porters."

Mallory turned to Pasang and said, "Will you climb the mountain?"

"Yes."

"There are demons there. Are you afraid of them?"

"I am not afraid because I have the blessing of Marepa," said Pasang as he placed his hand on the amulet that hung around his neck. "Marepa is the holiest monk in Tibet; his spirit moves through the mountains and the air. His prayers are captured in this amulet, and with each breath I take, they are repeated and flow across the mountain and into the frozen hearts of the demons, where the Buddha's loving wisdom, in the form of the prayers, renders them incapable of doing harm."

"Reverend Tutter, do you expect me to believe this?" asked Mallory.

"No. But I think you should recognize Pasang's belief as sincere."

Bruce said, "The reverend's point is valid. The history of Tibet is of one fantastic miracle after another, and for Englishmen to march in and call it all nonsense is narrow-minded."

"Think of all those Catholic saints; why, I remember one who survived naked on a frozen lake for days," said Irvine.

"Has the altitude made you daft? We're in a medieval theocracy, where the sex of an unborn child can be divined by a fly dancing on a pile of yak dung, and you're asking me to put our fate and everything the expedition stands for in the hands of superstition and ignorance. Rubbish!"

"That's ridiculous; we're not donning bearskins and picking up clubs simply because we acknowledge this Marepa chap. Why, we've been up to our necks in this mumbo jumbo since we left Britain. You didn't say a word about it previously. Why are you so bothered now?" asked Bruce.

"It hasn't been an issue until now. It is a matter of control. Acknowledging this Marepa fellow puts him in control. Suppose he sends word that the amulet is about to expire and he needs a few bob to keep it effective? Or suppose one of the amulets falls into a crevasse—do we just stop?" said Mallory.

Pasang spoke up. "To mention the saint and money is an insult to the hermit's vows. He has lived twenty years in isolation, so that others may know the purpose of life. He has no need of money or worldly power. His power is the path of true being."

"I didn't mean to insult him. In England, one often hears of parsons living lavishly, and I thought he might be the same," said Mallory.

"It is not the same," said Pasang.

"I see," said Mallory.

Pasang left the tent in silence.

"Well, we're in a pickle now," said Bruce.

"That we are," said Mallory.

There was a stomping of feet outside the tent, and then the flap opened and Odell entered.

"Word is that Colonel Norton has a couple of injured porters at camp V. Rockfall of some type. I hope it doesn't hold them back. I'm heading back up with Hazard to camp IV with a load of rations and fuel. There might be more information on them when we get there. Have you finalized your plan, Mr. Mallory?"

"We've a bit of an issue with the Sherpas."

"More of a rebellion," said Bruce.

"Seems they think all this rock and ice is a hell filled with devils, and the higher we go, the more dangerous it is. Our remaining porters are refusing to go, and I'm afraid I just offended Reverend Tutter's sirdar, Pasang," said Mallory.

Odell turned to face me. "Reverend, could you rally them? You've lived among them and speak their language. If you were part of the summit team, I'm sure they would support you."

"Possibly, I—"

"What? Are you suggesting that Reverend Tutter participate in the summit attempt?" asked Mallory. "He's not a climber. And he's not English."

"I'm not a climber either," said Irvine.

"You have talent," snapped Mallory.

"Who's to say the reverend doesn't have talent? He made it across Tibet in a novel way," said Bruce.

Odell said, "I didn't mean to say he had to go to the summit. But he could motivate the porters, leaving you and Irvine free to climb while he managed the logistics. Granted, he would be up there, and I suppose he might have a shot at the top. But should that unlikely event come to pass, would it be such a bad thing?"

"This is an English undertaking not an American or international endeavor. We have been through this before. Do you remember 1921? And 1922? There were a lot of problems because of Canadian and Australian members. The reverend was allowed to come along as an observer, with the possible opportunity to be a translator, but he was never considered a member of the climbing team. The fact is, he is here because of his generous donation to the committee," said Mallory.

"There needn't be a record," said Odell.

"What?" said Mallory, his eyebrows shooting up.

"No one need know if he climbs. We're all gentlemen here. There is no reason that a technicality can't be overlooked. As long as Noel keeps him out of the movies, who is to know? I'll speak to Noel about it at dinner. Oh, there is one more thing—rather important, I should think," said Odell as he turned to me. "Are you interested in participating, Reverend?"

"I'm willing to do what I can to help," I said.

"Mr.Odell, it's one thing to overlook something now and then, but intentional omissions from the record and personal journals would be completely unacceptable," said Mallory.

"I say, Odell, are you in there? Hazard wants to know if you want chicken bouillon with chipped beef or tinned fish and eggs," asked Noel as he stuck his head into the tent.

"I fancy the chipped beef," said Odell.

"Excellent choice. Chef Hazard recommends boiled potatoes and sauce with the main course, Is that acceptable?"

"Yes," said Odell.

As Noel started to leave the tent, Odell said, "Noel, have you any footage of the American?"

"Let me think. No, I don't. Should I? Actually, that's a wonderful idea: the reverend here in this wasteland, preaching to the last frontier. So American. I'll fashion a costume, add a touch of exaggeration. Like a good spice, exaggeration makes the most boring mush a fantastic memory. Pilgrim! That's it. I'll fashion a hat and ruff and have him standing, facing the sunrise. Optimistic American and all that," said Noel.

"My God, man, that's exactly what we don't want," said Bruce.

"Bruce is right," Odell said.

"You don't?"

"No. Actually, we think the reverend is in need of privacy," said Bruce.

"I don't understand," said Noel.

"A situation has arisen in which we need the reverend's help. It is in the best interest of the expedition to limit the publicity the reverend receives," said Odell.

"Is this Mallory's idea?" asked Noel.

"God, no. I only want to get to the top of this bloody rock!" said Mallory.

"Actually, we all do. It's just that the Committee is decidedly English, and if an American takes center stage, it will be cause for concern," said Odell.

"I see," said Noel. "I have nothing at the moment, and I suppose it would be easy enough to keep it that way. Reverend, why don't we replace that Rough Rider hat with something that won't be so conspicuous, should I catch a few long-shot frames of you with the others."

"I'm happy to accommodate," I said.

"Consider it done! God, country, and propaganda. Back in England, they'll never know what they missed," said Noel.

"I say, Noel, I'm not asking for deception, only a bit of discretion," said Odell.

"Understood, completely understood. Come, for I hear the horn of Chez Hazard calling."

"Ah yes, dinner," said Odell. He stepped out of the tent and then stuck his head back in. "Mr. Hazard and I are heading up after dinner to resupply camp IV and camp V. We'll do what we can to help you, Mr. Mallory, when you arrive."

It was silent for quite a while. I thought that perhaps Mallory was unhappy about what he considered cheating. Then he broke the silence. "Reverend, I reckon it's time you and Mr. Bruce find our Sherpas. Mr. Irvine and I will go over our kit. Do you have what you need to go to camp V? Do you have a replacement for that ostentatious Teddy Roosevelt chapeau?"

"That I do, Mr. Mallory," I said, and we all laughed.

It took the rest of the afternoon to find enough Sherpas. In spite of Bruce's good intentions, I found reasons to exclude all but two expedition Sherpas (Gulu and Tarmo) from the group of eight porters we needed. I chose Pasang, Chhamzi, and three others: Lha-mo, Jangmu, and Je-tsun, whom Pasang and Chhamzi both agreed upon. The sixth was Sonam. Neither Pasang nor Chhamzi wanted him along, citing his lack of experience. But it was really because he was a shepherd and not a Sherpa. Pasang was right about Sonam's experience, but except for Pasang none of them had any experience except for what they had learned in base camp. Sonam was the only person I could trust. I had to have him with me. I went to Mallory and Irvine's tent to let Mallory know that the porters had been chosen and were getting the loads ready. I found Irvine alone. He had an oxygen mask on and was taking a few test breaths. I realized that even though I had taken and hidden masks and tanks, I had never tried one.

"Is that the same model? I've heard you're a whiz at these things and have actually redesigned them here in the field," I said.

He started to speak with the mask on and then removed it. "Sorry, Reverend, you were saying something. Can't hear with the oxygen flowing."

"I asked if there were different masks being used."

"I've been working on them since we left Darjeeling, so there are some in different stages of development. They get misplaced. There were a couple that were experimental down in the hospital tent that we can't seem to find. They are probably being used by the Sherpas for a ghastly rite. Mallory and I are the only ones keen on their use, so there is no shortage of them. These two are my latest versions. They are much simpler and less prone to freeze up than the others."

Freeze up. Were the masks I had stolen worthless? "Wouldn't it be dangerous if someone were to use an older experimental mask by mistake?" I asked.

"Yes. And no. The freeze-up occurs only at a high oxygen flow. I've modified the orifice in these so the oxygen flow is less into the mask, but with the others, one has to manually set this valve to prevent freezing. If it does freeze, it may take a while to thaw, depending upon location and temperature. Why don't you take this one, just in case there is an emergency. There's time for me to modify another."

"Are you sure? I don't want to put you in harm's way," I said.

"No need to be concerned. Mr. Mallory is handling all the climbing matters. I've little to do until tomorrow morning, when we head up to camp IV, so I'll modify and test another one."

"I believe that oxygen is unnecessary and cheating, but perhaps I'll take this 'English Air' along in case of an emergency," I said.

Irvine said, "No oxygen. Is that because of your faith? I daresay you don't mind asking the Lord to help you; all we've done is ask a few scientists to help us."

"The Lord helps the individual who helps himself. Although I have no argument with science, I feel that it enables the lazy and indifferent to gain access to what in the past was the domain of the hardy and devoted."

"You must feel quite at home among these Stone Age Tibetans, then."

"Contemporary Christianity is a far cry from a feudal theocracy, Mr. Irvine. You paint me as a reactionary, which is far from the truth. I merely believe that man is at his best when he is in his purest state. I would set off naked, were it not for the fact that I would offend others and freeze to death," I said.

"'Long live the *Mayflower* and oceans wide / So men of all creeds may peaceably abide.' That's something my father said quite often. He didn't take stock in tolerance: He took stock in fences and distance. Pilgrims went to America and that sort of thing."

"An insular view," I said.

Irvine laughed and said, "Well, he does live on an island."

"Not just an island, Mr. Irvine. He lives in England," said Mallory as he entered the tent. "Have you found our porters, Reverend?"

"Yes, and they are a strong and reliable bunch. Six are part of my team and two are yours."

"Two from our group? How did you manage that? Magic charms?"

"The amulets? Yes," I said.

Mallory looked at the oxygen mask in my hand and then at Irvine.

"What are you doing with that?" he asked. "Surely you don't expect to climb. Are you and Mr. Irvine planning something that I'm not privy to?"

"Not at all," said Irvine. "There is an extra, and I thought it might be useful in the event of a problem."

"Problem? There will be a problem if there isn't enough oxygen for us. We are already in short supply. What type of problem do you anticipate, Mr. Irvine?"

"Nothing specific. But Finch claimed it saved his life when he was trapped by the storm," said Irvine.

I said, "I think Mr. Mallory is right. There is no need for me to carry extra equipment that is of doubtful benefit. All oxygen should be committed to the assault itself, not to the hypothetical." I handed the mask back to Irvine.

Mallory turned to me and said, "Reverend, I must say that there are rumors that you were a piker. But your candor just now has made it obvious that you are not. I'm glad you're here."

19

THE LETTER

We started off the next morning. Mallory led the way up the icefall, cleaning up a few steps with his ax now and then. It was more for our benefit than his. He was a natural on the mountain. The greater the challenge, the more energy he had. For him, balancing and swinging an ax was nothing but pleasure. In reality, he didn't need to do it, for Irvine had constructed a rope ladder for the tricky spots. When we arrived at camp VI, Odell was already there, along with Hazard and two Sherpas.

Odell said, "I think they've got a good shot at it. Norton has chosen to stay below the skyline and head toward that broad couloir that leads to the summit. They'll avoid that hideous wind, so the temperature will be balmy. Once they reach the couloir, I don't think anything will stop Colonel Norton, as it is the obvious route to the top."

"I hardly think the word 'balmy' is accurate for either Mount Everest or Tibet," said Mallory.

"You're quite right, Mr. Mallory. I let myself get carried away in my excitement about their ascent. Nevertheless, I'm optimistic," said Odell.

The climb to camp IV was relatively quick, but it was a steep and exposed location, requiring a couple of hours to find and clear a spot for the two extra tents that the Sherpas and I needed. I went with Sonam to make sure the hidden oxygen tanks were still there. They were. I had been able to switch Irvine's extra modified oxygen mask before I left camp III with the one I stole from the hospital, plus I had another, of uncertain vintage that I would give to the Sherpa who came with me. Tomorrow we would move up to camp V, where Mallory and Irvine would launch their summit attempt. There wasn't much else to do but rest and wait. I watched the afternoon clouds move in. The clear mornings had been the only inspiration for what was increasingly looking like a futile undertaking—the monsoon season was not far away, and once it arrived, there would be no chance.

I ate and went to bed. I shared a tent with the Sherpas, which the English frowned upon. But I had no choice, for I could not take the chance that they might find the oxygen mask or tanks in my gear.

"I say, Reverend, there is no need to sleep like a sardine, as there is room with Mr. Irvine and me," said Mallory.

"I should stay with them. They are understandably a bit anxious, especially the two Sherpas from your camp. I don't want a panic in the middle of the night to snowball into another mutiny."

"Snowballs on Everest! I've had enough of those," said Mallory. "I'm referring to the avalanche the last time I climbed this mountain. The snow was snowballing on the slope. I ignored it, with very unpleasant consequences."

"I remember hearing about that," I said.

"Frankly, I think your concern is well founded. I appreciate it, especially as we may have another crisis at hand."

"Norton?"

"Yes, it is getting late and there'll be no moon to speak of."

"Do you want me to stand watch?"

"No, Mr. Odell has moved up the mountain and is watching for them; he'll signal if help is needed. We should rest as much as possible. Good night," said Mallory.

That must have been around seven in the evening. A couple of hours later, I woke to shouting and the movement of lights outside the tent. Norton and Somervell had returned. Thanks to Odell, they had found the camp. Somervell was definitely the worse for wear. He could hardly speak and his every breath sounded like sheets of paper being torn apart. Norton was snow-blind and had to be led to Mallory's tent. Amazingly was quite lucid as he explained the route he and Somervell had taken in their quest for the summit.

"We stayed below the skyline and then took a diagonal to the yellow band until we reached the great couloir. I'm convinced it will go directly to the summit. There may be a bergschrund or crevasse, but I'm sure they can be surmounted, as the couloir is so broad. I felt as if it were right in front of me. If only I hadn't taken off my glasses!" said Norton.

Mallory said, "I see your point, but I've never felt comfortable in couloirs—they're too unpredictable. I'm going to stick to the ridge. Irvine and I are going up to camp V tomorrow."

"I'm afraid I've spoiled your chance. I'm blind, so I can't come with you as translator. It will be nearly impossible for you to keep your Sherpas organized. You do have your vocabulary booklet though, don't you?" asked Norton.

"We've had a stroke of luck, Colonel. The reverend is going with us to camp V. He has done a yeoman's job of organizing the Sherpas. We have eight who, thanks to the reverend's rapport with them, would march off the edge of the world if we asked them to. It's quite fantastic what he has been able to accomplish," said Mallory.

"The reverend? Are you serious? He's no mountaineer—and he's an American."

Neither man knew that I was standing at the door of the tent as Norton continued to lecture Mallory on the foolishness of having me along. Finally, Mallory, in his schoolmaster voice, said, "I have no argument with what you have said, Colonel. But you have forgotten that we have no other option."

There was a long silence. Then Norton said, "I see. Very well, then. Carry on, Mr. Mallory."

I had hoped that Norton would descend the next morning. Hazard was due to come up with a few items and was in good shape. He could easily escort Norton back down. But in spite of Norton's agreeing with Mallory's plan, he refused to descend to camp III. Instead, that morning he called me over to his tent for breakfast and conducted what amounted to an interview in the Sherpa language.

"Reverend, let me speak frankly. You are a leader of sheep by trade, and I am a leader of men by trade. There is only so much a man can do on his own. In spite of your Declaration of Independence, there is still rule of law in America." He tried to open his stuck and swollen eyes to emphasize the point but failed.

"Have you tried tea?" I asked.

"Of course I've tried tea."

"I meant for your eyes. A compress of tea leaves might help."

"Interesting idea. But as I was saying, man's greatest achievements are the product of organization and discipline, not dreams or prayers. Discipline: submission of the one to the order of the unit. That is the essence of success. Reverend, I am concerned that you are too familiar with these people and that your familiarity does not bode well. Mr. Mallory has told me of the charms that the porters are wearing. Reverend, are you really a Christian? Or are you or a Crowley-type charlatan? Or worse yet, a Buddhist, who insists that everything is an illusion and the ego should be abandoned."

"I am an ordained minister, and I take my vows seriously," I said.

"I should hope you do. I take my commission seriously also. Now here is my concern: I can't and won't have the porters being motivated by a bunch of hocus-pocus. You've impressed Mr. Mallory with the charms, but what will you do when the next shadow crosses your path? You may praise the Lord, but you must keep your powder dry."

Norton paused and started to rub his eyes but stopped.

"It's an insidious adversary, this altitude. One can never let down one's guard and forget that it is not only the lungs that suffer. I'm blind but it will pass in a few days, not like Jerry gas. I'm trusting you to do your upmost to get Mr. Mallory and Mr. Irvine to the top of this mountain. I also must inform you that no matter how creditable your actions, you won't receive any official recognition."

"I understand."

"Tea?"

"No, thank you. I need to check a few things and then speak with the porters about tomorrow."

"More amulets?"

"No. They can be fussy about the loads. I want to make sure they have them sorted out beforehand."

"You would have made a good soldier, Reverend. You've a keen eye for human weaknesses. By the way, Odell says four of the porters are women. Is that a good idea?"

"No doubt in my mind. I chose the best."

"No need to be concerned about romantic intentions, jealousy, or love triangles?"

"I think we took care of that when you sent Miss Joyell back to the monastery."

"Let's hope I did."

I heard the sound of boots approaching the tent.

"Colonel Norton, it looks like we've got good weather for a bit longer. A telegram from Calcutta says the monsoon is slow in moving into the Bay of Bengal," announced Hazard as he entered the tent.

"Excellent. Anything else, Mr. Hazard?"

"There is a note for Mr. Mallory."

"Then see that Mr. Mallory gets it."

Hazard cleared his throat. "It is from that woman, Colonel, that Miss Joyell."

"My God, man, is she returning?"

"No, sir, but she has left the monastery and is on her way to Darjeeling. Rumor has it she has written a scandalous account of her dalliance with Mr. Mallory and intends to sell it to the *London Times*." said Hazard.

"Give me the letter, Mr. Hazard."

Hazard placed the letter in Norton's hands. Norton took the envelope and held it as if to read it. He put it down abruptly. "Bloody eyes, bloody mountain, and now a bloody lunatic! Read it to me, Mr. Hazard," said Norton loudly. He waved the letter in his hand.

"Sorry, Colonel, I can't do that. It's personal correspondence; you understand it isn't allowed."

"Are you mad, Mr. Hazard? We're on the verge of conquering the greatest mountain on earth, and you are going to give a letter this totty wrote to Mr. Mallory without knowing what is in it!"

"Again, Colonel, it is private correspondence, and it needs to be respected as such."

"Reverend, would you be so kind as to read me this letter," said Norton as he turned to where he thought I was.

"Of course, Colonel," I said.

"Mr. Hazard, I suggest you inspect the ice axes," said Norton.

"Yes, Colonel," said Hazard as he left the tent.

"You may begin, Reverend."

I quickly scanned the letter. It was full of what could only have been plagiarized from Elinor Glyn.

"More of an excerpt from *Three Weeks* than a personal letter, Colonel," I said.

"And what is *Three Weeks*?"

"Erotic trash in the guise of literature."

"I see. Well, continue."

"My Dearest George, This morning I awoke with tears in my eyes, for I fear that I might never see you again. Yet strangely they were tears of joy. For those very tears had the shape of the dewdrops that clung so tenuously to the tent that morning after we first made love. The Tibetan dawn light moving through my tears cast the rainbow colors across your body as you lay asleep in utter prostration. I placed my lips upon your brow as I felt you move across your beloved mountains. My tongue tasting—"

"That's enough, Reverend. Is there any real news in there?"

I skimmed the several pages and then looked at the colonel.

"She says she is carrying his child and that she is leaving for Darjeeling, where she plans to have the baby and from where she will send excerpts of this and other letters to the *Times.*"

"I remember the horrors of the war: trenches, gas, and endless shelling. Yet the odd thing was that there was the underlying feeling that it was all rational."

"Rational?"

We were trying to win, and the Jerries were trying to win. We'd shell. They'd shell. We'd attack. They'd attack. What I am trying to say is that I don't understand. What does this woman want?"

"I doubt that even she knows the answer to that, Colonel," I said.

"Perhaps it doesn't matter. What matters is that this rubbish doesn't get to the press. We don't need a scandal. Someone will have to stop her. The problem here is that all I have are gentlemen and soldiers. I can't expect them to kidnap someone. Why, Hazard won't even open her mail. I'm afraid I'll have to ask you to go, Reverend. You know the culture, and you have spent some time with her. You'll simply have to detain her until we are back in Darjeeling."

"But Mr. Mallory is counting on my assistance,"

"I'm aware of that. But he has a dictionary, and the porters will be performing their usual tasks. An interpreter is a definite asset—but not a necessity. If you leave now, you can be at camp III before dark and be off the mountain in a day."

Stella had failed to stop the expedition, but she was trying to exact her revenge. Unwittingly, she was taking me down also.

"Pasang the Sherpa has a sister."

"Many men do, Reverend," said Norton.

"He has a sister who is a nun in a convent in Natu Buk. If we send him with a small donation, they would hold Miss Joyell for as long as needed," I said.

"Ah, the Tower. An excellent idea. And for few shillings, you can take her there."

"That is not what I had in mind, sir. If I am involved, then she will know that the expedition is also involved. But if we send Pasang, he can disguise himself and an assistant as bandits. They can kidnap her and take her to the convent, where she'll be held for "ransom." When you are in Darjeeling, you can send the ransom. Miss Joyell will never know the truth. And, I might add, she will no doubt find the kidnapping exciting, just like something she reads in novels."

Norton tried to open his eyes to look at me, but he couldn't. "Reverend, it is a plan worthy of Shakespeare. Can you trust this Pasang? And how soon can he leave?"

"We can buy trust. Do you have a five-pound note?"

"That's not something one needs on Mount Everest. We do have cash at the base camp."

"That won't do. I need the money now if he is to leave within the hour."

"Then we'll have to make other arrangements," said Norton as he scratched his head. "Wait, I do have a white fiver. Is my hat in here? Can you see it?"

"There is a hat behind you."

He turned, groped, and found the hat. His fingers moved around the inner band.

"Ah, here it is. I've always kept a fiver here. 'Expect the unexpected,' they always say."

Norton handed the five-pound note to me. I tore it in half and gave half back to him.

"Here is your insurance policy, Colonel. I'll go and give the other half to Pasang."

"Pasang, I must talk to you. There has been a change of plans, and I need your help."

147

"What change, sahib?"

"Come with me for a minute," I said.

We walked away from camp in a downwind direction.

"Pasang, a horrible thing has happened. We have just learned that agents of the British government are searching for Miss Joyell. They have information that she is a spy for the Russian czar. I found out this morning that Miss Joyell has left the monastery and is on her way to Darjeeling. If the English find her, it is possible they will kill her or, worse yet, turn her over to Chinese opium traders."

Pasang paled. "They will make her addicted to opium and then sell her as a prostitute to the Uighurs."

"That is true."

"Miss Joyell is no spy."

"I know she is not a spy, but the English government is very afraid of the Russians. They think she followed the mountaineers to help the Russians plan an invasion of India," I said.

"Why they think that?" he asked.

"Because of the Englishman Captain Hennessy's wife. She thinks her husband is in love with Miss Joyell so she started the story to have her arrested."

But she is a good woman. She is like a Sherpa woman, strong and honest."

"You are right, sahib. She is strong and honest like a Sherpa woman."

"Pasang, you are the only one whom I can trust to save her. If Miss Joyell can get to Darjeeling, then she will be safe, because her father has friends there."

"Why doesn't Reverend Tutter sahib help her?"

"Because every Tibetan will be watching. The English pay money for eyes," I explained. "I have a plan and only you can do it. Disguised as a bandit, I want you to pretend to kidnap her. Then take her to the Nata Buk convent. Have your sister hide her until the English have left Tibet. Then we will make arrangements to get her to Darjeeling."

He was silent for a long time. Then he said his place was with me, as he was the only one in my group with real mountaineering experience. He was right, but right for the wrong reason. I knew from Norton's description of his and Somervell's attempt that the effort needed was Herculean. Pasang would discover that. As a matter of fact, he would know early on that the attempt was most likely futile. I didn't want that. I wanted someone who would believe me if I said the summit was only one hour away or that there was no need to worry about the weather.

It took a bit of effort to get Pasang to agree to my plan. He was interested in helping Stella, yet he didn't want to lose his role as sirdar. I realized he was jealous of Karma Paul.

"If I go, Karma Paul will take my place," he said.

"No, he won't. He is in camp II and he is sick."

"How Reverend know Karma Paul is sick?"

"It was in the message to Norton. He ate bad food, English food from metal skin."

"English food make him sick? English do that on purpose?"

"Maybe. The English are never to be trusted. Look what they are doing to Stella," I said.

"Reverend very good man," said Pasang.

After kicking in another five pounds of my own money he agreed. He needed that money to get horses, noting that no real Tibetan bandit would make a captive Englishwoman walk.

"Pasang, two more things: You must not let Miss Joyell recognize you. And you must not say anything to your sister or anyone else about the English and Russians. It must be a secret. Do you understand?"

"Reverend Tutter is Pasang's friend. I will find Stella and take her to the convent," he said as he set off toward Rongbuk.

20

THE SUMMIT

Luckily, a couple extra of my Sherpas had followed us up to camp IV, so I would be able to replace Pasang, though in reality he tended to carry less than the others because he was a sirdar. Chhamzi was unofficially the new sirdar, so I set her to inspecting and prioritizing the loads of the others. She had a knack for it, and amazingly none of the porters complained.

We got a late start the next morning because Hazard and Odell had decided to make breakfast for Mallory and Irvine. It was a good thing though, for it gave me time to make sure the extra oxygen equipment was well hidden in the porters' packs. We were assembled at the edge of the camp, ready to leave, when Odell led Norton over to say a few words.

"Men, this is a great day. Some may be tempted to say it is one of the greatest days of their lives; others may say one of the greatest days in the history of mountaineering. I think both are acceptable, but as a soldier I have found that in a war, all days are equal because each day is a step toward that day that is the great day. The day that victory is achieved. I bid you Godspeed, knowing that we are but steps away from that great day, our victory over nature's greatest challenge to humanity: Mount Everest." Norton raised his arm as if he held a swagger stick, pointing off toward the clouds, until Odell aimed it toward the summit.

"Thank you, Colonel. Reverend, are your porters ready?" asked Mallory.

"Ready and most willing, Mr. Mallory."

"Excellent. Please take the lead; Mr. Irvine and I will follow. We're laggards at the moment. Remind me to avoid tinned trotters before noon in the future."

That was the last thing I wanted. "Are you sure that is a good idea?"

"Why wouldn't I be? Are you concerned about something? The porters aren't afraid, are they?"

The fact was that they weren't very experienced, and I didn't want it to be obvious right off the bat.

"To us, it's a climb, but to the porters it is a sacred journey. In their eyes, it is a formal procession," I said. "In spite of their pleasant and accommodating personalities, they come from a very hierarchical social system. They'll be more comfortable if you are first."

"Karma Paul never mentioned this," said Mallory.

"Probably because in his eyes it is the only way there is."

"Right you are, then, Reverend. Mr. Irvine and I will carry on. See you in camp."

The porters did better than I had expected. They had gotten on well with the expedition's team and picked up the basics from them while hanging around camp. We made good time to camp V.

Mallory approached us to look at what we had brought up. He was surprised at the lack of material. "I thought there would be enough for a second attempt in your run, Reverend?"

There would have been if I hadn't brought up the pilfered oxygen equipment. "Mr. Hazard insisted that they take lighter loads. He said he didn't want another evacuation disaster on his hands like the most recent time, when the porters were overloaded and driven to exhaustion."

"Really?"

"Those were his instructions."

"Mr. Hazard has a peculiar interpretation of the facts. We'll simply have to make do if there is to be another attempt. Now I'm sending two notes back with the returning porters. Do you have them sorted out?"

"I do."

"Excellent. So you and the remaining four are going with Mr. Irvine and myself in the morning to camp VI. After that, you and those four will descend."

"Yes, unless we are needed."

Mallory had a couple of notes, and he gave them to Tarmo. "Reverend, please tell Tarmo that one note is for Mr. Noel and the other is for Mr. Odell. He is to make sure that they get them."

I relayed Mallory's instructions to Tarmo and then told him and the other three to return to camp IV.

Mallory said, "In the morning, you and the porters will follow us to camp VI. After leaving the supplies, you will return to camp IV, as Mr. Irvine and I will descend directly to camp IV after the ascent. I intend to inspect our equipment and then get some rest. I'll see you in the morning, Reverend."

"We'll be ready," I replied.

I needed a reason to stay at camp VI instead of returning with the Sherpas. Illness would be the easiest excuse, but with Norton marching around snow-blind and Somervell pausing for a moment now and then to cough up the lining of his esophagus. it would have to be a pretty serious problem in order to stay in the camp.

"Reverend Tutter, are you ready? I say, Reverend, are you and the porters ready?" His intermittent and then rapid footfalls as he paced in front of our nonresponsive tent revealed Mr. Mallory's frustration.

"I'm afraid we're not, Mr. Mallory. Our boots are frozen. Sonam put them at the edge of the tent, and they froze. We're going to have to warm them up before we can get going," I said.

"Is he daft? The whole plan is in jeopardy!"

"It's my fault. I forgot he was a nomad and not a Sherpa. Nomads keep boots out of the sleeping area. So he kept them inside but just barely," I replied.

"I'll thank you not to make light of the situation, Mr. Tutter."

"I'm not. I just think that it is only a delay of an hour or two at most. It shouldn't affect your schedule," I said.

"I hope you are right. See here, don't dally. We may need to work to establish a proper camp up there, and it certainly won't be easier when the whole place is in shadow."

We got off to a slow start and didn't arrive till late in the day, so late in fact that it was too late to return to a lower camp. Mallory was unhappy about it and let me know.

"You'll find it hard going to pitch a tent here in these conditions. I suggest you do what you can though, for it is too late to descend. We are leaving at dawn. Remember to check our tent and make sure it is secure before you head back down. We plan to skip this camp if we can during the descent, but that may not be possible. Good night."

"Good night and good luck," I said.

At twenty-seven thousand feet, every movement took great effort, even for the Sherpas. We worked until well after dark to set up the tent in the shale debris. After a meal and tea, there was nothing to do but lie down and wait for dawn. I thought about tomorrow. I wanted Sonam, but he wasn't acclimatizing like Chhamzi. She was one those rare people who easily adapted to high altitudes. In addition, she was stronger than Sonam. She had a certain fanaticism about her; maybe that was the source of her strength. I decided to send Sonam down in the morning with the others. I would wait until Mallory and Irvine left and then follow them from a distance, maybe even to the summit. I had gone over my equipment and made sure that our boots were placed between the sleeping bags. Sonam and Chhamzi had also packed for the summit, as both assumed they were going to go with me. Finally, I tried to sleep, ignoring as best I could my irregular breathing. As I closed my eyes, Chhamzi lit a cigarette.

"What are you doing?" I asked.

"Smoke makes air heavy, heavy air stays in chest, more power, more sleep," she said as the exhaled smoke floated above our sleeping bags.

Even the thought of holding a cigarette seemed laborious, but I decided to try one. I remembered reading that Finch was a smoking proponent and had smoked when he was stranded on this mountain in1922 during a storm. He claimed that it made sleeping easier. I took a few drags and drifted off to sleep. Just before dawn, I heard Mallory and Irvine preparing to leave. There was a minimum of conversation, and in spite of Mallory's penchant for disorganization, it didn't take them long to depart. I waited until Mallory and Irvine left and then nudged Chhamzi.

"Time to go," I said as I opened the Thermos and poured her a cup of tea.

"I am ready," she said.

She was, for she had slept in not only her clothes but her boots. I put on my oxygen pack and then helped her put on hers. Chhamzi was resistant and agreed to wear it only if she didn't have to use it right away. Incredibly, we were on our way in half an hour. In the early light, we followed their tracks, which climbed up and across broken, tile-like rock slabs toward the ridge, and then through a snow-filled gully, which cut upward through a large yellow band of rock. Their steps in the deep snow made it easy going to the dark rock and ridge above.

We reached the ridge and started up, but after a few minutes a pillar of black rock surrounded by house-size boulders blocked our path. I could see that Mallory and Irvine had gone around it to the right. We followed. I knew better but kept hoping that each pitch was the last. I wasn't afraid of continuing: I was afraid that I would never return. I thought about great people. *Is that how they succeed? Do they think only of the goal, never the consequences?* I turned and looked at Chhamzi. She was only a few steps behind me and appeared unfazed. She still hadn't put on the oxygen mask, yet showed no signs of fatigue.

She brought her head close to mine and asked, "Sahib want Chhamzi to follow the Englishmen?"

I shook my head. "No."

We were now below a massive spike of snow and ice. The tracks left the ridge and went down and across a steep and exposed slope. How had they found the route so easily? Mallory's tracks never wandered or went to dead ends. He seemed to know exactly which way to go at every critical point. *What do I have to worry about? All I have to do is follow them. It's the exposure that is frightening. The climbing isn't that difficult.*

It was then that we reached what is now called the Second Step. I stood there and looked at what had to be thirty or forty feet of near-vertical rock. Their tracks led to ten feet of smooth vertical rock with a crack on the left side. I tried to find a handhold, but it was too smooth. The crack was such that my gloved hand slipped out when I put weight on it. How had they climbed it? Chhamzi stepped in front of me and tried. She even used English air. But her efforts were in vain. At this altitude and temperature, even with oxygen it was exhausting. How, on a twenty-nine-thousand-foot mountain, could ten feet be the deciding obstacle?

I felt a glove on my shoulder and turned—it was Sonam! Somehow he had followed us and without oxygen. He had watched my desperate attempts at the rock from below before coming up. He looked at me and then at the rock face. He placed his hands together and bowed his head three times. I watched as he removed his gloves and hat and took a knife from his backpack. He grabbed his long ponytail, wrapped it around his neck, and stuffed it into his coat. Then he took a Thermos from his pack and poured tea onto the fingers and palm of each glove and then put the gloves on.

"Sonam will be roots that wrap the cold stone, so that the branches may reach the heavens," he cried as he leaped forward onto the rock face, his arms reaching high above him and smashing the tea-infused gloves against the stone face. In seconds the gloves were frozen to the rock. He pulled himself upward until his feet were even with my waist and then locked his legs together forming a step.

"Climb, Wangdue, climb upon my shoulders!" he shouted between gasps.

I started to shout that his hands would freeze, but I was knocked to the ground by Chhamzi, who was up and over Sonam before I could get to my feet.

"Chhamzi, what are you doing?" I shouted as she continued upward till reaching the top of the Second Step.

"At last the nomad has found a purpose: a step for the strong. Are you coming or are you staying with the slave?"

With his injured hands, it would be nearly impossible for Sonam to return alone to a lower camp. Leaving him would be a death sentence. Why had he acted so foolishly and ruined my chance for the summit? It wasn't possible for me to both help him and go on. I needed Chhamzi's help to get him back to camp. I started to call to her, but she had vanished from sight.

"Wangdue, climb! I am protected by the blessing of Milarepa. My hands are blue because the goddess of the mountain has made them strong as ice."

Sonam was right. What could I do for him anyway, except return to camp with him after the damage had been done. I grabbed his coat and pulled myself up, and after stepping on his shoulders and placing one foot on his right hand, I had an easy scramble to the top of the Second Step.

Turning and looking down, I saw that Sonam had dropped to the ground and was clutching his frozen hands to his chest.

"Sonam will wait for Wangdue!" he shouted.

I remembered that I had extra gloves and started to get them out for him when a gust of wind hit me. *I'll need them,* I realized. I turned and looked down at him huddled against a rock. "Take off one pair of your socks, and put them on your hands before they freeze. Then put your arms in your pack!" I shouted.

Chhamzi was only a little bit ahead of me. She had stopped and it looked like she was trying to open the oxygen valve. We were on a large boulder-covered plateau that led toward what looked like the summit in the distance. I climbed up and joined her.

"Here, let me try it," I said. I gave the valve a turn, and the gas started flowing immediately. "English air," I said as I nodded to her.

She took a few breaths and then took the mask off. "Enough. Turn air off."

"Off?"

"Yes, off! The air is bad. It smells like breath of cows," she said as she removed the pack and dropped it to the ground.

"I don't see how that can be. It is only oxygen. But if you don't want it or need it, we should have left it with Sonam. By the way, you should have been more careful back there. You cut his face with your boot when you climbed over him."

"He is a little man from a little people. It is no loss. When a fool offers up his life for another, only a fool would not take it."

"That is not what I believe. Only through kindness to others will the world be a better place. That is why I gave him my extra pair of gloves."

"You gave him your extra gloves? Then you are a fool also."

"I see," I said as I looked toward the summit. "Are you ready to continue?"

She nodded and we started off.

The Third Step was ahead of us, and once again Mallory and Irvine's tracks showed no sign of hesitation as they veered down and to the right of the rocky obstruction. We dropped down a steep gully, and then after a traverse we climbed up and out onto a snowfield that led to the summit pyramid. It was steep, but it looked like there were no other obstacles. Two figures were moving slowly up the pyramid. They were Mallory and Irvine. The snow was soft and deep, and with each step they were sinking up to their hips. They were maybe a half hour ahead of us.

Suddenly I was gasping. I must be out of oxygen, I thought. I shoved my ax into the snow and stopped to discard the empty cylinder. As I raised my arm to undo a strap, I saw that Chhamzi was holding a knife. She had cut my line! In desperation I pulled off my mask and tried to stick the hoses together. As I focused on the hoses, I felt a blow to my chest and fell backward, sliding down the mountain face, head first toward the vast glacier thousands of feet below. My head hit a soft mound of snow, I flipped, then was thrown upright and finally stopped by being jammed into a large crack in a bergschrund. I looked up and there, thirty feet above me, stood Chhamzi.

"Help me! Use the rope, and come down and help me," I yelled in spite of the lack of oxygen.

"Help the great man of God? Where is your God now?" She laughed as she raised her knife to the heavens. "O goddess of Chomolungma, Mother of the World, I breathe the air of your limitless life, and with your power I will vanquish those who defile you." Then she turned to me and said, "I have given you the death you deserve, the death of a coward. Like the nomad's blood, your blood is not fit to touch the white snows of the goddess. But the blood of the two brave English—I shall offer it to the goddess. I had hoped your body would land below, where the goraks might feast upon your eyes as you lie broken and helpless. But no matter. Your acts of blasphemy have ended," she said as she turned and started toward the summit.

I cried for help again, but she was gone and I was jammed into an ice wall, unable to move. I screamed again and again, but there was nothing, nothing but the cold wind and loose snow that peppered my face. I struggled, but my arms could not reach the straps of the oxygen kit; at best I could only touch my waist. My waist! I had a gun in my waist belt! I had slept with it and forgotten to put it in my pack that morning.

I had only one chance though, for I had to remove my right glove to grab it. I stuck the frozen glove to my mouth and pulled. It slipped out and tore away part of my lip. I tried again and the glove came off. I reached for the pistol, knowing my hand would freeze to it in an instant; I had to keep my trigger finger free until the last second. I pulled the pistol from my belt and fired at my left shoulder. The ice shattered and I fell forward, knocking the gun from my hand. Dazed but OK, I found my right glove and put it back on my half-frozen, bloody hand. I found the pistol and tucked it into my coat. I took off the oxygen kit and looked at the severed hose.

The oxygen tanks were nearly empty because of the cut hose. I turned the valve off and looked around. I had fallen about thirty feet before being jammed into a pillar of ice on a ledge thousands of feet above the Rongbuk Glacier. The only way out was the way I had gotten there, up the vertical wall of ice and snow above me. It looked impossible. Even if I'd had an ice ax, I wouldn't have had the strength at that altitude to chop the steps needed to climb out without oxygen. "Sonam, Sonam! If only I had stayed and helped you," I yelled out. Then I sat down to die. There was a sharp, cracking noise and then another and another. A large block of ice landed at my feet before bouncing off the cliff and falling to the abyss below. It was followed by a couple more smaller blocks of ice. With each crack I tried to pull myself closer to the wall of ice I sat against in an attempt to ignore what was happening. I was cold. I closed my eyes and lowered my head. My world was ending and I didn't want to watch. Another hunk of ice fell, this time grazing my head.

Then I felt warm. I opened my eyes and saw that I was nearly in direct sunlight. There had been a break in the cloud cover., I looked up at the cliff above me; the icefall had created a couple of small ledges that were large enough for my feet. All I needed was one more to be able to climb back to the ridge. I looked at the broken hose. *If only I had oxygen.* Just then a drop of water fell and then froze as it hit my shaded boot. Water! I stood and stepped into the full sun. In the still air, I suddenly felt as if I were in an oven. I grabbed the oxygen kit, held the severed ends in the sunlight, and watched the ice start to melt. Then a cloud passed and before I realized what was happening, the temperature dropped below freezing. I looked up. Clouds were building up rapidly, but there was a small blue patch left. I held the ends of the hose and waited for the sun to return. I would have only seconds. Just then the sun reappeared and the frost-covered ends turned black as I spit on the hoses and jammed them together. Instantly the clouds returned with their frigid temperature. I gave the ends of the hose a slight tug. The connection held. I hoped that the pressure in the tank was low enough that it would not break the ice weld as I slowly opened the valve and took a deep breath. It held.

I took a few more breaths and then turned my attention to the cliff above me. I had nails in my boots, but I had nothing for my hands except a small pocketknife and the pistol. I opened the knife and, reaching up, jammed it into the ice. I pulled myself up to the first ledge, where a large crack filled with snow formed a ramp to the second, newly formed ledge. I was only a few feet from the ridge. While holding onto the knife, I jammed the barrel of the pistol into a crack in the ice and started to climb. As I did the blade broke, and I fell forward, dropping to a ledge six feet down. Without the knife I couldn't return to the upper ledge. I was trapped, for even though the present ledge actually continued to the snowfield, it was blocked by an overhanging fang of ice.

My breathing was becoming labored. I was nearly out of oxygen, and without it I was helpless. "Mallory! Irvine!" I screamed as I tried to pull the mask from my face. I panicked. The mask was frozen to my skin. My frozen gloves made it impossible to grab the straps. In a moment of insanity, I pulled the pistol from my coat, placed the barrel tip at the mask, and pushed the trigger with a frozen finger. The gun fired. The world went blank as the shot rang through my ears. I felt a stinging sensation across my face as numbness turned to pain. The mask was gone and I could breathe. The pain came from the skin that had been torn off with the mask. I pulled my balaclava down over my face, not caring if the open wounds froze to the hat. I took a deep breath. I could now die a peaceful, painless death from exposure. Or… I looked at the pistol in my hands.

There was a loud bang and then another. They were so loud that at first I thought it was the gun, even though I hadn't touched the trigger. Then a massive block of ice landed on the ledge before tumbling down into the glacial abyss. I heard another bang and looked up, expecting to see something about to hit me. Instead I saw the last of the fang of icefall. The overhang was gone and the ledge led straight to the snowfield! The bullet had gone through the mask and hit the ice, causing it to break loose.

I'm not going to die, at least not on the ledge, I thought as I crawled toward the snowfield. The wind had picked up and the weather had closed in. I wasn't certain if it was the beginning of a storm or just clouds—not that it mattered, for I had but one option: descend. I took a last look toward the summit and saw two figures. Chhamzi's tracks went off in the direction of the summit, but she was nowhere to be seen as I turned and headed down the mountain. Descent was difficult but possible. Even a little bit of climbing, however, was nearly impossible. Luckily, I was able to avoid climbing because I wandered onto a snow slope that led almost to the top of the Second Step. The snowfield ended in a chute that, after two or three steps, turned into a trap of loose, dry snow. I was swept down and tossed over a small ledge, and I came to rest in a patch of snow with my head against something hard. What little breath I had left was taken up by coughing as I struggled to clear the dry snow from my throat.

Finally catching my breath, I tried to stand up. As I did, my hand came in contact with the hard object: Chhamzi's oxygen kit. I stood up, pulled the kit from the snow, opened the valve, and took several deep breaths. The cold, the fear, and the isolation vanished as the oxygenated blood flowed through my body once again. *Sonam.* I could continue to the Second Step and descend. It would be difficult, but I had a short length of rope. Once down, I could have him back in camp in a short time. I guess I had assumed I would follow Mallory and Irvine back, for I realized I hadn't thought about the down climb when Chhamzi and I had ascended the Second Step.

I turned and looked toward the summit. It wasn't that far. I could make it, for, thanks to Chhamzi, I had three tanks of oxygen. As for Sonam, he wanted me to climb. I put on the kit and headed back up the mountain. In what seemed like no time, I reached the base of the final pyramid. My eyes followed the tracks until I saw Mallory and Irvine. At first I thought they were descending, but no, they were still climbing. Why weren't they descending from the summit by now? Then I saw tracks off to their right.

Unbelievably, Mallory must have made a mistake. He had gotten off route and they had been forced to backtrack.

There was another set of tracks in the snow: Chhamzi's! She was nowhere to be seen, yet her tracks followed Mallory's and Irvine's. Or I assumed they did, until my eyes adjusted to the bright but shadowless midday light and I saw tracks that cut off and headed diagonally across the face of the mountain. She had seen them turn right and tried to catch them by taking a steep diagonal traverse. But both sets of tracks disappeared around the right side of the pyramid before they met. At this altitude, how did she continue? She was strong and amazingly acclimatized, but there was something else: Like a Thuggee, a professional assassin, she was one spoke of a great, eternal wheel propelled by the blood of nonbelievers. She was both a slave and a protector of Chomolungma.

At some point Mallory had realized his mistake and turned around before Chhamzi's route crossed his. There was no way of knowing where she was. She might have stepped off a snow cornice or fallen into a crevasse. Whatever the reason, she had been unable to catch them and was now nowhere to be seen. *Let's hope it stays that way*, I thought as I started up the steep snowfield, Everest's final challenge. There was a lot of exposure. The face must have been 50 or 60 degrees, but the tracks—more of a rut-- made it seem like less. Mallory and Irvine were making slow, methodical progress with short switchbacks through the waist-deep snow. I had passed four spent and discarded oxygen tanks. They were on their last tanks. It was so slow going that I wondered if they had enough oxygen left to make it to the summit. Without oxygen, further progress would be out of the question.

But no, it wasn't *impossible* to climb without oxygen. At that instant I saw Chhamzi coming down the mountain, using long, floating plunge steps, until suddenly she stopped. She had seen Mallory and Irvine. She turned and climbed to the edge of a snow cornice above them and watched. They had just turned and started a new switchback, and their backs were toward her. There was a flash of light as she raised her knife and jumped. She landed on Irvine, knocking him down into the soft snow. Mallory was unaware of what had happened and continued his relentless plod to the summit.

I pulled off my mask as I screamed, "Mallory, look out!" No response. He couldn't hear me because of the oxygen flow. But Chhamzi did as she rose from Irvine's body with the bloody knife in her hand.

"Perhaps your blood is worthy of the goddess after all, coward!" she screamed at me before she started toward Mallory.

Mallory heard her, for at that moment he stopped and turned around. Irvine's body lay in the snow and Chhamzi was coming at him with her knife, but he just stood there, staring at Irvine.

"Use your ice ax," I yelled. But he just stood there as Chhamzi charged him. "You fool! Use your ice ax. Don't just stand there," I yelled again. Then I remembered my pistol. It was at least a two-hundred-foot shot, but it was the only chance. I pulled off my gloves, aimed, and pulled the trigger. *Click!* Nothing.

Chhamzi leaped at Mallory, missed, and fell headfirst into the snow below him. Mallory took the opportunity to try to reach Irvine as Chhamzi struggled to extricate herself from the fluffy trap. The cylinder hadn't rotated. My pistol was frozen. Again and again I tried to fire as I banged my ice ax against it, but it was useless. Chhamzi had gotten out of the snow, but I could see she had lost her knife and was searching for it. I had to thaw my gun, but there was no time to put it in my coat and wait for it to warm up. I tried my match, but it was too little heat.   Panicked, I searched my rucksack. Brandy! I poured brandy on it and lit a match. The gun began to warm, and then there was a flash and then another and another. The heat was setting off the bullets. I packed snow on the pistol, hoping to fire it before it refroze. I aimed and pulled the trigger again. Nothing, again and again. Nothing. Had the shells exploded? No, there had to be one left. I aimed one last time at Chhamzi as she grabbed the ice ax from Mallory's hands. The pistol fired and Chhamzi dropped to her knees, pulling Mallory with her as he held onto his ax. I dropped the gun and scrambled up the snowfield to help. Irvine was lying face down with blood-soaked snow and clothing around his shoulders. *Rest in peace*, I thought as I slogged past him to help Mallory, who was still alive. Then Irvine's arm moved. *He's alive!* I grabbed his shoulders and rolled him over; he had lost his oxygen mask and his mouth was full of snow. I rolled his head to the side, slapped his face to clear his mouth, and put the oxygen mask back on his blue-tinged face. In seconds, his color returned.

"You can't lie here. You'll freeze!" I shouted. Irvine grabbed my hand with his good arm and sat up. His right shoulder was covered with frozen blood, but the rest of his back looked OK. He rubbed his wounded shoulder and took deep breaths before turning to me and removing his mask.

"What in God's name just happened to me, Mr. Mallory? Wait, you're not Mallory. Why, you're Reverend Tutter. What are you doing here? Was that a banshee? Where is it? Is Mallory OK?"

"I think so," I said as I looked up to where Mallory had fallen. "He is on his way down. She attacked him also."

"She?"

"Chhamzi attacked you. She jumped you from above and then stabbed you. Then she attacked Mallory. I think she's dead. I shot her. Now let me see your shoulder," I said, dropping to my knees.

"You shot her?"

"Yeah, I got lucky," I said as I knocked off the frozen blood and ice and pulled the sliced anorak and other clothes apart. "You've got two stab wounds. I don't know how deep they are, but one is still bleeding. Hold on a second," I said as I stomped the snow with my boot. Then I put a piece of the compacted snow against the wound. "Don't move for a few minutes."

He nodded and sat motionless.

"Is he OK?" asked Mallory, pulling off his mask.

"I'm not sure. I'm just trying to stop the bleeding; he may have internal injuries," I said.

"You shouldn't have any trouble with the bleeding. Why, single-handedly you just stopped the conquest of Mount Everest, Reverend," said Mallory as he dropped down to inspect Irvine's injury.

"That's not true. I was trying to help. Chhamzi is part of group of fanatic monks, the Red Hats, who have sworn to stop any attempt to climb this mountain. Even Captain Hennessy is part of the plot. When I woke up this morning and found Chhamzi and Sonam gone, I followed them from the high camp."

Mallory let go of Irvine's anorak and grabbed his ice ax. "You lying bastard. I ought to run you through," he said as he held the tip of his ice ax against my chest.

"You don't understand! Please let me finish explaining."

He paused. Then using what air was left in his lungs, he said in a very calm voice, "You're right: I don't understand. I don't understand how lies, which substitute for a spine, can take a man to the top of the world when so many other good men have perished." Mallory pulled the ax away and turned back to Irvine. "Mr. Irvine, the bleeding has stopped. If you are able, we should return to camp. Are you ready?"

"You don't expect me to return without having reached the summit, do you?" said Irvine.

"If we don't descend immediately, you'll die."

"I fear not for myself. 'God shall be my hope, my stay, my guide and lantern to my feet.' But I fear for you and I fear for England, because you will die a thousand deaths if you fail in your quest. For whatever evil is in that man's bosom," said Irvine as he looked at me before turning back to Mallory, "it holds no candle to the might of English character. Do not, Mr. Mallory, surrender to the darkness at hand, but go now and stand on that summit, so that all the world may know that here first stood an Englishman and held England's banner high above the earth's dark clouds."

Mallory sat motionless for a few seconds. I think that he was wondering if Irvine had been hit in the head, for Irvine was an engineer and a mechanical whiz, not a poet. But at death's doorstep, he was quoting *Henry VI*. Mallory got up and started digging a hole in the snow with his ax. Then he took a sweater out of his rucksack and placed it in the pit. He checked Irvine's oxygen tanks and turned to me. "Turn around and let me check your tanks. Good. You've got two full tanks. I'm taking one for Mr. Irvine. Now have you got any extra clothes in your rucksack?"

"A sweater."

"Then get it out and give it to me."

"But I only have one extra sweater; suppose the weather turns."

"Give it to me, before I run you through with my ax."

Mallory turned to Irvine: "I think it is wrong not to take you down, but if you refuse to go, then I shall make your stay as comfortable as possible until I return. Come, get in this foxhole, and wait till I return. The reverend will stay here with you. Won't you, Reverend?"

I knew Mallory would kill me if I refused or offered an excuse. "Of course," I said.

"No, take him with you in case you need a belay," said Irvine. "I'll be OK here."

"Take this liar with me?"

"'There is some soul of goodness in things evil.' Surely he can help you break the trail to the top or secure you if there is a snow bridge."

"You actually believe that this piker can be trusted," said Mallory, turning to me.

"The only reason he is here is because he wants to get to the top, so in that regard he is entirely trustworthy."

"I think I'd better stay with Mr. Irvine," I said.

"There is no need to continue lying, Reverend," said Irvine. "You must go. Mr. Mallory may need you."

"Well, if you insist," I said as Mallory struck me with the blunt part of his ax blade.

"Lying bastard. Let's go," he said as he handed me the end of a rope. "Tie in; there is a small bergschrund up ahead, and I may need a belay."

We started up and in a couple of minutes reached Chhamzi's body. Mallory stopped and waited for me to catch up.

"You must have hit her heart, for though she dropped instantly, it took a few moments for her to loosen her grip on me. Do you have a eulogy for her?"

"I think not. We saw the world quite differently. One view of it is that it is static and needs to be protected. The other view is that the world is evolving."

"Interesting. Someday you'll have to explain which view belongs to which person. Now let's get moving. You lead and break trail. Let's take a slightly steeper traverse and head for that rock. If we're lucky, we can avoid the bergschrund. Use a bit of a kick. I want good, solid steps so we can use them on the way down," he said.

We made good progress and were soon at the base of the large rocks we had seen from below. Mallory had been right about the bergschrund: there was one just below the rocks, and we needed to cross it before we could continue.

"Stop right there and dig a pit—.be quick about it—while I look around. That's deep enough. Now wrap the rope around your waist and stand in it. You are going to belay me while I jump across," he said.

"I know how to belay, but why the hole?"

"Because I don't trust you. I want the rope wrapped around you and you in the hole, like a post or a tree, in case I fall in," he said as he made a few coils to hold in his right hand. "That should do it. Are you ready?" he asked as he turned to make sure I was standing waist-deep in the hole.

"I am."

"Very well," he said as he jumped up and across the crack in the ice and landed safely on the upper side. He moved upward a few feet and then over to the edge of the rocks. "This is it! It's a ridge that goes right to the summit. I can see it." He quickly planted his ax and motioned me to follow. "Hurry up. No need to worry. I've got you on belay; just jump across."

I threw my body forward and jumped. My right foot landed firmly on a patch of ice, but instead of falling forward, I lost my momentum and fell back on my left foot. It had landed on the edge, which failed immediately. Instead of using my ax, I panicked, dropped it, and tried to grab the rope. It was slack! I looked at Mallory. He had the rope but wasn't taking it in. He must have untied it and was letting me fall. I was tumbling head first into the abyss. I yelled so loud that my mask came off, and then there was a jolt. I stopped and fell forward, landing in snow. Moments later my ax was thrust into the snow, inches from my head.

"One should never drop one's ax, Reverend. It's bad form and occasionally leads to fatal consequences."

I knocked the snow from my mask and took a few deep breaths before getting up. "I thought you were going to let me fall just then," I said.

"I was. Then I realized I would lose the rope," he said. He untied me, coiled the rope, and placed it over his shoulder. "Don't worry. I haven't any plans to abandon you, at least not until Mr. Irvine is safe. Let's go. We won't need the rope for what's ahead—that is, as long as you mind where you put your feet," he said as he turned and followed his tracks, which led around the rocks.

I followed him around the rocks and up a short slope that led to the summit ridge. Mallory was putting something under a rock when I reached the top.

"Well, at least she'll know I made it," he said to me.

"Who will?"

"My wife. I promised her I would leave her photograph here if I made it. But as for the *Times* and the rest of the world, they'll simply have to take the word of an English schoolmaster, for I forgot to get the camera from Irvine and I have no idea where the Union Jack is. Any chance you brought one along?"

"A Union Jack?"

"No, a camera."

"I didn't."

"Pity," he said as he took something from his rucksack. "Care for a bite? It's mint cake."

"Thanks," I said.

"Queer, isn't it."

"What?"

"Well, look around. Here we are on the summit, only a few clouds in the sky above, yet a thousand feet down is a layer of clouds. Noel can't film us. Odell and the others can't see us. It's just you and me. In the war we had trophies or the occasional prisoner as proof, but here there's nothing."

"I'm your witness."

"No one will believe you. Frankly, *I* can't believe you made it. And you're not someone the Royal Geographical Society would believe, even if you had proof. The best I can do is to memorize the view, make a cairn, and wait." Mallory began to gather rocks for his cairn.

"Wait for what?"

"Wait until the next fellow gets here and tells the world what he found. Only then will my children know that their father was the man he claimed to be. Now that I've made it, I want to return to England as soon as possible. But you knew all that, didn't you?"

"I knew what?"

"Why, that I hated Tibet, but I hated the idea of failure even more than this miserable place. I had no intention of giving up in spite of Mr. Irvine's injury, of returning a defeated and soon-to-be-forgotten man. I left a man behind, and only the devil is witness to my standing on top of this mountain. I sold my soul to conquer this mountain. 'Men at some time are masters of their fates: The fault, dear Brutus, is not in our stars, But in ourselves, that we are underlings.'" said Mallory as he stacked the last rock on his cairn.

I took a bite of the candy and watched as he stood and surveyed the endless clouds, which hid us from the world below.

"Time to be going. I suspect Mr. Irvine is getting cold, and we need to descend that second step before dark," said Mallory. He removed his oxygen kit and tossed it over the edge.

"What are you doing?"

"Best to toss it. My last tank is empty, and the kit is useless now. Mr. Irvine's calculations were spot on: just a bit less than three tanks to get to the top. No sense carrying the kit, as each step down the mountain means a bit more air. Besides, the extra weight makes one top-heavy on the descent, and that's very unpleasant."

I had a half tank left and knew it was still easier going with oxygen than without. But Mallory's point about being top-heavy was a good one, so I tossed my kit over the edge also. The instant I threw my tanks over the edge, I realized our mistake. "We should have left them here by your wife's photograph."

"By God, you're right, Reverend. Must be the air. Can't seem to think very clearly today," he said, and then started down the mountain.

21

DESCENT

We made good time. The snow was firm but not icy, and it wasn't long before we came to Chhamzi's body.

"She died implementing her god's will; she's at peace," I said. I noticed that the tip of a red hat was protruding from under her scarf, so I took it out and placed it over her head. "She might appreciate that on her journey," I said as I stood back up.

"What journey is that?"

"The journey through the bardo. It is the soul's stage of existence after death and before rebirth."

"Very considerate of you. Shall we continue?"

We found Irvine still sitting in his foxhole.

"I trust all went well and the Union Jack is waving for the world to see?"

"I'm afraid the world will have to take our word for it, Mr. Irvine, for I left the camera with you. And as for the Jack, I simply don't know where it is, except to say that it won't be found on the top of this mountain. Are you ready to return to England?"

"That I am, but shall we have the reverend take a snapshot of you here before we descend?" asked Irvine.

"Why not, though no sense in it being only me," said Mallory as he stood waiting for Irvine to hand the camera to me.

"You'll have to get it. My right arm is rather stiff, and I can't remove the rucksack."

"I see," said Mallory giving me a quick glance before reaching into the rucksack and handing the camera to me.

"Reverend, do try to get the ascending tracks into the picture," said Mallory.

I took the camera and moved down the mountain. "It won't be much for evidence," I yelled. "All I can see are your heads, your shoulders, and the rocks above. The trail isn't visible because it's so steep." I snapped the photograph.

"It will do," said Mallory as he helped Irvine to his feet.

"What about the banshee?" asked Irvine.

"The reverend said she is already on her way home," said Mallory as he put Irvine's ice ax in his left hand. We started back down the mountain.

Our ascending tracks proved to be a godsend, giving us firm and secure steps in the snow. Had they not been there, we would have had to cross the now-freezing snow slopes with a "bit of the kick and pick" as Mallory was fond of saying. At the Second Step, Mallory set up a belay and lowered Irvine down the face in the twilight. The only problem was that it was impossible for Irvine to untie himself when he reached the bottom of the step.

"Damn, why didn't I put a bite on the end of the bowline," snapped Mallory. "You'll need to slide down and help him. I can't leave the rope here."

"Slide down?"

"Abseil. Rappel, as you Americans say. Surely you know how to do that."

"Of course. It's just that I haven't done it for a while."

I tied my ax on. Then I stood over the rope, grabbed it, placed it over my shoulder, and backed to the edge.

"You're stepping on the rope! Lean out or your feet won't hold. Don't grab the rope—use your right arm to control your speed!" shouted Mallory.

I was starting to remember the technique. But I was nervous. And the more nervous I got, the more I gripped the rope. I made it down the first section of rock and plunge stepped through the steep patch of snow that lay just above the last section of the step, using the rope as a makeshift handrail. I stood above the last section of the step. It wasn't large, maybe twelve feet. I knew I could do it, but as I went to step over the rope and place it around my shoulder, it wouldn't budge.

"What are you waiting for?" yelled Mallory.

"The rope is stuck. It's wedged in a crack."

"Well, get it out!"

I tried to pull it out but failed. Then I got on my knees and tried to fish it out, but my gloves were in the way. I took off my right glove and managed to free the rope, but as I stood up I kicked my glove over the edge. "Oh no," I cried, "my glove! It's gone. I need something for my hand or I can't go on."

"You bloody well *have* to go on! Now go!" screamed Mallory.

I grabbed the rope and had gone about halfway down when my foot slipped out from under me. Alarmed, I let go with my lower hand and grabbed the upper end of the rope. In an instant I was at the bottom of the pitch, on my feet. I was actually OK, except that I had burned my right hand."

"My hand, my hand! I can't move it; it's bleeding," I cried.

"Shut up and help Mr. Irvine untie," yelled Mallory.

"I need my glove. My hand is freezing."

"Please, it won't take but a second with your help, Reverend," said Irvine. "You can do it with your gloved hand. It's only a silly bowline, but I can't seem to get my fingers around it enough to release it. Your glove is just over there. I saw it fall," he said as stepped toward me.

"Where is it?"

"It's just over there," he repeated as he grabbed my hand and placed it on the coil around his waist. "Now hold, please, while I pull." The knot released and Irvine yelled, "All clear." Mallory immediately took up the rope and then abseiled down.

"We must get a move on," said Mallory as he coiled the rope. "We have to get through that yellow band before it's completely dark. With your incapacitated arm, Mr. Irvine, I may need to belay you down the chute."

"I'm ready," said Irvine.

"I can't go. I haven't found my glove."

"Then use a sock, use your hat, use something—we don't have time to wait for you to find it," snapped Mallory.

"It's not to be taken lightly. His hand will freeze without it," said Irvine. "We should help him look for it."

"Mr. Irvine, I have no intention of risking you or myself in order to help this lying bastard. I needed his help to get you over this step, but I can manage alone from here. I am not abandoning him. I am simply stating we will not wait for him."

"But isn't that the same thing? Putting one's interests before the group's?" asked Irvine.

"We are the group, Mr. Irvine, you and me," said Mallory just as I found my glove.

"I found it," I shouted.

"Then let's go," said Mallory.

We hadn't gone far when there was a voice.

"Wangdue! Wangdue! Sonam has waited for you," he said as he limped from the shelter of a crack in the rocks. He put his arms around me and began to recite prayers.

"What in God's name is going on? What is he doing here?" demanded Mallory.

"He said he got worried and followed the tracks," I replied.

"My God, his hands! Look at his hands!" cried Irvine. "His hands are frozen stiff."

"Alone? He came up here alone with no experience?"

"That's what he said. It seems impossible but he's here," I said.

"Ask him where his gloves are," said Mallory.

"Can you walk, Sonam?" I asked. "We need to get to camp quickly."

"I can walk, but my hands are useless. I am sorry, Wangdue."

"He said he lost them when he stopped to eat something."

"Tell him we must get going. You need to rope up and keep a belay on him. He's walking death. If he falls, he won't be able to stop," said Mallory.

"Maybe we should leave him and send up a team to get him in the morning; it would be a lot safer," I said.

"Reverend, this is no time to be kidding around," said Irvine.

"He isn't kidding, Mr. Irvine. His priorities are rather specific, aren't they, Reverend?" said Mallory as he took my rope and tied me to Sonam. "Now get his ice ax and tie it to his pack. You will need it for an ax belay at the yellow band. Tell him that he will follow Mr. Irvine and me and to keep in our tracks at all times. Should he fall or lose his balance, he is to shout that he is falling, so that you can begin the arrest. You are to keep the rope taut at all times. Is that clear?"

"OK, we understand," I said.

"We *understand*? You *know* he doesn't understand me! Tell him! Tell him what I told you, now!"

I translated Mallory's instructions to Sonam while Mallory observed carefully. "Do you understand?" I asked Sonam.

"Yes," he said.

"He understands," I said to Mallory.

"Very well, now please repeat them," said Mallory.

"But—"

"Just repeat them," he said.

I repeated the instructions and then turned to Mallory. "Anything else?" I asked.

"No. I wanted to hear if your instructions sounded the same and they did. I think you followed my orders. Let's go. We can still make the yellow band before dark if nothing else goes wrong."

Amazingly, nothing went wrong. In spite of their injuries, Irvine and Sonam were able to move rapidly, with the help of a few quick belays to negotiate the last real climbing section, the First Step. Then the only remaining obstacle was the Yellow Band. We hoped the snowfall and wind during the day had not covered our tracks. There was maybe fifteen minutes of light left when Mallory stopped.

"We going to drop down here; there isn't enough time to get to where we came through the yellow band. This chute should put us on Colonel Norton's route. It's steep but once we are down the chute, it will be a straightforward traverse to the camp. We'll hold our elevation till we find the camp or hit the ridge. If we hit the ridge, then we'll turn round and work our way down a bit and traverse back. It's the safest bet, considering the moon won't be up till half past eleven. We can't afford to be too low, for none of us has the energy to climb should we find the camp above us," said Mallory. He banged his ax against his boots before instructing Irvine to start. Then he addressed me: "Keep the rope taut and have a good grip on your ax, Reverend. If Sonam falls and gets any momentum, you're dead men."

"Perhaps the reverend should go first," said Irvine.

"I don't know if I'm up to it. Maybe you should take Sonam. I'd hate to see something happen because I wasn't capable. It's better if I go alone and see if the route is passable. Then you can bring them down," I said.

"Three on a rope, two of them invalids left to my care, while you descend alone! I'll be quite happy to be rid of you, Mr. Tutter, and let God and the devil decide your fate. But while I live, I will decide the fate of these two brave men. Their survival is paramount. They will not be abandoned or endangered by foolish behavior. Our descent will be two to a rope or three survivors and one lost," said Mallory as he grabbed my ax and prepared to throw it down the chute.

"No, no, don't do that. I was only trying to do what I thought was best. But you have more experience, and now I see that you are right. I wasn't trying to leave anyone. I was just trying to help."

"My God, you're nothing but a filthy, lying coward," said Irvine. "What a fool I've been to think that you were a man of character."

"Why, Mr. Irvine, it seems that your mechanical genius is surpassed only by the ability to evaluate character," said Mallory with a schoolmaster's sarcasm. "Time and tide wait for no man. Mr. Irvine you may begin. Keep to the center of the chute if you can, and remember to shout 'Fall!' should you lose your footing. Reverend, you will wait till we are at least a rope length below before you begin your descent, and of course you will notify us should you or Sonam fall."

"Understood," I said.

"Very well, then, it's back to camp and tea, Mr. Irvine, at your leisure." And with that they started down the sliver of snow that disappeared into the steep chute and near darkness. "Oh, here is your ax," said Mallory, plunging it into the snow.

It wasn't more than rope length before they were out of sight. The light was almost gone. With my fatigue and with the terrain changing between snow and rock and scree, it was hard to keep a good pace, that pace where the mind goes blank and the feet continue, almost as if they have a different source of energy. As for following, I remember hearing them move over different sections, the scraping and sliding on the scree, the clanging ax on rocks, and then the silence when they were on snow. Every now and then, we saw Mallory and Irvine's faint silhouettes in the distance when they crossed snow. Mallory was amazing: How could someone, by dead reckoning, be so sure of where he was going in the dark. In the faint starlight, something white lay below us. At first I thought it was a cloud; then I knew it was a snowfield, the large snowfield that lay beneath the Yellow Band. Mallory had gotten us down. All that was left was the traverse. The sound of their voices grew louder. They had stopped, and I soon found out why.

"Why did you stop? We're almost there," I said.

"Because of this," said Mallory. I heard him toss a rock into the silence before it eventually hit something below. "We're at the edge of a cliff, and we need to find a route down."

"I knew this was a mistake. We should have followed the ascent route. Now we're doomed. We're going to die here!" I cried.

"You can die if you choose to, Reverend, but I expect you to get Mr. Sonam safely to camp before doing so. Mr. Irvine, you are to stay close and mind your feet. We are going to traverse to our right and look for a chute that will lead us to the snowfield below. Reverend, if you shut up, then you will be able to hear us and follow," said Mallory as they started off through the darkness.

We followed, each step a gamble—but not much of a gamble, because with Mallory's genius, the odds were in our favor. It wasn't long before we stood at the edge of a finger of snow that cut through the invisible blackness of rock and headed down toward the faint glimmer of the snowfield below. *Maybe we'll make it after all*, I thought as I stopped to listen. I heard Mallory and Irvine below. It wasn't the sound of plunge steps going into soft snow: It was the sound of boot nails on ice and the chipping of Mallory's ax as he sought to anchor himself and Irvine as they moved down the icy gully.

Then I heard Irvine say, "The snow, actually it's ice, is quite hard here. I'm going to try to step to my left and use my arm to brace against the rock so as not to slip. Do you have me?"

"Belay on."

"Odd. It feels a bit slack, but if you've got me, I'll just give it a go. Climbing," said Irvine. "Just a matter of getting my left foot—fall! fall! I'm falling," he cried, his voice echoing up the chute.

"I've got you," shouted Mallory, and then there was a thud, followed by the sound of Mallory tumbling down the chute.

I don't think I ever heard him come to a stop. All I remember is that after a few moments there was only silence. Cold, darkness, and silence. I hadn't noticed the silence before. There had been so much noise: shifting rocks, crunching steps across the frozen snow, clanging axes, and even breathing. And now there was nothing, absolutely nothing, just like the sky above and the emptiness below.

"Death?" asked Sonam.

"I don't know," I said as I cupped my hands around my mouth and shouted, "Mallory! Irvine!" again and again.

I felt a bump. It was Sonam. "Death," he said.

"Yes, death," I said. We had three options. We could follow Mallory's route and die. Or we could continue a blind traverse until we found another chute, try it, and probably die. Or we could bivouac and freeze to death while waiting for dawn. I decided to bivouac. In the faint light, I saw a patch of snow to our right surrounded by darkness. It was probably a drift that had filled in a big crack. I poked it with my ax. The surface was frozen, but under the breakable crust was soft snow. If I could tunnel under the crust, I could make a cave and we could huddle together and try to keep warm. I explained my plan to Sonam as I stomped a pit in the snow: "It is our only hope. I don't have any extra clothes, though we can use our packs as big socks for our feet." It was exhausting work because I had only an ax and my hands to dig the snow. The ax was worthless for making a cave. I had to use my hands. It was slow going. My gloves were getting wetter and my hands were starting to freeze, I had extra dry gloves, but they were thin. If I kept digging, I would lose my hands. Sonam! His hands were already frozen—what more could he do to them. I backed out of the hole and had him crawl in and dig. His frozen hands were like shovels as he bored his way into the drift. In no time he had created a cave big enough for both of us. I chopped a vent hole through the crust and then crawled inside. I sat on my pack and shivered as I took off my frozen gloves and stuck my hands into my armpits. I noticed that Sonam wasn't shivering. "Sonam, are you warm?" I asked.

"Yes, Wangdue, because I am covered in bird skin."

"What's that?"

"The feather coat that Pasang got from a father climber. Pasang said before you came, others came; they are father climbers, no?"

"Oh, the earlier expeditions. You've got the coat that Finch gave to Pasang. Why did Pasang give you the coat?"

"I bought the coat. I gave Pasang my tribal knife for it. He said that he was going with the English lady and not climbing mountains any longer. He was a warrior now and had to protect her. My knife was useless against the demons, but his coat is very warm."

"You were smart. I laughed at him when I saw it. And now my laughter has become shivers. I guess there is a lesson there. Could we shift positions? Let me move in against the rock and you sit with your back toward the opening?"

"Of course, Wangdue."

We squeezed past each other in the darkness, and I made myself as warm as possible as I curled against the rocks. In a matter of minutes, I heard Sonam snoring! How could he sleep up here? My envy only made me more miserable as I constantly shifted to keep the cold at bay and waited for the dawn. I wished that, like Sonam, I could sleep and make time disappear, but I wasn't that lucky. If I was going to die, then why couldn't I just fall asleep? Why did I have to have insomnia? It wasn't fair. I decided to wake up Sonam. If I was miserable, then he was going to be miserable. As I rolled to my side and kicked him, there was an odd vibration in the snow. Then a roar. And before I knew it, I was upside down with my face packed in snow. There had been an avalanche. I struggled to clear my face and free my arms before the snow froze, and in a couple of minutes I was standing a few feet below where the snow cave had been.

"Sonam! Sonam!" I cried, but there was no response. In the dawn's light I could see that our cave had been against a rock outcropping, and when the avalanche rolled over us, I had been spared, but he had been swept away. I stood on a vast rubble and a snow-covered slope and shivered as I traced the path of the avalanche, which had swept Sonam off the North Face and carried him all the way to the Rongbuk glacier, thousands of feet below. The avalanche had had a narrow path, but we had experienced the misfortune of being in it. *Maybe Mallory and Irvine were spared*, I thought. *They could be just below in the chute.*

I shouted, but there was no response, and from where I stood, I couldn't see down the chute or where it ended, but only farther below. *They could be there, but they would be dead*, I realized. It was pointless to look for them, and even though I was the sole survivor, I still had to get back to camp. Luckily, the avalanche had hit just before dawn. The intense morning sun was the only thing that kept me from freezing. I found my ax and pack. I could see that Mallory had gotten us to the traverse point, as planned, and that his decision to descend the chute had been a mistake, a mistake that had cost two lives. I would let Odell and the others know where they had vanished. I took my handkerchief and placed it under a rock, and then I headed   east   across   the   face   toward   the   camp.

22

SALVATION?

The morning had started off clear, and I headed east toward what I thought were familiar landmarks. The fact that I was so close to the camp and safety energized me more than food and water, which I had lacked in the past sixteen hours, could have. *I'm going to make it*, I thought. *I just have to keep going east.* I hadn't been under way for very long, however, when patches of fog started to appear. The next thing I knew, I was in a whiteout. Suddenly I had no idea of direction except for the glow from above, indicating the sun's approximate location and the slope of the face. As I wandered across the face I only knew I was going eastward, moving though occasional pockets of soft snow and around ice-covered rocks. It would be easy to miss the tents in the fog and end up on the Northeast ridge with no alternative but to turn around—and I didn't have the energy to turn around. Suddenly my euphoria was gone. I started to grow cold and stopped after every couple of steps. The only thing I could see were rocks and my feet; everything else was fog. I had to find the camp.

Then I saw a tent; it was Mallory's. I had made it! I had survived! I took a deep breath and told myself I could make it without a rest, but after ten steps I stopped, exhausted. And when I looked at what had been the tent, it was only a rock. A voice from behind me said, *"Do not despair. Though you wander through the putrid breath of thousand-year-old demons, I will watch over you. Be resolute in your faith, my son, and you will survive. Your Lord will not forsake you."*

It was the voice of God. He was with me; he was going to guide me through the fog of death. "Yea, though I walk through the valley of the shadow of death, I will fear no evil: for thou art with me; thy rod and thy staff they comfort me," I whispered to myself as I turned around and looked into the fog. "God, O my Lord and Savior, you have not forsaken me," I cried out as I lowered myself to my knees and bowed my head before God in the loneliest place on earth. "You know that I have never lost faith, and now, because of that, you have come to guide me to safety. Praise the Lord! For I am saved."

"And so I have, Morton Tutter. As your Lord, I have come to guide you home to the palace of a million lotus blossoms."

"Oh yes, home to the palace of a million lotus blossoms," I repeated.

"Rise and follow me."

I stood up, lifted my head, and opened my eyes. It wasn't Jesus—it was Chhamzi! She was standing a few feet away. Actually, she wasn't standing, she was floating above the snow and rocks, surrounded by a soft yellow glow.

"Chhamzi, you're dead!" I screamed. "I saw you die."

"O feeble liar and wart on the sole of the blessed feet of the goddess. Do you think that your god is mightier than the infinite wisdom of the boundless universe?"

"I believe in my Lord and Savior, the Son of God. He will never forsake me."

Chhamzi let out several bursts of laughter, and with each burst her head multiplied in size until it seemed one hundred feet high. *"You are not forsaken, little wart, you will live a million million eons in the boiling acids of my stomach,"* she roared as her giant tongue extended and tried to curl around me.

"No," I screamed, "no!" as I tried to escape by turning and running down the mountain, but I was too weak to manage more than a slow stumble. Her tongue followed along, continuously extending no matter how far I went until I came to a ledge. I was trapped and the tongue began to encircle my feet. "No," I cried, "no!" as it retracted, pulling me into the cavernous black mouth and the acids of infinite suffering. I swung my ice ax frantically at the throbbing tongue. I had to chop it off; it was my only hope. But with each cut another tongue appeared. I was surrounded by a dozen tongues. "No, no!" I screamed as I took the ax and jabbed it into the tongue, which wrapped around my legs. I felt a sudden pain and then an odd warmth, as if my foot had suddenly returned to my body. I looked down. I had stabbed my foot with the tip of my ax. There was no Chhamzi or giant tongue. It had been a hallucination, and I had stabbed myself.

Exhaustion and the intense yet shadowless light of the fog were driving me insane. I was hot and cold at the same time. I barely knew up from down and was so tired I no longer cared. I dropped my ax but was too weak to bend over and pick it up. I needed to sleep. If I could sleep for just an hour, then I would have the energy to find the camp and everything would be fine. "The fog was my blanket and the snow my pillow," I thought as I sat down. "Everything will be OK after a nap." And then I fell asleep.

I had to answer the door; someone was knocking. It was a timid knock, more of a tapping. Why did they have to bother me now, why didn't they go away? Maybe that was why they were tapping. They didn't want to but had been ordered to do it. Was it Mrs. Hunt the organist? She never wanted to ask for anything, but choir members made her responsible for everything. Yes, it must be her. Not timid, just tapping "Come, Thou Fount of Every Blessing." She knows I love that hymn:

Come, Thou Fount of every blessing,
Tune my heart to sing Thy grace;
Streams of mercy, never ceasing,
Call for songs of loudest praise. . .

Ow! my face. Ow! what is going on? Where am I? Mrs. Hunt? There was a loud, almost clapping sound as I shook my head and opened my eyes in time to see a gorak fly away. I wasn't at the church. I had been asleep and "Come, Thou Fount" was the gorak pecking at my goggles. The fog was gone. I stood and looked around. I saw the northeast ridge, with clouds slowly rising behind it. The Yellow Band was above me.

The camp had to be to the east, and so I went east. In half an hour I found a tent. "Hello, hello," I mumbled as if I were a lost stranger knocking on a remote door. What was I doing? I opened the tent, crawled inside, and collapsed. After a few minutes, I opened my eyes and looked around. Though the tent was abandoned, it wasn't empty. There were a couple of sleeping bags, a thermos, biscuits, unopened bully beef, and the frozen yet unmistakable odor of rancid butter. This wasn't Mallory's tent. It was one of the tents used by the Sherpas who supplied the camp.

It didn't matter. I smashed open a can of bully beef and pushed a frozen chunk into my mouth. It froze to my tongue. I needed water more than food. I searched but there was none, only a couple of thermoses that were frozen solid. I took my ax and smashed a container, covering the tent floor with glass, but I had two frozen hunks of tea—something other than tasteless ice and snow. I wiped the glass from the hunks, broke the tea into pieces, and popped some into my mouth. It also froze to my tongue. Where was the stove? How could they leave a complete tent and not the stove?

Angry, I threw a frozen hunk of tea across the tent. There was a tinny noise when it hit the tent wall. Was it the cooker? I jabbed the pick through the tent canvas, tore a hole, and dug through the snow. My glove hit something—the cooker! It was in a bag, complete with matches and fuel. I filled the pot with cubes of tea and waited. When the tea was finished, I melted snow with pieces of the bully beef. I felt better as a bit of warmth returned to my feet and hands, even though the wind outside the tent reminded me that I was alone. I shoved one sleeping bag into the hole I had made in the tent and then crawled into the other to rest before continuing on to camp V.

As I lay there I thought about Mallory, Irvine, Sonam, and Chhamzi, the four people who had just died on this mountain. No one would believe that I had been to the top and returned, but Mallory had died. *How did you do it?* they'd ask. And when I told them—if I told them—I'd be blamed. After all, I was the only survivor, like Mr. Whymper on the Matterhorn. If only Mallory were alive! No, he hated me; it was better that he was dead. I had reached the top and survived. No reason to be ashamed of that.

23

ODELL

"Yodel-Ay-*Eee*–Oooo, Yodel-Ay-*Eee*–Oooo. Yodel-Ay-*Eee*, Yodel-Ay, Yodel, Mallory, Mallo, Mal, Mm, Irvine, Irvin, Irvi, Irv."

"Splendid, isn't it. And to think that Whymper climbed it by simply going round the backside. Yodel-Ay-*Eee*–Oooo, Yodel-Ay-*Eee*–Oooo. Yodel-Ay-*Eee*, Yodel-Ay, Yodel. Go on, Reverend, give it a try. Pretend you're calling the cows. Eh, I suppose sheep in your case," said Mallory as we gazed at the Matterhorn from a hilltop.

"Well, I would never yodel to call my flock. But here goes: Yurdel-hay-seed-no, Yurdel-hay-seed-no.'"

"A bit more from the chest; you've almost got it."

"Yogel-nay-seed-tow, Yogel-nay-seed-tow."

"My God, man, stop! Rats! You're calling rats; we're going to die. We've got to get into the tent."

"Mr. Mallory? Mr. Irvine?"

There was a flash of light and a rush of wind. The tent was open and there was someone in the door. "Mr. Mallory? Mr. Irvine?"

"What? Who is it? Who's there?" I cried.

"Reverend Tutter, is that you? What in God's name are you doing here? It's me, Odell. I heard you answering my yodel and found the tent. I had no idea you were here."

I was confused. I had been dreaming again. "I was yodeling?"

"Well, for lack of a better term. I think you were answering my yodel."

"I was dreaming I was in Switzerland with Mr. Mallory. We were looking at the Matterhorn and yodeling."

"I suspect you heard my yodeling, and it triggered an associative dream. It's a sign of extreme fatigue. Saw it a lot in the trenches. One chap fell asleep and thought he was swimming the English Channel when actually he was lying face down in the muck; don't remember what kept him from

178

drowning. Another fellow dreamed he was at the Derby when actually he was nearly trampled by cavalry. I had no idea this tent was here until I heard you. Not to be rude, but might you know where one could find Mr. Mallory and Mr. Irvine?"

"They are probably lying on the Rongbuk glacier."

"Are you saying they are dead?"

"Yes, they fell. Or rather Mr. Irvine fell and took Mr. Mallory with him."

"And how do you know that?"

"I was there."

"You?"

"Yes, we were returning from the summit. It was dark, but Mr. Mallory insisted on continuing. He knew we weren't far from camp and decided to press on. When they fell, there was an avalanche. I had begged them to bivouac, to make a cave, but they insisted on continuing. That's why they died."

"They made it to the summit? Then I *did* see them! I was sure I saw them on the ridge before the clouds came in. Oh, but this is an awful turn of events."

Odell sat down abruptly on the floor of the tent. He bowed his head for several minutes. When he looked up again, his eyes were red.

"At least they made it." His voice was choked.

"Actually, only Mr. Mallory made it. Mr. Irvine was injured, so I went with Mr. Mallory."

"You!"

"Yes, I said I was with them."

"You did, but I didn't think that was what you meant. I must go and see if I can find them. Where exactly did they fall?"

"Exactly? I have no idea, only that it was a chute below the Yellow Band at about this elevation, maybe an hour from here. I did leave a handkerchief there though."

"I'll go and have a look-see. Matter of respect and honor, you understand. 'Go tell the Spartans, passerby. That here, obedient to their laws, we lie.'"

"Laws?"

"The Lacedaemonians, never surrendering, dying on the battlefield. I'll honor our fallen comrades as best I can, perhaps by placing their axes at their sides, death in battle. Everest is where they made their last stand and Everest is where they fell, and so I say to this monstrous pile of sedimentation, ossified fragments of life, ye shall not be rid of thy conquerors even in death. These men stood upon you and shall forever remain upon you. These lions shall not be caged in crypts for schoolboy tours but remain here for the entire world to look up upon. Their memory will spawn ever mightier Englishmen and ever greater glory. Oh, but let these warriors rest where they fell! Well, enough of the talk. I'm off and when I return, we'll drop down to camp IV in time for tea."

Drop down to camp IV? I thought. How did he do it? Climb up and down the mountain without the least sign of altitude sickness. He made the descent sound like getting off a bus.

"In time for tea, perfect," I said. "Good luck."

Maybe an hour passed before I heard Odell return.

"Time to be going, Reverend."

"Did you find them?"

"No, not a trace. I've never learned to appreciate the scale of these mountains. Things always seem so bloody close until… until one tries to go somewhere or find something. Well, it is nearly impossible. I've signaled Colonel Norton that they're dead. We can head down now if you are ready."

"I am."

"Very well. Do you want a rope or can you manage?"

"A rope. I can walk, but my mind—it's as if it's no longer with me, and I'm afraid I might just wander off for lack of concentration."

"Ah, still basking in the glory, no doubt," said Odell as he tied me in.

I turned and stared at the summit. I was there yesterday. Or was it the day before? I didn't know when, but I had indeed stood there.

"Fantastic, isn't it? She pulls one in like a beautiful woman, alone and beckoning. I'd swear at times I've even heard her sing."

"It's a siren's song."

"Ah, a siren! Luring men to their deaths. A tragedy with the exotic touch of both the sacred and the forbidden."

"Sacred to the Tibetans. But the goddess didn't kill them. That's superstition. What killed them was the mountain: the rock, the ice, the wind, and the cold. We are in the most desolate spot on earth. If there is a goddess, then it is the goddess of nothing and nothing more than that."

"Reverend, have you forsaken your God?"

"No, I'm sure God is by my side. I've just never been somewhere so alone, so remote, so otherworldly. For a while I did consider the possibility of there being nothing except what lay under my feet."

"I must say I'm surprised you did make it to the summit with those sorts of ideas running through your mind. Chaps like you are usually the first to go in a pinch. Are you ready?"

"Yes."

"Very well, next stop camp IV and tea. That is, if Mr. Hazard has managed to get out of his sleeping bag."

Odell was a rare man in the world of mountaineers: He had infinite patience combined with relentless plod. He took me down the mountain, leading when appropriate and belaying when necessary, never rushing yet never letting me stop, for he knew that should I stop I'd fall asleep, regardless of the location. When we arrived, around five, Mr. Hazard had tea ready. Odell filled Hazard in on what he had found.

"The reverend says he and Mallory made it to the top. Have you got any brandy for a toast?"

"I'll toast to the fallen but not to a liar," said Hazard as he shoved a cup of tea into my hand.

"Why on earth do you doubt him?"

"I rather think the question is why on earth you believe him, And in any case he's not an Englishman, so there is no reason to recognize what he's done."

"But he was with Mr. Mallory."

"So he says. Now see here, Odell, we've got a man of questionable integrity who goes up the mountain with four others and returns alone. I know what we called that at the Battle of the Somme. Does it have a different name in Tibet?"

"Mr. Hazard, you should at least let him speak before you condemn him."

"All right, Reverend, why didn't Mr. Irvine reach the summit?"

"He was injured."

"How?"

"He had fallen and hurt his shoulder; he could walk, but had a difficult time with his ax."

"I see. And where are the Sherpas?"

"Died in an avalanche."

"And you didn't?"

"No, it was a matter of luck. We were in a snow cave, and I was closer to the mountain. The others were swept away."

"That was convenient."

"Convenient? Two human beings die and you call it convenient. What are you getting at, Mr. Hazard?" asked Odell.

"I hardly think he has the wit to plan something like that, even though I'm sure he would if he could. Not only does he return alone, but there is no trace of the others. Is this what it means to be a man of God in America? Return from battle alone, uninjured, and expect to be treated as a hero? Why did God let them die? I'll tell you why! He let them die because they were doing his will. They were no doubt helping each other when this bastard was thinking only of himself! Why, I ought to run you through, you coward," shouted Hazard as he seized Odell's ax.

"My God, man, stop it!" shouted Odell as he grabbed the ax.

"So this is what it comes down to: the greatest mountain on earth is conquered not by the fearless, but by a liar. Is that how it is to be, Mr. Odell?" said Hazard as he let go of the ax and walked to his tent.

"Mr. Hazard, Mr. Hazard," Odell muttered. "Pity. He's a fine man, but something happened to him during the war, and he tends to get upset when the conversation turns to that subject."

"I never said anything about war. It was Mr. Hazard," I said.

"He did? Yes, that's right, he did. You probably should avoid him for a time. I'm sure he'll get over it. What say we eat something and then you get some sleep?"

We ate and then I went to an empty tent and fell asleep. When I woke late the next day, I climbed out of the tent and found a note pinned to the tent door:

Reverend, very sorry that camp abandoned. Urgent that we return to base camp. Orders from Colonel Norton. All things considered, thought it best you rest. Mingma to remain. Route to base camp well-trodden. Will ensure provisions left as expedition retreats.

Odell

Hazard and Odell had left without me. I wasn't surprised that Hazard had left, but I had felt that Odell was willing to give me the benefit of the doubt. What was so urgent that they could not wait for me? I looked around; it was probably well past noon. The snow was soft and the temperature was warm enough for just a shirt. I had slept a long time, but I was still exhausted and had a ways to go if I wanted to survive. Where was Mingma?

"Mingma! Mingma!" I called loudly. No reply. *The coward probably left after they were out of sight. Why would he risk his life for me, especially now that the expedition has retreated.* There was nothing in my tent except my gear, so I decided to check the other tents to see if there was anything to eat before I started down.

Opening the last tent, I found Mingma sound asleep; so he was a good soldier after all. I reached in and touched his shoulder. He didn't move, so I tried again. Nothing. As I got on my knees and tried to shake him, my hand hit something beside him—an empty bottle of brandy. He was dead drunk. I tried again to rouse him but to no avail. He was worse than useless; he was a burden. But not my burden, for I wasn't going to carry him down the mountain. If Odell and the others cared about him, they could return for him. How dare they leave me and then expect me to care for a drunken fool. I looked around the tent. It had several cans of bully beef and tins of biscuits. Well, at least I had found something to eat. I reached across Mingma to take the food, but as I did so he rolled over and grabbed my arm.

"Mingma waits for you, but you steal Mingma's food. You are not like English. You are bad man."

"Nonsense. I tried to rouse you, but you were too drunk to respond. I was simply getting something for breakfast, which I was going to make for both of us before I tried to rouse you again."

"Reverend is liar," said Mingma as he pulled a knife from his sleeping bag and held it at my chest. "Hazard told Mingma to kill Reverend," he growled as he tried to push the knife into me. "You are a ghost sent by the evil long noses who want to enslave the Tibetan people. Hazard sahib said you have cast a spell on the other Englishmen and that you killed Sonam and Chhamzi.

"Let me go, you fool!" I shouted as I tried in vain to get away. I had one hand on his knife hand, which was inside the sleeping bag. My other arm was held by his arm. He was incredibly strong. And why shouldn't he be, having spent his life being a beast of burden. I couldn't break free, but the fact that his arm was partially bound by the sleeping bag prevented him from delivering a fatal stab. It was a stalemate between two elk with locked antlers.

"I didn't kill anyone. Mallory and Irvine died in a fall."

"You killed them."

My strength was failing. Soon I wouldn't be able to resist, and he would kill me. *To come so far and then die because a drunken fool thinks I'm a ghost! And yet he is trying to kill me. No, he actually doesn't think I'm a ghost, for if he did he would be frightened.*

I thought of my early Sunday school lessons in which I deliberately frightened the kids with my impression of the devil. I turned and stared at Mingma, letting my eyes roll back in their sockets. I flared my nostrils, made a deep gurgling sound, and then exhaled through my open mouth into his face. "*Gowon tubor gowon rorum rorum pestus mortus,*" I mumbled.

"*Aiiee! Om mani padme hum, om mani padme hum.* By the light of the blessed Buddha, may this dust-blown chaff be spared eternal suffering!" cried Mingma as he flung me across the tent. He jumped up and ran barefoot out into the snow. I got up, gathered my things and his boots quickly, and headed down the mountain, stopping only to toss his boots into a crevasse. *That will teach him to threaten a ghost.*

24

MISSING PRESUMED DEAD

The best I could hope for was to reach camp III, but what hopes I had for succor were dashed when I arrived at what had been the camp, for it had been destroyed and burned. I was about to continue on what would have been a freezing night march when I saw a piece of paper fluttering under a rock.

It was a note from Odell, telling me where to find supplies:

Colonel sees us at war. Leave nothing for the enemy (whomever they might be). Sorry for ruins. No need for a cryptogram, natives can't read. Kit is third big rock as you look to summit. Then twenty feet to left behind lone rock.

Odell

True to his word, Odell had left bully beef and biscuits, along with a sleeping bag and tarp—definitely enough to keep me going. When I finally arrived at base camp, all I found were more charred debris and empty cans. There were no notes or hidden supplies.

As I left the camp, I passed a large stone cairn adorned with prayer flags. Some of the stones were inscribed with the names of the dead: Mallory, Irvine, Kellas, and the dozen Sherpas who had died in the three expeditions. *At least they didn't count me as dead.* Then I noticed a stone lying on the ground beside the cairn: *Tutter (American) 1924: missing, presumed dead.* In a fit of anger, I picked up the rock and threw it into the other rocks that made up the surrounding moraine.

I had climbed the mightiest mountain in the world, and now I was the loneliest man in the world.

The End

ABOUT THE AUTHOR

Stan Huncilman started mountaineering over forty years ago when he was a Peace Corps volunteer. Since then he has worn many hats: parade float designer, farmer, fire investigator and sculptor. He has always used his hands to earn a living and express himself. That changed when a friend suggested that he use his sculptures to illustrate a story. He took to writing like cats to cream, or maybe it's just that by writing, an aging sculptor needn't struggle so much with gravity. He lives in Northern California and still enjoys peak bagging.

www.ingramcontent.com/pod-product-compliance
Lightning Source LLC
Chambersburg PA
CBHW060105260626
47160CB00005B/1811